PRAISE FOR #1 *ESSENCE* BESTSELLING AUTHOR PATRICIA HALEY AND HER IMPOSSIBLE-TO-PUT-DOWN NOVELS

Let Sleeping Dogs Lie

"The story grabs the reader from the beginning, drawing you in . . . and keeping you on the edge of your seat as the plot takes unexpected twists and turns."

—*Romantic Times*

Still Waters

"Haley's writing and visualization skills are to be reckoned with. . . . This story is full-bodied. . . . Great prose, excellent execution!"

—RAWSISTAZ™

"A deeply moving novel. The characters and the storyline remind us that forgiveness and unconditional love are crucial to any relationship."

—Good Girl Book Club

No Regrets

"*No Regrets* offered me a different way, a healthier way based in faith and hope, to look at trying situations."

—*Montgomery Newspapers*

"A must-read. . . . Highly recommended."

—APOOO Book Club

Broken is also available as an eBook.

Also by Patricia Haley

Broken

Patricia Haley

G
GALLERY BOOKS
New York   London   Toronto   Sydney   New Delhi

G℡

Gallery Books
A Division of Simon & Schuster, Inc.
1230 Avenue of the Americas
New York, NY 10020

First Gallery Books trade paperback edition August 2011

GALLERY BOOKS and colophon are registered trademarks of Simon & Schuster, Inc.

For information about special discounts for bulk purchases, please contact Simon & Schuster Special Sales at 1-866-506-1949 or business@simonandschuster.com.

The Simon & Schuster Speakers Bureau can bring authors to your live event. For more information or to book an event, contact the Simon & Schuster Speakers Bureau at 1-866-248-3049 or visit our website at www.simonspeakers.com.

Manufactured in the United States of America

10   9   8   7   6   5   4   3   2

Library of Congress Cataloging-in-Publication Data

Haley, Patricia.
   Broken / by Patricia Haley.—1st Gallery Books trade paperback ed.
      p. cm.
1. African Americans—Fiction. 2. Family-owned business enterprises—Fiction. I. Title.
   PS3558.A35772B76 2011
   813'.54—dc22

                                                          2011004797

ISBN 978-1-4165-8064-5
ISBN 978-1-4165-8352-3 (ebook)

To my oldest brother,
Reverend Frederick Lane Haley

Thank you for the years of love, support, and conversations
(which have been many). When I was a shy young girl in
school, you were my constant protector. Not a day goes by
that I don't appreciate you and the heart you have for our
family. If God had allowed me to pick my oldest brother,
out of all the choices in the universe, it would still be you.
Gloria, thanks for being a great wife and friend to him.

Happy 50th Birthday, Fred

With all my love, from your "only" sister

The Lord is close to the brokenhearted
and saves those who are crushed in spirit.

—Psalm 34:18

Broken

Broken

Prologue

Joel, you can't be serious. You've had tougher fights and never once were you interested in quitting. Madeline and her son have tried and tried to drive you out of the company, to make your life miserable. You've beaten them every time."

"Not this time, Mom. I've lost." He glared at the financial report. "We're twenty million dollars short again this month. DMI is in a free fall. I've lost two of our four divisions. Fifty percent of the company now belongs to somebody else." He was too disgusted, remembering his father's admonishment to keep the company as a solid unit and never allow DMI to be split into pieces. The words seemed fresh, yet he hadn't heeded the warning and the results were final. His father's company was no longer. "I don't have the inspiration to get this turned around in time."

"You don't have to give up. I won't allow it. You deserve your father's company. Okay, I understand. You're going through a tough time, but that's no reason to quit."

"Face it. This has been a good ride and now it's over," he said, standing and tapping on the desk before walking toward the door.

"No, Joel, no. At least wait a few days."

"No need. My mind is made up. I'm tired." Saying the words gave him a surge of relief. The war was over. He'd lost to a seasoned warrior.

His mother left, dejected. Joel swallowed his pride and prepared to wave the white flag. He decided not to call ahead as he pulled into the valet parking area. Joel went inside and approached the front desk. "I'm here to see Don Mitchell."

"And you are?" the security guard asked.

"Joel."

"What's your last name, sir?"

"Just Joel," he said, eager to get in, take care of business, and get out. Sharing his last name might raise questions he didn't feel like answering, such as how they were related. How was he supposed to answer a question like that? They were brothers to the degree that they shared the same last name and their father's DNA, but that was the extent of their connection. It was definitely best to leave the last name tucked away. "He'll know who it is, trust me."

The guard proceeded to call Don. It wasn't too late, Joel thought, anxious. He quelled his urge to bolt from the building without Don knowing he was ever there. The security guard got the clearance, just in time. "Mr. Mitchell has given you the okay to come on up. He's on the thirty-fourth floor, unit number eight."

"Thanks." As he entered the elevator, Joel planned to dash in, get the task over, and split. When the doors opened he froze. There was no changing his mind. He had to move. Standing in front of door number eight, he regrouped and collected his thoughts, relying on his dignity. He knocked hard and fast.

Don opened the door right away. He stood in the doorway with a befuddled expression.

"Your face says it all."

"I'm shocked to have you standing at my door. It's been, what, six or seven years since you've been here?" Don said, standing with his shoulders back, arms folded tight across his chest and hands tucked under them. He appeared too intense for Joel.

"It's been a while, let's just say that. But don't you worry. This is a very short visit. I'm here to tell you that it's yours."

"What is mine?" Don said, standing directly in the middle of the doorway.

"DMI. It's yours."

"Man, I don't have time for games."

"I'm serious. Believe me, this is not a game." Joel felt like dirt—the kind people had no use for and shook off their shoes. He wasn't delusional. Joel wasn't expecting a warm reaction from Don or an invitation to come on in and have a seat. They weren't that kind of brothers, never had been and never would be. "I'm resigning."

Don erupted in laughter. "I know you're not serious now." The laughing stopped abruptly. "I don't have time, Joel. You need to hit the road, my brother," he said. Don must've thought Joel was getting some type of sick pleasure from tormenting him, which was far from the truth.

"I'm telling you this is no joke. Seriously, I'm stepping down. I've had enough. I'm tired and it's time to quit." He heard "quit" roll across his lips and wanted to leap forward to snatch the word back, but it was too late. It was gone, much like his reign as CEO. Joel hoped Don wasn't going to ask any questions. He wasn't going to share his personal, marital, and financial problems with his opponent. His mission was to get out of the condo. Leaving with a remnant of dignity would constitute a personal victory and keep the day from being a total disaster.

"You want me to believe that you're walking away?"

"Just like that," Joel said.

"Nope, not possible. Come in," Don said, taking a few steps from the doorway. Joel entered but stayed close to the door after it was shut. "You have fought me and my mother for three solid years, almost four, for control of DMI. What gives?" Don asked.

"Circumstances and situations have changed." The helplessness dominated him. He had to seek refuge. "The transition has to be effective today."

"Today's no good," Don told him, but Joel was firm.

"Today I'm offering you the top spot. I can't speak to how I'll feel about all of this tomorrow. If you want the position, you must move on it today. Do you want it or not?"

"Of course I do, don't you worry. I'll hammer out the details."

Worry was a close friend these days. "Hammer away," Joel said with grim humor. "So, that's it, done," Joel said, turning to leave.

"I have to ask: why are you doing this? It doesn't make sense. You love being CEO."

There was plenty to tell, to explain, to justify, none of which mattered. He opted not to publicize the source of his anguish and disappointment. "I have to leave." The space was confining and getting tighter.

"You know there will be changes," Don told him. Joel couldn't find the words to respond. He nodded in affirmation. "I can't keep the company you bought from your wife's father," Don told him. "Their principles, especially the religious ones, are in conflict with those at DMI."

"Sell it," Joel said, letting his gaze plummet to meet his dignity, which was squirming on the floor. "I can't tell you what to do with the company. You're in charge now. But I do have one request. I hope you can find a way to let my wife purchase Harmonious Energy. Like you said, it belonged to her father. It's his legacy, and now that he's gone, it should belong to their family."

"No problem, I'm certainly willing to work with her on a fair deal. On another note, what about the West Coast division? How can I reclaim ownership for DMI now that you've sold it?"

Joel's shame was mounting. "My wife owns it. I can convince her to sell it to you only if you cut her a fair deal on Harmonious Energy." It was difficult to keep standing there taking the onslaught of humiliating questions. He reached for the doorknob.

"I have to ask about the Southern division too."

"You'll have to speak with Uncle Frank about that one." Joel had to go now. Staying longer meant more humiliating questions intent on highlighting his failure. He turned the knob, lurching into the hallway.

Don called out to thank Joel, but he didn't respond. Joel kept hustling to the elevator or stairwell, whichever came first. The deed was done, and so was he.

chapter

1

The English light filtered into the cramped flat, distorted by the haze overshadowing the few windows located throughout the studio. Her last home, the one-bedroom flat in the South of France, had been more spacious but admitted no more light. The one before that had been in Spain, and the one before that in Scotland, and the one before that in Italy; each had been larger but similar. Filtered light had become Tamara's reality, darkness her faithful companion. Day and night, flooding her thoughts, her hopes, inescapable. She'd tried time after time to shake the past, set it aside, and start over, but the crippling trauma of her childhood in Detroit wasn't easily shaken. Fourteen years had passed, and the grip of despair was as strong today as it had been the day she ran away from home. She'd been mastering the art of running ever since.

Being alone with her thoughts was something Tamara vigorously avoided, but she hadn't figured out how to run from them too. The cell phone rang, jerking her consciousness back into the apartment. It rang and rang, yet she made no attempt to answer. There was a brief peaceful pause and then it started ringing again. The pattern continued for nearly five minutes until she grabbed the phone and belted out, "Why don't you stop calling?"

"Because we must talk," Remo responded in his Italian accent.

"There's nothing to talk about. How did you find me anyway?"

"You've never been lost to me."

Tamara had hoped she had eluded Remo with the move to the English countryside several months ago. The phone hadn't rung, with the exception of several calls from her brother Don. He was the only one she'd given the new number to, careful not to let it get in the hands of Remo. Somehow, yet again, he'd found her. Between Remo chasing her around the world and her mother relentlessly tracking her down, the strain of running had grown tiring. She shouldn't, wouldn't, or couldn't anymore. But her options were limited. "Remo, you have to let me go."

"That I cannot do. We belong together."

His accent had once been a soothing melody. That was four years ago. Now the sound of his voice served as a constant reminder of how vile men could be, demanding, defiant, disrespectful, living with no regard for the emotional damage they forced upon others in pursuit of what they wanted. "We've had this conversation, over and over. Nothing is going to change my mind. We're over, done, *finito.*"

"We're not over. We'll never be over, not as long as we're alive."

"What is that supposed to mean? Are you threatening me?"

"Of course not, why would I threaten my love, *mi amore*? I am only reminding you of the love that we share. It is worth protecting with my life."

"Remo, you can't keep doing this, hunting me around the world. You have to stop this. I won't let you do it anymore." Weariness was determined to speak up for her when she didn't have the strength. "I don't love you anymore."

"I can't accept that," he said, elevating his tone. "When I pledged my love to you it was on my life, and I will honor it until death." He spoke with a sharp edge of seriousness.

"You don't have a choice. I'm done. Let me go."

"Never. I will see you soon so that we can talk in person. I'll get you to change your mind. I'm sure of it." She disconnected the call, refusing to hear any more.

Tamara panicked. She didn't know what to expect from him. She recalled the time he'd climbed up the trellis and tried barging through the window of her third-floor unit in either Italy or Scotland. She couldn't remember exactly; forgetting unpleasant details was a critical item in her survival kit. Thank goodness it was the one day she had locked the window. She was certain that he was capable of doing anything to her with some twisted idea of protecting their shattered love affair. Second-guessing herself, she briefly considered packing up and heading out, not sure how far away Remo was.

Twenty minutes passed and a rap on the door sent Tamara into a fury. She was terrified. Calm down, she thought. Get it together. Get a plan quickly, think, think. The narrow window didn't offer an exit path. Besides, there was little probability that she'd survive the four-floor drop to the ground below. Another knock and she froze in her steps. She wasn't considering calling the police. That would put her in the metro police system and possibly make her whereabouts public. She couldn't take that chance. Tamara had sacrificed years of stability for anonymity, but the weight was heavy.

chapter 2

There was no more time for preparation. This was the defining moment. "Tamara, are you in there?"

"Don, what are you doing here?" he heard his sister shout in a tone that sounded like it had a glimmer of enthusiasm, or at least he hoped it did. She opened the door rather quickly. "Come on in," she said, guarded and seemingly a little nervous. Her reaction appeared normal to Don, given his impromptu visit. He knew how much she valued her privacy and was prepared for her discomfort. It was something he was willing to risk if the visit could foster reconciliation between his mother and Tamara.

"I'm not alone," he said, reaching for his mother. Madeline stepped into view.

Tamara stood still. Madeline did too. Fantasizing about their reunion didn't compare to watching it play out live.

Mother greeted Tamara, seeming standoffish for a person who hadn't seen her child in such a long time.

"Mother," Tamara responded.

Don didn't expect Tamara to welcome them. They had invaded her space without notice. He was glad she'd opened the door. Don recognized the strong possibility she might not have, especially if she'd known Mother was with him. Thank God for His many blessings, he thought. His mother and sister continued standing and staring at each other. Neither made an effort to talk or budge from her position of strength. The gulf between them remained.

"I knew you'd find me sooner or later."

"You did?" Mother said.

"Yes, I did."

"You haven't made it easy."

"Ditto," Tamara said.

"Did you want me to find you?"

Tough question. Don suspected it wasn't going to be easily answered by Tamara. Her feelings could range between an emphatic no and a gleeful yes.

"I bet everyone wants to have at least one person in the world who will never give up on them."

"My darling girl, I'll never give up on you," Madeline said, closing the gap between her and Tamara. "You are my only daughter, and I will always, always love you," she said, stepping even closer.

Mother grabbed Tamara and held her. Don squeezed past them, determined not to disrupt the reunion that had been fourteen years in the making. Don was content. He'd lit a spark. He expected the journey to total family restoration to be long and bumpy, with many sections unpaved, but the first step had been executed with perfection. The ladies were talking without fighting, which was a great sign. His abilities were limited. Keeping the flame of restoration burning was up to them. Don eased out the door to tell the cab driver to go on, since it looked like they would be visiting longer than planned.

He hustled back up the four flights of stairs to Tamara's flat. Her phone was ringing. Tamara and Mother were both sitting on the sofa sleeper.

"Nice place," Madeline said, glancing around the room. It was so small she didn't have to get up from her seat to take in the entire flat.

"Oh, come on, your master bedroom closet is larger than this condo," Tamara said. Don knew it was true but it didn't really matter.

"At least you still remember a few things about home."

"There's a lot I remember, and most I'd like to forget."

Don could feel the harmony evaporating. The mere mention of home had Tamara sounding irritated. "I'm so glad to have both of you together," he said, fanning the flame, unwilling to watch it burn out so quickly. Mother and Tamara were cordial. Both seemed to avoid personal topics, as if they were maneuvering through a minefield. Thirty minutes into the visit, they were still chitchatting, and Don was pleased.

The phone rang, interrupting the conversation for the second or third time. "Your phone has been ringing off the hook," Don said. "Go ahead and answer it. We don't mind."

Tamara cleared her throat. "I-it's okay, whoever it is will call back."

"They have been calling back, over and over," Madeline said.

"It's okay, really. I'm not bothered by the phone. I'm busy and that's that," she snapped.

Okay, Don thought. He'd leave the subject alone. Stirring up unnecessary unrest was to be avoided. The visit was going relatively smoothly, better than he expected—almost too well.

"How long are you planning to stay?" Tamara asked.

"Why? Are you ready for us to leave already?" Mother asked. Tamara didn't offer a response. "I guess that's our answer, Don."

"I didn't say anything," Tamara snapped again. "Don't put words in my mouth."

Mother's neck stiffened and her eyes widened.

Don could feel a storm brewing. He had to jump in to facilitate calm. "We did come unannounced. So, if you have other plans and need us to go, we understand."

"If we go, I'm hoping that you're coming with us," Mother said.

"Where?" Tamara asked.

"Home, of course, Detroit. Three tickets and we'll be home together, finally. I really am excited about us being together."

"I'm not coming back to Detroit," Tamara said, leaping to her feet. The phone rang again and she ignored it again.

Mother stood too. "Don told me you were ready to come home. That's why I'm here."

Don stepped between the ladies.

"Did Don tell you the terms that I want?" Tamara blurted. Madeline crossed her arms and reeled back on her four-inch-high stilettos. Don had hoped the conversation wasn't going to deteriorate so drastically. The first half hour had given him a false sense of security. "Don, didn't you tell her what we discussed?" Tamara yelled, becoming increasingly irritated.

"Yes."

"Then tell her nothing has changed."

Before Don could respond Madeline was talking. "You

don't have to pass a message through Don to me, at least not today. I'm standing right here. You can say whatever you need to say to me directly."

"Fine, I'm not coming back to Detroit or to DMI unless you leave," she said, standing firm.

"Why do you hate me so much?"

Tamara looked away briefly and then back at their mother. "Why do you always have to push and push? Why can't you just leave some things alone?"

"Maybe I could if I knew what you were talking about."

Don was totally dejected. The two rams were locked in a duel that neither could win or was willing to lose. It was brutal watching the two go at it. He wanted to stop the disagreement but knew there was little chance of his succeeding. They were both too pigheaded to back down. He could only watch from the corner.

"Let's not do this," Tamara said. "I'm not rehashing twenty years of family problems. I've spent the last fourteen years getting away from you and the nonsense, and I don't appreciate you popping into my place acting like we're one big happy family when you know good and well we are far from it."

"Maybe, but what have I done to you? What have I personally done to hurt you and cause you to be so bitter?" Madeline asked, pointing her finger into her own chest. Tamara's ringing phone was barely noticeable anymore. "I might not be perfect, but I won't apologize for loving my children and trying to protect each of you."

"Funny, look around, Mother; do I look protected?"

"This is your choice. I have an eight-bedroom mansion back in Detroit, but you prefer to live on the run in a place like this," Mother said, stretching her hands out and framing the small room.

"Now, that should tell you something. I'd rather live in this pit than stay in your big house. So, back to your original question, no, I'm not coming back to Detroit unless you're gone."

"Let's all calm down and take a breath," Don said. He'd heard plenty. Their conversation wasn't headed anywhere good. He had to intervene and restore what could be saved. "We can work this out. Maybe you can go on a long vacation while Tamara returns and gets acclimated. After a month or so of cruising down the Mediterranean, you can come home and we'll take it a day at a time."

"No way, Don, I've laid out my terms. All or nothing for me," Tamara said.

"Don, stop," Mother replied. "Don't beg Tamara to change her mind. It's not necessary. I've already decided to leave. So, you see," Madeline said, letting the palm of her hand brush over her hair and her gaze slip to the floor, "there's no more discussion needed. If you want to come home, then come. I won't be a problem. I'm out of there. Give me two days to get home, packed, and on my way."

Don was disappointed but had no energy left to intervene further. Some fires were so large they had to burn out on their own. The one raging between Mother and Tamara was one of those.

"Can you go now?"

"I'll go, but can you at least tell me why you're so angry with me, to the point of staying away for fourteen long, painful years? You've punished me and Don. All I'm asking is for an explanation. Why? Help me understand so that I can walk away with some peace."

"Mother, I don't know what peace looks like, feels like, or smells like," Tamara said, spitting the words like nails at their mother. "How can I give you something I've never had?" Then for a moment she seemed to be cracking. "You know what? The whole thing was a bad idea. Just forget about the whole thing. You stay in Detroit, Mother, and I'm going to stay here. I've survived this long, and I can go another fourteen years without your help. Now, can you just go, leave, please go?"

At first Madeline seemed like she wasn't budging, but Tamara was too riled up. She snatched her jacket and yanked the door open. Don didn't immediately decide whether to stay and comfort Tamara or run and console Madeline. His grand idea of uniting the two hadn't completely failed. At least his mother got a chance to see her daughter in person. That constituted a miracle and had to provide some sense of relief.

chapter

3

Tamara was relieved watching Madeline walk out. She had said what needed to be said.

"Come on, Tamara, why does it have to be all or nothing?" Don asked her. "Do you honestly need the whole state of Michigan cleared out to feel safe? Can't you let her stay in town while you're there too? We are talking about Detroit, a pretty big city, big enough to hold both of you comfortably."

"Don, I don't want to create confusion, but you're putting too much pressure on me. I didn't create our family problems. I'm just finding a way to survive with the situation that I was dealt. Is that so wrong?" she said, plopping onto the sofa. Don was her only ally. She felt awful putting him in the middle, but she couldn't let her allegiance to him compromise her judgment. Letting her guard down one time could be a fatal mistake with Madeline and Remo hanging around.

"I can't speak for you, but I'm tired," he said, appearing frustrated. "When will the fighting end? First it was Mother and Sherry over Dad. Then it was me and Joel over DMI. Now it's you and Mother, over what? I don't get it."

"I don't expect you to get it," Tamara belted out, unable to contain her agitation. She'd stayed out of everyone's way, removed herself from the drama. That wasn't good enough. They had to track her down in the English countryside and drop a guilt trip in her lap. She wasn't going to accept it. As imperfect as her life was, Tamara wanted to live it out on her terms.

Don came to the window and stood next to Tamara. They saw their mother pacing along the walkway in front of the building.

"So what's the deal? Are you putting an end to this distance and coming home with us?"

"Nope, can't do it," she said with her back against the wall, one knee bent and her foot on the wall behind her, her gaze locked on the walkway below. "I'm staying right here. Let Mother do whatever she wants to do, go wherever she wants to go, so long as she lets me do the same."

Don didn't answer. He schlepped to the door and turned toward Tamara. "I guess we'll see you next time."

She watched Don reach the steps out front and begin talking with Madeline. Tamara sobbed, wanting to reach out but unable to fully reconcile. Aches and unresolved emotions overcame her. The irksome sound of the ringing phone didn't draw her from the window.

Madeline watched Don come outside, appearing glum.

"Tamara won't change her mind. She's not coming back with us. Nothing I said made a difference," he said.

"Why is she so mad at me? If somebody could answer

my question, then maybe I could understand." Madeline could feel the mixture of hurt and anger stirring. She was not going to shed a tear. There was no need to apologize for being a mother. The label of "imperfect" she could accept. Being Tamara's enemy she could not. Madeline had spent years fighting her husband's illegitimate son and was worn out. She refused to fight her own child. "I'm ready to head back to the U.S. Let's go," she told Don.

"Are you sure?"

Madeline remembered each of Tamara's words. "Positive. Let's go."

"Let me run upstairs and tell Tamara that we're going." Madeline fluttered her hand in the air a few times, indicating that he should hurry. The sooner she could get out of London the better. She was grateful to have seen and touched her daughter. The other chaos wouldn't overshadow her dream come true. She leaned against the building, just to the left of the door, feeling empty. Her heart was in unit number twelve.

Tamara had finally moved away from the window. It was too hard. Watching Don and Madeline on the street below and being unable to reach out to them created an ache she couldn't soothe. Each time she considered going to them, images of the rape, her parents constantly bickering, and her marred childhood threw up a concrete roadblock on her path to restoration. She tried maneuvering to the left and right with no luck before finally giving up. The roadblock was too wide, too tall, the childhood trauma too deeply rooted for her to get past. A knock at the door caused Tamara to shriek. Fearing who it might be, she didn't respond.

"Tamara, open up. It's me, Don. I know you're in there."

Relieved that it was Don, she made her way to the door and opened it, a bit frazzled. She leaned the side of her face against the door. "I came to tell you that we're heading to the airport. Mother is ready to go home." Tamara continued letting the door support her weakened body. "I'm asking you again, will you consider coming with us? We'll find a way to make it work. I believe in prayer, and God can work this out."

"I've already had to deal with our mother. Please don't beat me over the head with God too. Both in the same day is too much for anyone, especially for me," she said, letting her hands slide down and grab the doorknob, one hand on each side.

"Can't blame me for trying."

"I don't," she said. Tamara wanted to tell him how glad she was to see him but expressing too much joy would have given the mistaken impression that the impromptu visit was welcome. Her world was small and controlled with no room for expansion.

Madeline popped up in the doorway, prompting Tamara to release the door and take a step back. Mother didn't come inside. Tamara didn't go out. Don stood near the door, in the middle.

"I came back to tell you that DMI belongs to the two of you. That's the way I want it and that's the way it is."

Tamara couldn't stand Madeline telling her what to do, still trying to control everything. Tamara wasn't a child depending on a distracted, bitter mother to protect her. Madeline hadn't done a good job eighteen years ago when it counted. Tamara didn't need her now and didn't care to hear her barking out orders. Perhaps Don could live with it but not Tamara. "I told you that I've changed my mind. I'm not sure if I want to go to Detroit, at least not now."

"Whether you accept it or not is up to you. Before I leave this place, I want you to know that I love you unconditionally. I've never stopped loving you. My heart breaks every day knowing you're out here in the world without a mother's love."

"I've done just fine without a mother."

Madeline's hurt showed. Tamara could have tempered her statement, she thought, but it was already out. The words were true—painful, but true.

"Regardless, I will always be your mother and I will love you and all my children until the day I die." Madeline shot her gaze toward Don. "I've said my piece. Let's go."

Don approached Tamara. She tensed. Affection remained a challenge. At times she'd experienced several breakthroughs with Remo but nothing consistent. She shut her eyelids tight and steeled herself for her brother's embrace, prepared for old wounds to be reopened. The sooner they left, the sooner she could return to her normal state of being.

chapter

4

They were gone and Tamara could breathe easy again. She'd reclaimed her space. The walls were no longer closing in. She heated a teakettle, replaying the words exchanged during the visit. Mixed emotions filled her. Madeline was her mother, an undeniable, piercing reality. She was born to love her, but that didn't mean she had to like her, not with her constant pushing and attempts to force Tamara to accept the Mitchell family on Madeline's terms. Mother made it hard to like her, but it didn't stop Tamara from loving her. Seeing Don was comforting—honestly, seeing her mother was too.

She poured the water into a cup, constantly replaying the words like a recording set on repeat. The anger had vanished and a pinch of loneliness was setting in. Having her family there wasn't so bad, she thought, taking a seat on the small sofa. The phone rang but she didn't answer, unwilling to release the warm feeling she was experiencing toward her family. It was rare, unexpected, but welcome. The euphoria forced her to rethink her decision about going home. The more she reflected, the less eager she was to push her mother away. She had to forget the whole idea. When Don first asked her to consider returning home, there was interest. Seeing how distraught her mother was changed her mind. She wasn't out to crush Madeline, not really, although there were times when the pain carved deep in the pit of her soul cried out to be shared with the perpetrator. Andre clearly was her rapist, but he hadn't been alone in crafting the destruction within her mother's mansion. There were many contributors who helped create the perfect environment for hell to dwell on earth.

The phone rang so much that it wasn't readily noticeable to her anymore. Whether it was Don, Madeline, or Remo didn't make a difference. Her brief slice of euphoria was certain not to last, but she'd cling to it for as long as possible by blocking out the sounds and smells around her. Tamara was simply trying to survive.

The phone wouldn't stop. Caving to reality, she snatched it up, consumed with frustration. "Remo, what do you want?"

He spoke in English mixed with Italian. His dialogue was as random and confusing as his actions. He spewed demand after demand at her. The frustration she felt at the beginning of the call quickly converted to tension.

"You can't walk away from me. We are for life. I won't let you go so easily with my heart." His ranting was fueled by escalating rage. She could feel the heat.

"I'm not going to let you control me anymore. I can't do it. We're done, Remo. You have to accept this. It's over for good," she said, mustering her courage but not sure how he'd accept her betrayal.

"We can't solve this on the telephone. I need to see your face when you tell me these things. The telephone won't work. I can jump on the rail and be in London by afternoon. I'll see you. *Ciao*," he said, and disconnected.

Tamara held the phone, unable to move, scared. She hadn't told him her new address. How did he know? she wondered. Probably the same way that Madeline had, by hiring a private investigator to keep track of her, selfishly violating her space. Her thoughts swirled out of order with no continuity. She jumped to her feet, realizing that getting out of the flat was critical. Remo was unpredictable and she couldn't take a chance on letting him catch her. She scurried around the tiny space desperate for a plan. Peering at her cell phone again, she realized she didn't have much choice. Maybe it was time to go home. Her brother had made the offer and she couldn't discount it this time, so long as her nonnegotiable term was honored. Her mother couldn't be anywhere near Detroit or the state of Michigan, just to be safe. Mother wasn't a physical threat like Remo, but her ability to orchestrate emotional despair was just as deadly to Tamara.

She fumbled through a small stack of papers on the two-seat table and stopped when she got to her checkbook. Seeing the equivalent of a $1,314 balance was sobering; she couldn't run too far with that amount. A plane ticket alone was around $600, which didn't leave enough for an apartment deposit and the first month's rent. Tamara plopped down on the sofa sleeper, fingering through her hair, searching for answers that weren't falling from the ceiling, no matter how she stared. There was only one option. As much as she hated the notion of going home to Detroit under duress and to her dysfunctional family, it didn't compare to the trauma that could come from

Remo running around somewhere out there ready to do her harm.

Tamara removed her luggage from the wardrobe. She checked the time, careful not to let two hours catch her in the flat. Remo was definitely on his way, taking every possible shortcut to get to her. If he was going to be there in a few hours, she had to be out in one. Twenty minutes had already evaporated while she was calculating the remaining dollars in her skimpy account. Although she desperately needed help, Tamara was not going to let Madeline or Don know the full extent of her troubles.

She scrambled to get packed, constantly peering out the window and keeping a tight grip on every second. Clothes were scarce. Carrying excess from town to town had grown exhausting, and each move shaved away some of her belongings. Upon leaving France, she'd opted to bring only the two pieces of free checked luggage allowed on her flight to London. After ten or eleven moves, Tamara was sure she was at the core of her existence and had only items of value remaining. She looked around the room, a stark contrast from the plush accommodations that enveloped her childhood. Tamara stuffed the suitcase, not quite able to get in all five pairs of pants, eight shirts, her jacket, and her underclothes. She'd take along only one of the larger suitcases, plus the smaller knapsack as a carry-on. The other suitcase, along with a few shirts, would have to be sacrificed and stay behind. What else? she thought, looking around, combing the room while simultaneously keeping track of the time. Forty-five minutes gone. Her nerves were flaring up. Remo couldn't be taken lightly. She had to hurry. Suitcase zipped, knapsack latched and tucked under her arm, she was ready. Tamara opened the door and began pulling it shut. *Wait.* She rushed back in and snatched open the wardrobe, dropping the knapsack. She didn't have her passport.

Tamara rustled through the papers and trinkets left behind. She got to a huge clasped envelope and breathed a sigh of relief, drawing in a long stretch of air and slowly releasing it. She pressed the envelope to her chest. This represented the grand sum of her independence—passport, birth certificate, a copy of the first check she'd received for one of her paintings, and her Swiss bank account details. She extracted the papers partially, checking to make sure none were missing. Focused on her travel documents, her key to freedom, Tamara was unprepared for the photo at the bottom of the stack. She looked away, letting her bottom plop down to the floor. There was the family photo taken at Disney World with Dave, Madeline, Tamara, and her three brothers, Sam, Andre, and Don, right before her father left them. She held it, peering at the strangers on the paper. She was five years old when it was taken. The memory was raw, like it was yesterday. The time represented one of the rare moments when she recalled being happy, safe, and normal. The rest was a blur. Tamara shoved the papers and photo into the envelope. Fifty-five minutes gone. Time had run out. She dashed out of the flat with her suitcase and knapsack. Move number twelve was under way. She'd feel more secure when the plane was taxiing down the runway and there was no sign of Remo on board.

chapter
5

Reconciling was a priority, but the cab ride was sobering for Don. There had to be a reasonable solution to this fresh family catastrophe. Don wasn't delusional about the monumental task he was undertaking, trying to restore a family that had endured nonstop destruction. If he allowed himself to fully grasp the magnitude of this undertaking, he would have given up right there, but hope catapulted him forward. If God could miraculously put DMI into his hands, a seemingly impossible feat, then certainly He could reconcile a mother and daughter. The fight they'd just had didn't shout reconciliation, but Don refused to give up.

This was supposed to be the beginning of a new era for the Mitchell family, which had imploded over the past forty years. Gobs of forgiveness and grace laced with time would be the building blocks necessary for their healing. He'd already taken the first step. Less than forty-eight hours ago he'd asked his stepmother, the woman who made his childhood miserable, to stay on board at DMI. Nobody could have predicted these events, that Joel would resign or that Don would reach out to Sherry. He didn't want her to leave. Don hadn't told Madeline yet, but it was time for healing all around.

Don wasn't able to gauge his mother's feelings. She gazed out the window as the cab rolled along the country-side on its way to the airport.

"She's too thin. You see how thin she is?" Mother said, and mumbled a few more incoherent statements.

Don would keep her as calm as possible. "I noticed, Mother, but I'm sure she's not sick."

"Life is funny," she said, continuing to stare out the window. "I got what I wanted but not the way I wanted. I never expected that you and Tamara would be in Detroit, working at DMI without me. We were this close," she said, pinching her thumb and index finger together, "yet this far away," she added, spreading her arms. "I can't do this again, get my hopes up only to have them crushed time after time."

Don realized sacrifices had to be made to get to the good part, but if he could spare Madeline any extra hurt today, he would. She'd suffered loss upon loss, starting with his father's affair with Sherry. The tragic death of Madeline's two sons followed, planting roots of bitterness deeper than his love could reach. She deserved a break.

"Mother, before we came to London, you were pack-ing up and planning to leave Detroit and DMI." Madeline nodded in confirmation. She didn't speak but he wasn't surprised to see her dab the wet corners of her eyes. "I don't see any reason for you to leave, not now."

"Why not?" She spoke barely above a whisper, continu-ing to pat the corners of her eyes with a tissue.

"The only reason you were going was to make Tamara happy. She's the one who wanted you to go, so she could come home without any conflict. Personally, I don't think you have to completely leave the state to give her space. Detroit and DMI are the two constants in your life. Honestly, neither would be the same without you."

Madeline laughed. "You're a good son," she said with a tempered grin. "But there comes a time when you have to recognize that it's time to leave the dance. This is my time."

"No it's not. Tamara has changed her mind. She doesn't want to come home, and if Tamara isn't coming back, you don't have to leave. Plus, remember, the main reason I asked her to come back was to join forces with us, combine our stock, and vote out Joel. Now we don't need her stock. God has given us the company without it."

"I've been known to pull a few underhanded moves on Joel and that mother of his, but I've never backstabbed my children. I won't start now."

"Mother, you're not backstabbing Tamara. She changed her mind. You heard her say that she's not coming home, and if she's not, you don't have to leave Detroit."

"All right, all right, how many times are you going to repeat that?"

"As many as it takes to get you to change your mind."

"All right, I'll think about it. I mean, I guess you do have a point. If she's not coming home, that does change the situation." Don watched as his mother pondered his request. "I guess you could use my help fixing the mess your father's baby boy has made. You'll need all the help you can get."

"Is that a yes?"

"I guess so," she said.

Don rushed in with a hug. Whatever joy his mother could muster was well earned. "Cool. Once we get to the airport, I'm taking a flight to Cape Town, just to check in with my business." His phone rang. "I'll plan to see you in Detroit by early next week." Don excused himself and answered the call. It was Tamara. "Hello, Sis. I was planning to call you once we got settled in at the airport, but you beat me to it. Are you feeling any better since we left?"

"Depends on who you ask. I've changed my mind again. I am taking up Mother's offer." Don didn't respond, avoiding eye contact with his mother, intentionally shifting his gaze out the window and across the field. "Can you hear me?" Tamara asked, probably because he was quiet.

"I heard you. You've changed your mind," he said, keeping his gaze away from Madeline. He couldn't bear to look at her.

"You don't seem too excited. Is the offer still on the table?" Tamara asked.

Don finally had to face his mother before answering. "I'm sure the offer is still on the table." Madeline's head bobbed up and down in confirmation.

"Great, because I need to come back. But there is one problem. I haven't been able to find my credit card since I moved in. Could you loan me the money for a ticket until I can get funds moved around in my accounts?"

A ticket was going to be less than a thousand dollars. Don was surprised Tamara needed help with such a small amount of money but didn't see it as a problem.

"I'll make sure you get a ticket," Don said. Madeline heard him and perked up. "Do I need to get you some cash too?" he asked.

Mother got the gist of the conversation and grabbed the phone. "Tamara, there will be a first-class ticket waiting for you at Heathrow Airport. I'll pay full fare on the next available British Airways flight with no restrictions. You can change the time or date to whatever you want. Just know that the ticket is waiting for you, and if you give me your account number, I'll have fifty thousand dollars wired, no questions asked. If you need more, let me know. It's no problem."

"The ticket is all I need. It's just a loan until I get my funds rearranged. Since it's after hours, I can't get much done until after the weekend, but don't worry. I'll give you your money back."

"Don't worry about the ticket. No matter where I am and no matter what's going on between us, I'm still your mother. If you ever need me for anything, I will be there, no strings attached. You remember that. I love you," Madeline said, and quickly handed Don the phone without allowing Tamara time to respond.

When Don took the call, he heard nothing. Tamara hadn't responded. He didn't expect her to tell their mother she appreciated her but a kind word or gesture would have been refreshing. None came. Don realized the amount of work that had to be done between them. Madeline appeared willing but Tamara was not. He ended the call and faced his mother.

"It's not too late for us, Mother. Give Tamara a week or two and I'll talk to her again. She might listen."

"No, no," she said, raising her voice slightly but tapping Don's hand simultaneously. He figured it was her way of letting him know it was okay. "I gave her my word, and I will keep it, even if the commitment literally kills me. She deserves this, and if it's in my power to give her a small slice of happiness, then it's done."

Don didn't respond. He read the resolve in her response

and knew that no exceptions would be considered. Her decision was final.

Madeline braced herself. The remaining cab ride to the airport was going to be filled with mixed emotions. She was boiling over with satisfaction at having both of her children finally heading to Detroit to run their father's company. It was why she'd fought so vehemently against Joel and Sherry, year after year, to reclaim their rightful inheritance. Heaviness lay on her shoulders. Never had she dreamed that the cost would be so high—that she'd be barred from witnessing the happy reunion. Disappointment had become her soul mate. God had finally given her a taste of redemption and victory over her adversaries, her husband's other family. Yet the celebration wasn't long-lived. Hers never were.

chapter

6

Don was drained. He was accustomed to Madeline and Joel constantly fighting over this and that, but the dueling between the two had taken its toll. Watching the reunion between his mother and Tamara disintegrate was too much. He craved a mini-retreat, some time out of the line of fire. South Africa, his home for the past three and a half years, was the perfect spot. Don let his head lean back against the seat of the cab and shut his eyelids, just for a brief time. Madeline was uncharacteristically quiet, too quiet. "Mother, Tamara was overwhelmed by our surprise visit. This whole thing is my fault."

"No, it's not. I don't blame you, not one bit."

Witnessing the distraught look on Tamara's face and the hurt feelings that his mother was experiencing didn't make him feel good about the impulsive decision. "What can I do to help you?" Don said just as his phone vibrated on the seat. He glanced at the number on his PDA, expecting it to be Tamara. Instead it was from LTI, his office in

South Africa. Don ignored it, wanting to give Madeline his undivided attention. It continued ringing.

"Answer it, that's what you can do for me." Don was about to push the off button when Madeline grabbed his hand. "Answer your phone; please do that for me."

Reluctantly he answered and heard Naledi on the line. She was the encouragement he needed. Her perfect blend of Indian, French, English, and South African speech never grew old. "Naledi, it's good to hear from you." Madeline turned away from Don and peered out the window. He attempted to keep her in his line of sight while concentrating on the conversation with Naledi. Managing LTI and DMI business spread across two continents required many adjustments, sacrifices, and a mound of help. Naledi was a godsend at LTI.

"Don, some of our clients from Nigeria will be here tomorrow, and they would like to meet with you. Is it possible?"

"I wasn't planning to be there tomorrow," he said, gazing at the back of his mother's head. "I'm heading to Detroit first and then home to Cape Town in a few days."

Madeline turned toward him. "Go," she whispered. "Go," she said again, flicking her hand toward Don repeatedly.

He muffled the mouthpiece on the phone. "I'm not letting you go to Detroit alone, not after what happened with you and Tamara."

"And I don't want a babysitter," she yelled at him.

"Okay, if that's how you want it. I won't push. The last thing I want to do is upset you more than you already are," he said, covering the phone more tightly, not wanting Naledi to hear. He had to live with the Mitchell drama daily but didn't want Naledi subjected to the darker side of his world. "Looks like I am coming to Cape Town. I'll see you tomorrow."

"Wonderful, I look forward to seeing you," she said, her voice softening with each word. He melted. "I'll text you my travel details after I get to the airport. Cheers," he said, and ended the call. He shifted his attention back to Madeline, who had eased back in the seat and appeared to have lowered her protective shield.

"Don, I apologize for yelling at you. I'm on edge but I can't take this out on you. Please forgive me," she said, locking her gaze on him. "This is your time."

Three years had skated by and now look where he was: assuming the CEO position at a bankrupt company. Despair wanted to lay claim to his victory, reminding him of how poorly Joel had managed the company and what an awful state it was in. Why couldn't he have received it in the same condition in which Joel had received it from their father? But Don couldn't let old resentment toward his brother, their father's favorite, slither in. He refused to let his victory be overtaken by vengeance.

"Apology accepted. Now, let's get down to business. I need you in Cape Town with me. Besides, you can't find a more peaceful place on earth to regroup." It had worked for him nearly four years ago and it would serve as a good retreat for her too. "I promise."

She slowly shook her head.

"Seriously, I could really use your help with LTI. I have a boatload of projects going on there, and Naledi has been an angel with holding it down. But she could use the help, especially now that I'm going to be spending so much time in Detroit pulling DMI together. Don't misunderstand, I'm not complaining, but it's going to be a bear over the next six months. Joel left the company in shambles and it won't get fixed overnight, not without a miracle, and not without you."

"Don, stop right there." She shifted her body in the seat and completely faced him. "It's easy to see what you're trying to do. I appreciate you trying to find a place for me since Tamara has kicked me out of DMI." Don didn't interrupt. He didn't have the solution for comforting his mother. Nothing he'd said or offered so far had worked. "I'm doing exactly like I planned before our little rendezvous in England. I'm packing up and heading out of town and that's final."

"But—" was all Don could get out before Madeline interrupted.

"That's all there is to it. Nothing in this world is more important than you and Tamara are to me." She sat tall in the seat, smoothing the side of her hair as the tone of her voice grew firmer.

Don wasn't going to argue with her. He took comfort in seeing her regaining strength. She was human and subject to hurt and rejection like anyone, but admittedly, the sight of the fearless Madeline showing vulnerability wasn't something he hoped to ever witness again. Her relentless pursuit of her dreams had primed him to be the man he was today; his father had been less of an influence. Madeline was the one who'd poured love and support into his life from childhood, never wavering, always the perfect mother to him, despite her countless flaws. In her time of need he was determined to show her the same level of support and unconditional love. She deserved it. Maybe Tamara didn't see it, but he did. "Well, my offer stands. As much as Tamara wants you out of Detroit, I need you to work for me. I could honestly use your marketing expertise. Nobody can run an operation like you."

"True," she said, continuing to brush back her hair as a grin began to manifest, one she couldn't hold back.

The sign of joy creeping into her heart was sufficient for him. The cab pulled into London's Heathrow Airport. He chuckled. "If you change your mind, which I hope you do, the offer is open. Whenever you want to start, whatever you want to do at LTI is fine with me." He gave Madeline a hug and got out at South African Airways.

chapter

7

Tamara squirmed in her aisle seat. Comfort wasn't the problem. Madeline had taken care of that detail with the first-class ticket. So many images, conversations, and feelings pounced on her.

"Ladies and gentlemen, those of you on the right side of the plane can catch a glimpse of the Mackinac Bridge, one of the longest suspension bridges in the world. Enjoy the rest of the flight and we'll have you on the ground in thirty minutes," the voice blared over the intercom system.

Thirty minutes wasn't nearly enough time to get ready for Detroit. She'd been there several months ago as a favor to Don. She'd come to town, briefly, with the intent of signing her stock ownership over to Don, which was a bust. She was uneasy during that trip. At least she had a return ticket then. This was a one-way fare. Her palms sweated as thirty minutes clicked down to twenty, fifteen.

"Flight attendants, please prepare the cabin for arrival," the captain announced.

Ten minutes, five. Tamara braced for the impact. The landing was bumpy but not as bad as she expected. In a few minutes the door would open and she'd have to get off. The load of passengers exited the plane person by person until the cabin was empty. Tamara didn't budge. Finally the flight attendant came to her seat. "Ma'am, is everything all right?" Tamara gave her the okay sign. "Do you need help getting off the plane?" She needed help with more than getting off the plane.

"No, I'm okay," she said finally, sliding to the edge of the seat and collecting her items. Once in the Jetway, she didn't move along any faster. After clearing customs, she exchanged her British pounds for American currency. Tamara grabbed a chair away from the foot traffic. Hiding wasn't the long-term solution but it would allow her time to prepare.

Hours came and went. The baggage area filled and emptied several times. Tamara decided she was ready to venture on. The sinking feeling of being alone plagued her. There weren't family members waiting on the other side of the arrival ropes. The reality sank in. Returning alone was her choice, but it didn't make the loneliness feel better. Tamara reached into her pocket for her phone. At least there was Don. She could call him. A few taps on speed dial and Don was on the line.

"Where are you, Sis?" Don asked.

"Detroit."

"You're kidding. Wow, you were serious. I had no idea you were getting to Detroit so soon," he said.

She'd had to get out of London fast. Her life depended on rushing from the flat to safety. There was no desire to tell Don the details behind her abrupt change in plans. Remo had to remain a secret.

"Had I known, I would have met you there. But now I'm on my way to Cape Town. You just happened to catch me on my layover."

"It's not a problem," she said.

"Yes, but I would love to have been there to welcome you home. Unfortunately, once I get to Cape Town, I'll need to stay there several days before I can get back to Detroit. Realistically, we're looking at early next week before I'll see you."

"There's no hurry. Take your time. I'll be fine until you get here."

The words flowed, representing filtered truth. Don was the only person she trusted, as much as she could trust anyone. There was uneasiness she couldn't digest. Tamara had literally traveled the world, lived in many countries, tiny towns, and villages. She'd spent most of the past two decades isolated from family, avoiding friendships, and tackling life independently. Remo had been the only relationship she'd allowed, and that hadn't worked out so well. She ended the call and would toss the phone into the first trash can she saw. There was no one else she wanted or needed to talk with.

Tamara pulled her small suitcase behind her and walked through the airport. Being in Detroit, her birthplace, was more awkward than being in the rural village she visited in Uganda. Her heart was cold to the place; she felt no connection. Finally, after what seemed like an endless walk, she was outside, standing on the sidewalk, with no more distance to go.

"Are you in line?" a young man asked.

"Oh, no, no, I'm not," she said, not sure what to do. The few hundred British pounds she'd gotten from the money machine in London converted to almost four hundred dollars. She contemplated where to go. Don wasn't return-ing for at least four or five days, forcing her to find a hotel. There was another nine hundred dollars or so in her ac-count but that was purely for an emergency. Some kids grew up having to keep enough coins to make a phone call. Their parents insisted. She'd evolved to the point of having to keep enough to hop a flight. First-class was nice, but economy had become the new standard as her funds dwindled.

"Excuse me, are you in line?" someone else asked. She stepped away from the taxi stand after a third person asked if she was in line.

Tamara had to think. Transportation, a hotel, and food for at least a week were going to cut deeply into the four hundred dollars. She contemplated using the fifty thou-sand dollars Madeline had offered and quickly discounted the notion. She wasn't looking for a handout. The airline ticket was great, but Tamara wasn't about to trade one prison with Remo for another. She was never going to be indebted to Madeline. A long-term lease at a no-name motel, a can of beans, and a bus pass would come first.

She stood out of the way as people moved briskly up and down the sidewalk. They had purposes, places to go, and reasons for being there. Jealousy whisked in, followed by a flood of memories, causing her to rethink her deci-sion. Perhaps coming to the States wasn't her best idea. It wasn't too late to ditch the plan and run away. She could turn right around and get a flight to London, or maybe Brazil. She always wanted to spend more time in South America after taking a trip there a few years ago. Tamara stood still and let the tiny meltdown fade without over-reacting. Rational thinking took over. There was no way she could go back to London with Remo on the loose. He didn't know all the details about her tragic past, and what Remo did know wouldn't steer him toward Detroit. That's the last spot on earth he'd look for her, because no one expected her to go home, not even Tamara. Best to stay put. Detroit was the safest place right now, especially with her mother out of the way.

She moved to the taxi line. When her turn came she was ready. "Downtown, please."

"Where?"

Downtown was good enough for now. She'd select a hotel after they arrived. The Ritz-Carlton wasn't an option. Motel 6 wasn't either, not yet. That would come next week. Something in the middle would work until she figured out a better plan. "You can drop me off at Cobo Hall or the Renaissance Center, whichever ride is cheaper." It didn't matter where she landed; she'd be walking the rest of the way.

Joel sat in his office, reliving the whirlwind events. Over and over he tried sorting the pieces with no success. Three years of busting his behind to build DMI, and in one weak moment, it was gone. Poof. Gone. The loss was numbing but the strike against his intelligence was brutal—crippling and difficult to discount. Looking back, he could see the company was going through a slump. Sales and morale were down, but he was a winner. The same tenacity he'd used to triple the value of the company in three years could have served him in restoring DMI to its rightful place on the leaders' board. He was angry at himself for giving up so easily and handing DMI over to his half brother and to his nemesis, Madeline, the most horrifying stepmother on the face of the earth. Yet, in all of her attempts to destroy him, his credibility, and his success, she had failed repeatedly. It wasn't Madeline who made him a quitter. He held that title exclusively. No sane person would have willfully handed over the CEO position of a multibillion-dollar company.

The reality of his decision continued digging into his consciousness, eager to wreak ongoing havoc.

Joel flipped a handful of paper clips around, intrigued by them for no reason. Attempting to clear his thoughts wasn't working. He needed a much more significant distraction. Sheba was the first image that came to mind, his muse. The few hundred miles to Chicago were nothing; they hadn't been in the past. She was the one constant source of relief that he'd relied on from the moment they met three and a half years ago. Her magnetism had captivated him then, and the allure of her presence still raised his heart rate. There wasn't a particular aspect of her personality that explained the attraction. It just was. What the heck. He picked up the phone, holding it for some time without dialing, until the beeping became annoying. Zarah poked her head into the doorway of his office.

"I've been looking for you," his wife said, still frail.

He hadn't quite determined if her recent episode was truly a suicide attempt or purely a loss of will to live. Maybe they seemed the same to most, but to Joel, suicide was actively taking control of death, while losing will was equivalent to quitting. He had a preference, and quitting wasn't it. Regardless, Zarah had a ways to go before fully recovering. He returned the phone to its cradle. Sheba couldn't be in the picture. He had to give Zarah the full attention she needed. Their marriage was initially a business arrangement between him and her father in an attempt to combine their two companies, yielding a large international conglomerate. She came with the deal. At the time, Joel was comfortable with the agreement. Now that he had a wife who didn't have much of a personal life outside of their relationship, he felt the sheer weight of his decision. On paper it made sense. In his house, it was bitter, but he had to find a way to make it sweeter if there was any hope of her surviving. Truth be told, he wanted out, but Zarah had nowhere to go. Her family was a thousand miles away in India. Joel got up from the desk and went to her. She tensed.

"It's okay, just relax."

The irony sank in for him. Here was a woman who spent every second she was awake struggling to win his affection. To have him cast an endearing glance her way. To bear his children. Yet, as he pulled her close, Zarah wasn't receptive. Joel didn't give in. He knew she was frightened and fragile. He would go slowly with her. Perhaps there was a remote chance of salvaging the makeshift marriage. Zarah was his wife and for the second or third time in their marriage, he was interested in intimacy. Taking her hand, he led Zarah from his office in the back of the house, down the hallway, and up the grand staircase to the master bedroom. Each step he could feel her hand relax into his. By the time they'd reached the bedroom threshold, she was firmly gripping his hand and pulling closer. Joel shut the door, turned out the lights, and let the natural flow of their union lead without resistance. He didn't know what tomorrow was going to hold. He didn't know what Sheba was doing. All he knew was that Zarah was his source of comfort tonight.

chapter

9

Sherry was up and about early, which was easy to do given her constant worrying about her son Joel's predicament. Her nights weren't completely sleepless, but to say she was well rested would be a lie. After Joel abruptly stepped down from running DMI, Sherry had decided to leave too. There wasn't a compelling reason to stay. She had been willing to endure the years of torture at the hands of Madeline, her deceased husband's first wife, for the sake of Joel. The years had passed and the ribbing mellowed, or at least the layer of tolerance she developed softened the jabs. At times she felt like a gazelle darting from the clutches of Madeline. Oddly, Sherry respected Madeline's fearless commitment to protecting her children. Too bad Sherry and Joel had to be the primary targets of her relentless attacks.

As of a few days ago, the battle between her husband's two families was over. Unfortunately her son was on the losing end and perhaps wouldn't recover. Sherry pulled onto the grounds of Joel's estate, not stopping until she was parked in front of his house's double doors. She glanced into the mirror on the visor. Vanity wasn't important but the distraction did allow her a few more seconds before she had to enter the house. She slowly opened the car door, preparing for the fallout from the recent family upheaval.

Sherry knocked, simultaneously anxious to get inside to check on her family while dreading the despair that awaited her there. Her dilemma was cut short when the housekeeper answered the door.

"Good morning, Mrs. Mitchell. Please come in," she said, stepping aside.

Sherry entered with heart racing. "I know it's early but I was up and about and figured I'd stop by for a visit." Anxiety dominated Sherry, causing her to fidget.

"Mr. Mitchell isn't up yet."

"I'm up," Joel said, descending the stairs in a pair of silk pajamas covered with a matching robe. The housekeeper left them alone. "What are you doing out so early?" he asked his mother as he reached the bottom of the stairs and gave her a peck on the cheek.

She couldn't tell him the extent of her concern. He had enough of his own problems. She wasn't going to be another addition to his list. Besides, she was the mother. He needed her to help fix what was broken in the family, for a change, and Sherry intended to deliver. She rested the palm of her hand on his cheek. "How are you doing?"

"I'm cool."

"No, really, how are you?" she asked as Joel linked arms with her and gingerly stepped to the kitchen.

"Let me get you some breakfast," he said without answering her question.

Normally she would have left the discussion alone, sensing he didn't want to talk about it, but not this time. Joel and Zarah were in a crisis and she wasn't going to let the topic drop. She would push as she'd seen Madeline do so many times to get the results she wanted. Perhaps that's what Sherry had to do to save her family. Whatever was required, she was going to do it.

"Joel," she said, taking a seat at the counter. "I'm not worried about eating. I'm worried about you. This can't be an easy time, walking away from DMI. I know how much the CEO position means to you."

"I did what had to be done. With Zarah falling apart and nearly dying," he said, almost whispering, "I had no choice."

"I understand you want to nurse your wife back to health, but I worry about how you're going about it."

Joel pulled a pitcher of fresh-squeezed juice from the fridge, gathering and filtering his thoughts before responding. His mother couldn't know the depths of his failure. "Mom, you don't need to worry about me," he said, pouring the juice without making eye contact. He didn't want to take the chance of her seeing through his concocted answer. "I'm a big boy. I will recover from this fiasco and get back on track. Trust me," he said, resting his hand on hers, "me and Zarah will be just fine. Don't you worry."

He lifted her chin and looked her in the eye this time. He had to be convincing, otherwise she wouldn't let the issue go. Piecing together the fragments of his humiliated existence wasn't her job, and it definitely was not her burden to bear. It was his exclusively. Besides, there wasn't much she could do. She couldn't barge into DMI and reclaim the top spot for him. Madeline would eat her alive. Mom couldn't regain the Southern division from Uncle Frank's silent partners.

"It's my job to worry. You are all I have left, you and Zarah." Tears swelled in her eyes, weakening Joel's stoic disposition. He couldn't cave in front of her, but watching his mother cry was tough.

"Mom," he said, taking a seat on one of the bar stools next to her and draping one arm over her shoulder. "I have this in check. I have a few ideas brewing on another business opportunity," he told her, which wasn't true, but it was what she needed to hear. "Once I get Zarah settled down, I'll put some things in motion. You'll see. This kid is not out of the game. I had a rough run these past couple of quarters with DMI, but I'm as sharp as I was three and a half years ago when we put DMI in the spotlight. I did it once and I can do it again." That part he believed.

Sherry sighed. He took that to mean her fears were subsiding. So he continued painting a positive outcome. "You know Zarah owns the West Coast division of DMI. There is a real possibility that I can take that seed and build it into a viable business."

Joel could feel his mother's hand tense underneath his. "I thought you were expecting Don and Madeline to reclaim that division and fold it back into DMI. If you keep it, won't that cause a problem between us and them?"

Eager to maintain the ground that he'd gained with his mother, Joel quickly retracted the statement. "You're right, I'm not trying to re-ignite a war." He felt her hand relax. "Who knows, I'm just tossing ideas around to let you know that I have plenty of options. So you don't have to worry about me."

"What about money? You've spent almost everything

you have, between purchasing Harmonious Energy from Zarah's father and pouring cash into DMI for the past two or three months, trying to save it. You can't have much left."

That was an understatement. If it wasn't for Zarah's modest two million that came from her father's estate several months ago, he'd be broke. "I'll be okay," he said.

Mom turned to him. "If you need money, mine is yours."

"No way."

"Really, I want you to have my money. I checked with my accountant. I have sixty-seven million dollars in liquid funds, another hundred and fifty-three million in investments and other assets. It's yours, all of it, except my DMI stock. I have to keep that. You understand."

"No, I'm not taking your money."

"Take it. Besides, I don't need much. I have the estate and, if necessary, I can sell it and move into a smaller condo somewhere."

"No way, I'm not letting you sell our family home or your investments. That's crazy. I'm not that desperate." Actually he was, but she couldn't know. There was a limit to how far he'd go to rebuild. Selling his childhood home or taking his mother's security wasn't a remote consideration. He'd dig a way out of his pit of failure but not on his mother's back. Not an option. "Enough about me. Now that you've resigned from DMI, what are you planning to do with your time?" he asked.

"Don't know, maybe I'll become a true lady of leisure," she said, letting a glimmer of humor poke through the depressing façade. Joel's heart warmed. "Oh," she said, becoming chipper, "I almost forgot to tell you. When I went into the office to turn in my resignation, Don was very kind to me." Joel was confused and his expression must have shown it, because Mom went on with an explanation. "I was shocked too. He asked me to stay on board."

"Really? Why?"

"I guess he truly wants to end the feud between Madeline's family and mine. It was shocking but I sensed that he was sincere."

"Well, stranger things have happened. To think that Madeline wants you to stay on board is crazy after all she's put us through."

"Wait, I didn't say Madeline wanted me there. I said Don."

"Oh, no wonder, now, that makes more sense. I bet Don didn't get permission," Joel said, erupting in laughter.

"He told me not to worry about Madeline. He said he would handle her, and I actually believe him."

"Sounds like you're considering his offer."

"Absolutely not. I couldn't stay at DMI while you're out of the company. I wouldn't betray you like that."

Joel was out but not necessarily permanently. He didn't have a detailed plan, but DMI was like a drug. A few days of withdrawal and the pull to get back in there was intensifying daily. Sherry didn't have to know his intentions; no one did. But having her at DMI, on the inside keeping watch, was an opportunity worth considering. "I think you should take Don up on his offer."

"Absolutely not," she said, letting her hand flail in the air. "I'm not staying on without you."

"Mom, you have worked hard and established yourself as a serious publicity manager. Don't walk away from your accomplishment because of some loyalty to me." He rested his hand on her shoulder. "You're my mother and your loyalty is without question." Her gaze dipped but he lifted her chin. "If you really want to make me happy, then you be happy," he told her.

"I'm trying."

"I have only one question, Mom: do you enjoy your job?"

"Yes, actually I do. I'm pretty good at it," she said with glee in her tone.

"Then that settles it. Tell Don you accept his offer and go to work. Don't worry about me. I'll be just fine. If you're happy, I'm happy."

Joel appreciated his mom. He wanted her at DMI, not just for selfish reasons, but mainly because she deserved to be there. She was the wife of Dave Mitchell, founder of DMI. She had as much right to stay on board as Madeline, the woman who had stayed years after she divorced his dad.

"Zarah, I didn't realize you were up," Sherry said as her daughter-in-law entered the kitchen. They exchanged greetings. Joel went to get more juice from the fridge. "How are you feeling, my dear?" Sherry beckoned for Zarah to come and sit next to her.

"I'm feeling stronger."

"Please let me know if there's anything I can do to help."

Joel saw Zarah ease her gaze toward him. "My husband is taking very good care of me."

"Good, good," Sherry said.

Joel knew Zarah was referring to their time together last night. It was satisfying but not expected to be a regular occurrence. His job was to nurse her back to health, not to build false expectations for long-term fulfillment, especially since he couldn't predict the future. Supporting Zarah as she rejuvenated from her frail condition was the extent of his marital commitment. Anything beyond that was purely speculation.

chapter

10

Madeline eased the convertible Bentley through the twelve-foot-high iron security gates and ignored the ringing phone. She stopped the car right before entering the street. Memories rushed in like a flash flood, rapid and overwhelming. She swallowed the taste of sorrow, blinked away the tears, and breathed a deep sigh, releasing the air slowly. She pushed the gas pedal without looking back at the mansion that had been her home for twenty-seven years, ever since the divorce was final. One day, when the time was right, she would return.

Madeline crept down the road with the midday sun piercing the windshield. Had she been completely present during the ride, the bright light would have been irritating. Numb, Madeline didn't notice the inconvenience. Memories darting in and out had a lock on her attention. A horn every few blocks was the gentle nudge she needed to keep the car on the road. The ride to the DMI office normally took thirty-five minutes, but today it took her an hour and a half. She wasn't bothered by the delay. There was no urgency in getting on her way to nowhere. Madeline let the car crawl into the executive parking lot. She rolled past Joel's empty spot and smirked. At least her fight hadn't been fruitless. She pulled into her space and killed the engine. Her neck rested against the seat and she allowed the sunlight to spread across her face, eyelids closed. The memories had slowed from a surging flood to a light, manageable series of showers. The phone beeped again. There were only two people on earth she was interested in talking to. Tamara definitely wasn't calling. It had to be Don. The phone stopped beeping for a moment and then started again. He meant well. She'd ignored his calls all morning but had to answer this one. Worrying him wasn't the objective, but rehashing a bittersweet decision wasn't necessary either. She rummaged through her Louis Vuitton bag and pulled out the phone. Without taking a glance at the incoming number she immediately began speaking. "Okay, Don, I already know what you're going to say. Thanks but no thanks."

"Where have you been?" he said in a curt tone. She wasn't offended. Most likely he was concerned because he hadn't heard from her sooner.

"I was packing and getting the house ready to leave."

"Come on, Mother, you were so busy that you couldn't answer the phone?" His tone didn't soften.

"I'm sorry, Son. I guess I got so caught up in my own little pity party that I wasn't thinking straight. I really am sorry."

"See, this is exactly what I've been afraid of. You're over there suffering alone when it doesn't have to be this way. Why don't you reconsider and come to Cape Town, just for a while?"

Madeline had finally corralled her personal torment and didn't want to open the floodgates again. "I'll think about it, but at this moment I have to run an errand. We can talk later."

"So long as you promise to answer your phone."

"Don't worry, I'll call you later." They exchanged good-byes.

Madeline pulled down the vanity mirror. She patiently touched up her lipstick and patted down her hair. After a second glance she decided to add some extra makeup. She didn't dare let the staff see the truth. She plucked a pair of sunglasses from her purse and eased them on.

Showtime. Madeline strutted through the doors, bypassing the standard security check.

"Hello, Mrs. Mitchell," the guard said.

She managed to give a halfhearted greeting in return, continuing her stride to the bank of elevators. Many went out of their way to greet her while she waited for the door to open. Madeline wanted to be invisible. Of all the days for the elevator to take forever . . . She'd hoped to slide in undetected, pop into her office one last time, seal her lifetime of work, shed a few tears, and escape unnoticed. Hellos and good-byes would be too much if she was going to stick to the promise she'd made to Tamara. Tears formed on the brims of her eyelids. Madeline let them rest. The sunglasses would provide cover. The elevator stopped on the executive floor and opened. Madeline was poised in the back corner. The doors were just about to close when she swung her bag in between them so they'd spring open again.

She managed to slip off the elevator and into her office undetected, shutting the door quickly. She had to avoid running into more people. Leaving the company was painful. Having to explain the circumstances would be far worse. Madeline stood in the center of the room, the place that housed some of her greatest joys and sorrows. Her homes, her title at DMI, her administrative assistants, and even the carpeting had changed over the years. Her status as Mrs. Dave Mitchell had too, at least on paper. But her prime office had been the same from the day Dave opened the doors of DMI. She recalled the fall breeze teasing through her hair and tickling her face as they cut the red ribbon and entered the building for the first time. They walked hand in hand, prepared to take on the future with excitement and wild dreams.

Madeline gingerly traced the rim of the oversized mahogany desk, then plopped into the seat and let the chair twirl around to face the long windows. She wondered if this was going to be the last time she entered DMI. Maybe Tamara would have a change of heart, but Madeline wasn't hopeful. No tears, no regrets with her decision. If this was the way Tamara needed the arrangement to be in order to quit running and come home, then there was no other decision to be made. Madeline stood, taking in the view one last time.

Everything had a beginning and an end on earth. Dave had completed his cycle of life and had stepped down from DMI when the time came. Now it was her turn to complete her run there. She'd come full circle, birthing her children and DMI in partnership with her beloved husband. Now both had fully matured, their company and their children. Her heart mellowed as she acknowledged that she'd fought a good fight. She had held Joel and Sherry at bay until her children were able to rightfully assume their place in their father's company. The sweet bonus was having Joel and Sherry out of the company and on the streets, where they belonged. Relishing the notion boosted her mood. Her departure was softened to the point of being palatable. Madeline turned the doorknob, not sure which flight she'd grab once she got to the airport but certain that the day would end better than it had begun.

One step into the hallway tempered her renewed zeal. Three doors down stood Abigail and Sherry, laughing and seeming awfully jovial. Would her luck hold out one more time, allowing her to exit undetected?

"Madeline," Abigail called out. For a split second Madeline contemplated hustling on out of there, taking the stairs if necessary to escape the duo. Her four-inch heels might have hindered some women, but they were like sneakers to Madeline and she could move quickly in them. "Madeline," Abigail called again, approaching this time. There was no escape. Abigail had her in the snare. Short of chewing off her foot to escape, Madeline was caught. She braced for the impact. "I didn't expect to see you here," Abigail said.

"I'm short on time. I had to make a quick stop here, and I'm dashing right back out," she said, pushing the elevator button, not wanting to extend the awkwardness a second longer than necessary. Abigail was fine, but Sherry's presence was the source of her nausea.

"Are you still leaving? I know you packed your office a few days ago." Out of her peripheral vision, Madeline could see Sherry going into Abigail's office. She was relieved that Sherry wasn't crazy enough to join the conversation. Their battle was over.

Madeline pushed the down arrow on the elevator several times more in rapid succession. "Yes, I'm still planning to take an extended vacation. I could use the rest. Now that Joel and his mother are out of here, it's safe for me to

leave." Madeline peered up at the illuminated floor numbers above the elevator door. The light was stuck on three
but her floor should be coming up shortly, though not
soon enough. Madeline glanced Abigail's way, not wanting
to appear totally rude. Abigail suddenly seemed to tense,
blinking quite a bit. "What's wrong with you?" Madeline
asked.

"I guess you don't know."

"Know what?" Madeline said, looking up at the elevator
light, which was still stuck. She pushed the elevator button
again.

"Sherry has decided to stay on."

"What did you say?" Madeline bellowed, forgetting
where she was or simply not caring.

"Sherry is staying on board."

"No, she is not," Madeline said, drawing back and locking her arms across her chest. "You must be crazy. I know
she's crazy, but you sound crazy too."

The elevator door opened. One person already on the
elevator asked if anyone was getting on.

"No," Madeline barked out, causing the person to shrink
into the rear of the elevator, letting the door close without
any new passengers.

Madeline headed for Abigail's office to confront Sherry.

"Stop," Abigail said, jumping into her path, which was
like jumping in front of a runaway train. "Don asked her to
stay on board. Apparently at first she wasn't sure, but Joel
talked her into staying on."

"Huh, you have to be kidding me. This is a joke."

"I thought you knew."

Don had mentioned something about forgiving Sherry
and letting her stay on. A blur. At the time Madeline was
saturated with glee from Joel stepping down. She didn't

take the gesture seriously. Don had temporarily taken leave of his senses, or so she assumed. Sherry was flat-out crazy.

"I'm walking out of my office maybe for the last time and that conniving, home-wrecking bimbo is going to be walking around my company. Oh no she's not," Madeline said, pushing past Abigail this time. Don's betrayal would have to come later. Dealing with the issue in person was paramount. Abigail's last attempt to stop the collision failed. Madeline burst into Abigail's office and found Sherry sitting in one of the guest chairs. "Who do you think you are, showing up here?" She approached Sherry, allowing little room between them. Sherry tried to stand but there wasn't enough space. "Don't you get it? Your son is out of here. He was a failure and almost took DMI down with him." Sherry attempted to speak, but Madeline talked over her, rendering Sherry silent until she finished. "Thank goodness he had one act of decency in him and stepped down before he was kicked out."

"I'm not going to do this with you," Sherry said, pushing the chair back so she had space to stand. "Don asked me to stay on and I am. If you have a problem with it, talk to him. Personally, I've heard enough of your rantings and ravings to last a lifetime."

"You haven't heard the best of it yet, trust me."

"Whatever, Madeline, I'm not going to argue with you. Don was right, it's time to let go and start healing this family."

"So now you know what's best for my family? You didn't care about my family and children thirty years ago when you seduced their father away from them."

"Here we go, back to stuff that happened thirty years ago. Abigail, I'll talk with you later. I'm heading out until Madeline is gone."

"I bet you like that, don't you? I'm out and you're staying. Huh, we'll see how that works out."

Sherry stopped before reaching the doorway and turned to face Madeline. "Face it, you won. My son is out of a job. Your son is in charge, which is what you've always wanted. You've won, whoopee. Now, can you please leave me alone?"

Madeline felt the dagger of fate twisting in her heart. The blow of defeat couldn't have been crueler.

Madeline dashed from the room, furious. She couldn't stay there with Sherry another second. Watching her sit smugly in that chair and act like she was in charge drove Madeline far beyond frustration. She was ready to fire bullets of rage. Each time she realized a degree of calm and considered moving on, life jerked her back into conflict. She longed to get outside and draw in a breath of fresh air. She pressed the elevator button incessantly.

"Madeline, wait, I need to talk with you," Abigail said, hustling to catch up.

Madeline wasn't waiting. When the elevator opened, she planned to get in. Abigail could come along if she could jump in. Before her thoughts were fully formed, the doors sprang open. Madeline stepped in, pressing the ground-floor button without hesitating. Abigail followed.

"What do you want, Abigail? I have no interest in your

Mother Teresa lecture." Madeline extracted a lipstick case from her purse, unsnapped the latch, poised the mini mirror in view, and applied color to her lips. "I don't want you telling me why I need to be nice to Sherry. Don't bother with the lecture. Save it for someone who cares," she said as the doors opened.

"I'm not here to talk about Sherry. I'm here for you, to see if there's anything I can do for you."

Madeline stepped out of the elevator more composed than she had been six floors up. She slowed, letting Abigail keep pace. "Thank you, but I'm fine."

"I feel awful about what's happening," Abigail said, seeming embarrassed. "I hate to see you walk out. We all rely on you. I know it and you know it."

"Life goes on. You don't need me. You will be just fine. So will Don and DMI too."

"There's nothing I can do?"

"Nothing," Madeline said, preparing to exit the building, possibly for the last time. She turned to face Abigail. "There is one request that I have. It's extremely important to me."

"Anything, name it and it's done."

"Look out for my son. Don has his hands full with fixing DMI and keeping his own company together. He will need a huge amount of help. Naledi can only do so much from Africa, eight thousand miles away. He could use a friend right here in town." Madeline rested her hand on the bar of the revolving door. "I'm hoping that friend is you."

"I'll be here to do whatever I can."

Madeline winked at Abigail and pushed through the revolving door. When she reached the outside, she drew in a nice breath of air. Free. She put on her sunglasses and extracted a cell phone from her purse. A few pushed buttons and Don was on the line.

"Mother, where are you?"

"At DMI," she said, numb. The air teased her face. "But I'm on my way to the airport."

"Flying where?"

"I haven't thought that far ahead."

"What do you mean? Come on, Mother. Don't play this game with me. Where are you going?"

"I honestly don't know."

"So you're really going to do this to me?"

"Do what?"

"Make me guess where you are in the world with no immediate way to reach you. We've been through this with Tamara. You of all people know how horrible it's been."

She hadn't quite thought about her departure in those terms or the personal effect it would have on Don. He did have a valid point but she had to go without a trace. "I'll let you know when I get to wherever it is I'm going."

"Don't do this. Come here and save me the worry." She didn't want to torture Don but Madeline couldn't comfort him. She had to gain perspective first, to reassess her decisions, reconcile her past, and craft a future. They exchanged good-byes and she affirmed her love. Madeline wanted to cry out but held her emotions. No time for pity. The airport was calling. On the way to her car, Madeline turned her phone off and stuffed it into her purse. She claimed the space to think, plan, and hopefully recover. This was a new day, a new existence, a new normal, and she had to figure it out—her new life, void of what she loved. She hopped into the Bentley and drove it into the DMI covered garage. No sense letting the car sit at the airport indefinitely. She'd give her keys to the guard in case Don or Tamara wanted to use the car. Madeline parked and walked inside, dialing the private car service along the way. In no time she'd be at the airport and then to somewhere far, fun, and free of the Mitchell curse, the one refusing to let those with her last name savor happiness for longer than a brief moment.

chapter

12

Sherry didn't want to gloat, but the reaction was natural, long in coming. She tapped keys on her laptop, feeling stronger than usual. Finally there was a sense of redemption and validation. Madeline wasn't the only Mitchell wife who was a valued member of DMI. Sherry was no longer on the sidelines begging to be counted. Sparks in her renewed spirit were charged, although she wasn't about to let her guard down with Madeline. She had made that mistake too many times in the past. Abigail broke her train of thought as she entered Sherry's office.

"Are you busy?" Abigail asked.

"Not really." Sherry pulled off her reading glasses and set them on the desk. "Actually, I don't have much to do until Don returns. Since I was Joel's personal assistant and press secretary, I guess my job will be the same supporting Don? I'm not exactly sure, but it doesn't matter. As long as I'm needed and treated fairly, I'll stay around."

Abigail took a seat. Sherry was prepared for her to bring

up the incident with Madeline. "What is Joel planning to do?" Abigail asked.

"He's not sure. I can't imagine him sitting around the house every day. He has to be busy all the time. I just don't know what he wants to do." She pushed a button on her laptop. "For the immediate future he has to concentrate on his wife's recovery." Once she'd made the statement, Sherry felt awkward and wanted to reclaim it. "I'm sorry. That was insensitive, bringing up his wife. I'm sorry."

"It's okay, really. There is nothing left between me and Joel. I asked about him only out of curiosity. There's no love between us, but I do care about him as a person." Abigail seemed convincing but Sherry doubted her ability to get over Joel that quickly. His abrupt marriage was a shock to everyone, especially Abigail. Joel's moving Zarah into the house that Abigail designed was crushing. Women didn't purge those feelings of rejection so easily. Madeline hadn't. Sherry hadn't. She didn't believe Abigail had. But if that's what Abigail had to say to get through the heartache, Sherry wouldn't deny her the right. It was the least courtesy she could extend.

"I've had my share of heartache, maybe not the same kind as you, but I understand," Sherry said, filled with compassion for Abigail. She liked her and would have been honored to have her as Joel's wife. It would have been nice, but it didn't happen. She wouldn't dwell on "what if." There were plenty of real troubles percolating to hold her attention. "Don't get me wrong. I accept my daughter-in-law and adore her. Zarah and Joel are the only family I have. But I understand how his relationship with her must hurt."

Abigail crossed her legs and shifted in her seat. "That's water under the bridge." Sherry could tell that Abigail didn't want to discuss it any further. "But I have to admit that I miss the days when Joel was on top of his game and really running this place. Those were the good old days," Abigail said.

"It wasn't that long ago. That's sad." Sherry's hope for her son dipped.

"Joel lived and breathed DMI for almost four years. It was his top priority. He gave up everything and everybody for this place." Abigail's voice softened.

Sherry knew why. Joel had sacrificed their romantic relationship, refusing to allow anything that took his time, passion, and commitment away from DMI. He worked hard. Did well, and deserved better. Sherry was willing to accept his defeat so long as it didn't destroy him. "For him to just walk away scares me. I don't know what he's going to do to fill the void."

"I don't know either." Abigail sighed and let her head drop.

Sherry collected her thoughts and contained her emotions. There had been an abundance of sadness and despair for months. A break would be nice. "Joel will be fine. He's a smart young man. Maybe he'll start his own company like Don did. Why not? After all, they have the same father, and we both know what a dynamic businessman he was." Abigail nodded. "So, that settles it. Joel will be just fine." Sherry wasn't as confident as she appeared but Abigail didn't have to be saddled with her family's issues. Abigail had already suffered plenty.

chapter

13

Don wondered what he'd gotten into. He was convinced God had a plan for him when Joel had handed over the family business. Don jotted down a few notes on a legal pad, periodically peering out the window. The days of sitting back in his office chair and letting his thoughts soar past the Cape Town skyline and out onto the bay were no more. He organized the stack of papers marked up everywhere with red lines. DMI was practically bankrupt. He dropped the papers onto the left side of his desk and shifted to the right side, where the LTI documents were. A sense of calm flowed over him. At least his company was doing well. He rested his head on the stack of papers.

"What are you doing?" Naledi asked.

"Resting, I guess." Her presence had maintained the same effect it had the very first day he'd met her, when the bronze-skinned lady glided into his office over three years ago interviewing for a job in his struggling new company. The radiance in her almond-shaped eyes spoke to him then and continued to this day. Time had passed; the company had grown, and so had their friendship.

She was a blessing. Naledi had come into his life when he was lost, angry with God and his father, and bent on getting revenge on his brother. Solitude on a distant shore had enabled him to return to sanity, repair his shattered soul, and establish a renewed relationship with his spiritual beliefs. The man he left in Detroit was no more. He'd learned to forgive and to let go of the pains of the past. The new Don had a zeal for life, love, and a restored family. Naledi had been a safe haven during his time of despair. She'd supported him and allowed him to operate without the constant threat of her wanting more than he could deliver.

"You must be exhausted after such a long flight. How can I help?" she asked, soft-spoken.

"Your being here is already a help. What would I do without you?" he said, and then tossed the stack of red-covered DMI papers in the air. "I haven't figured out where to begin." Work was one problem; Tamara and Madeline were another. He wanted to blot out the turmoil, but if he did, there would only be Cape Town and Naledi left. That wouldn't be such a bad consolation prize, but abandoning Madeline, Tamara, and even Joel would be tough. Don kept thinking that God had gotten him into this situation and he was determined to rely on Him to get him out.

"How about lunch?" she asked.

Don pined over the stack of papers, calculating the hours of work needed to make a dent. Fifteen, twenty, forty, he wasn't sure. The burden of his impending workload threatened to dampen his waning spirit, the little of it his mother and sister had left him. He mulled a little longer before popping to his feet. "Lunch sounds great." The work wasn't going anywhere. It would be greeting him at the door for days, months, possibly years to come. He didn't want to pass up a perfectly good South African afternoon with Naledi. "Even better, let's have lunch at the cape," he said, gently and temporarily placing his hand on her shoulder. She didn't pull away. The reservations Naledi once had continued vanishing as they grew closer. "We'll take our usual drive along the coast."

"Is there time?"

"I'm the boss," he said, grabbing his jacket from the closet. "I can make time. Besides, it's two hours up and two back." They left his office not quite hand in hand. Decorum in the office was fitting. Letting his heart have free rein outside the doors of LTI was also fitting. He couldn't help it. Being home with Naledi, his business partner and devoted friend, allowed Don to feel temporarily shielded from the shambles of DMI, his father's fractured legacy.

Naledi and Don strolled outside. She reached for his hand and gladly he responded. At the threshold, he stomped out the flurry of family strife and separation existing with his mother, sister, stepmother, and half brother. If there was a chance of staying put and never having to return to Detroit to face the chaos, he would. However, his yearning desire to save his family at the leading of the Lord was inescapable. But this afternoon was off-limits. They could ravage his solitude tomorrow.

14

Joel pulled the Lamborghini into the garage. He sat in the car and turned up the music, blasting away his troubles. He rolled his shoulder several times, unable to fully stretch it out. The two-hour session at the gym had worked out some of his stress but the tightness in his shoulders remained. Joel let his back relax, tapping the steering wheel to the beat of the music. His body was positioned to relax, at least as much as it could in a sports car, but he couldn't free up his thoughts. He moved his neck to the beat of the music, trying every technique he could to let go and ease into some form of contentment, yet it wasn't for him.

He couldn't help thinking about Sheba. How many times had he been stressed out and hopped in the car or gotten on a plane to see her? She had a way of bringing down his anxiety and pumping him up like a king. He missed Sheba, craved time with her. Immediately, he shut the visions down. He had to; otherwise the Lamborghini would be backing out and hitting the road, Chicago bound. His conscience didn't usually get to decide, but today it had to.

He groaned, killed the music, and opened the door. Slowly dragging one leg at a time, he meandered to the door, claiming every step of freedom, acknowledging that as soon as he went inside, Zarah was going to swarm him like a bee to pollen. He drew in a few more breaths of space before succumbing to his doom. He paused and turned the knob, entering the house through the mudroom. He considered sneaking into his office, which was closer to the rear of the house. No sense bothering. Hiding now would only prolong his responsibilities. He pushed past his spirit of procrastination and sought out his wife in the kitchen.

"Joel, I didn't hear you come in. I'm very glad to have you home so early," she said, rushing to him.

He wasn't repulsed by her touch, nor was he inspired. It wasn't her fault. When they married, she was a virgin. Unless he counted a handful of times they'd been together as husband and wife, intimacy wasn't an area of familiarity for Zarah. Her chipper disposition made him feel better. Watching her battle depression and suicide wasn't anything he was proud of, especially when he was the cause. She didn't have to say it in direct terms, but he knew, she knew, everybody knew that he was the reason she'd wanted to die a few weeks ago. "You look good. Have you been eating like you should?"

Her eyes widened and color flushed her cheeks. "Yes." She looked away like a timid little girl. At times like this, he felt awful pulling Zarah from her family and not being able to love her like a real husband should. But they weren't a true couple, not really. Her father had to accept some of the blame, too. After all, the marriage was his idea from the beginning.

As Zarah was an only child, her welfare was critical to her father. Musar wanted to make sure his daughter had a husband to look after her and their family business once he transitioned to his next stage of life. To Joel, the next stage was death, but he wasn't going to debate Zarah's or Musar's religious beliefs. Joel was concerned about the present, and from his perspective, he had done the Bengali family a favor taking Zarah. Looking at her now, the gesture didn't seem so clear.

He grabbed her hand, causing her to drop her gaze to the floor. Business was business, no one appreciated the concept more than him, but he couldn't discount the human standing next to him. He felt passion in the moment and pulled her close. Feeling her body tense, Joel let go of her. "Are you afraid of me?"

"No," she whispered, giggling like a teenager. The passion that had rolled in was sailing out. He didn't feel right pushing her, but he also didn't want the burden of teaching her how to be a wife. The investment wasn't there. Images of Sheba crawled in. This time he wasn't quick to dismiss them. She was the refuge he longed to see. "Can we eat dinner together?" she asked.

"I guess so." Joel had lost his appetite. Food was the least of his concerns. He had no job, no passion, no direction; these things were ahead of food on his list of issues, none of which Zarah could help him with, not like Sheba or Abigail could. Zarah continued speaking. Joel didn't process a single word. He needed more. If his personal life wasn't going to quench his thirst, he'd have to get it done on the professional end. The odds of getting back into DMI weren't great, but it was possible, especially with his mother on the inside.

chapter

15

Tamara paid the taxi driver, shorting him on the tip. Limited funds didn't allow for excessive generosity. A few more nights at the Hilton Garden and she'd have to move to a motel. The credit card she'd used to check in was tied to her checking account. A low balance translated to a short stay. She'd consider other accommodations soon. A shelter was far off in the distance if she wisely managed the remaining three hundred dollars in cash and the nine hundred in her account.

She stood in the parking lot, staring at the six-story building. When she was there a few months ago, for the first time since fleeing, Madeline had spooked her. She'd come as a monumental favor to Don. He'd asked for her stock ownership in an attempt to oust Joel. She agreed, at first. Tamara remembered hauling out of the building and booking the first flight out of the country. She felt tired just thinking about how long it took to get home that time, three connections and a total of ten exhausting hours of layovers. Ugh. This time, she wasn't going to be spooked. Madeline was gone and the truth was that she needed a job.

She entered the building, amassing a burst of energy. After her fourteen years of aging, most people in the company weren't going to recognize her. Exactly as she hoped. Tamara sliced through the lobby, not garnering extended stares from anyone. She was just about to push the elevator button when the guard called out to her. "Excuse me, ma'am, but you have to sign in."

Tamara froze and then loosened. What was the big deal? She couldn't overreact and raise suspicion. Signing in was fine. It wasn't like Remo was chasing her onto the elevator. He didn't know where she was, not yet. She would have to learn to relax, act normal, and not always be on alert for impending danger. Not every man was out to hurt her. Rationally she understood. Reprogramming her natural reaction would take time. Consistent safety would eventually enable her to rewire her instincts.

She approached the security desk, avoiding direct eye contact. She wrote *T. Mitchell* on the guest log, hesitating before filling in the "Employee Visiting" box. The guard must have detected her uneasiness and asked, "Are you a vendor or do you have an appointment?"

"Neither, really. If I have to pick one I guess I have an appointment."

"With whom?" the guard asked. He was awfully serious. It wasn't like she was trying to break into the White House to steal international secrets. This was DMI, a locally owned company with no major security risks. She wanted to express her disdain but elected to maintain control. This was day one. Never knew when down the road she'd need the security guard to help her. She'd play it cool for now.

"I have an appointment with Don Mitchell."

"He's out of the office until next week."

"I know that," she snapped at the guard. "He's in Cape Town."

"Well, I can't let you in unless he comes down and signs you in."

"I guess he can't do that from Cape Town, now, can he?" The guard didn't respond. Tamara didn't quite know why she was so irritated. It wasn't like the guard had insulted her. He was just doing his job. She got that. Maybe it was the notion of having to sneak into her family's business and having to be signed into her parents' building? She'd chosen not to have any connection with the family or DMI. It was solely her decision, but there was an inkling deep within that said she belonged here, had a right to be here, should be here. "Who's in charge while he's out? That's who I'll want to see."

"Ma'am, you'll need an appointment or I'm going to have to ask you to leave."

"You don't want to do that. My brother wouldn't be very happy about that, and I can guarantee my mother wouldn't." Tamara had absolutely zero intention of calling her mother but she knew her name carried weight far beyond the walls of DMI. She was a good ally to have at times so long as a person was willing to pay the hefty price tag. Tamara wasn't. An airline ticket was the extent of the debt Tamara was willing to carry with her mother.

"Who's your brother?"

"Don Mitchell," she said, pausing. That was plenty to get in, but for added measure Tamara laid down the trump card because she could. "And Madeline is my mother."

"O-oh," the guard stammered. "Who are you? The only

Mitchells that I've met are Don, Madeline, Joel, and Sherry. I'm sorry, but I didn't know there was a daughter."

"Tamara Mitchell. I was just here three months ago. You don't remember me?"

"I've only been with the company two months. I'm so sorry," he repeated vehemently.

"No worries, so long as you let me get on my way."

"Sure, sure," he said, rummaging through papers and visitor tags. "I'm supposed to ask for ID since I didn't recognize you."

Tamara couldn't be angry at the guard for being thorough. She flashed her passport in his face so quickly that there was no way he could read the print. "I need to go."

"Okay, yes, no problem, Ms. Mitchell. Can I get you an ID badge and key card?"

"Why would I want that?"

"That way you can enter the building any time you want with the electronic sensor."

Tamara quickly thought about her depleting funds. Having a key to the building might be the answer to her housing dilemma. "That sounds good. I could definitely use a key card." She was amused. If security was this tight, Remo was no longer a threat, not as long as this guard was around. She was pleased with her lodging possibilities and the added security, and her decision to come home seemed better and better. "How long will it take to get the card and ID?" She didn't have plans, but hanging around the lobby wasn't her idea of an exciting time.

"Depends on how long you're staying."

Good question. "It all depends," she said, stopping short of telling him it was based on a day-by-day assessment. No commitments, no disappointment.

"Well, here's a temporary card you can use. We'll also

order a permanent ID card in case you're here more than thirty days."

Never know, she thought. "By the way, what floor is Don's office?"

"Sixth."

"You didn't have to look it up. Impressive."

The young guy blushed. "Everybody here knows where the offices are for the Mitchell family members, all except yours."

She giggled and peered at the key card. "Maybe I'll start with the CEO's office." She giggled some more. He joined in. Tamara thanked the guard and headed upstairs, ready to move on.

Sixth floor. She stepped out of the elevator pretending to know where she was going. She walked past several administrative-assistant stations and closed office doors. One lady sitting behind a station stopped her. "Excuse me. May I help you find someone?"

"Sure, can you show me where Don sits?"

The assistant wore a troubled expression. "He's out of the office. The security desk should have told you before sending you up here." The lady placed a call to security. Quickly she was off the phone. "I'm sorry, Ms. Mitchell. I didn't recognize you."

"No worries. I'm the missing Mitchell. I don't expect anyone to recognize me here."

"Since Don is out, is there someone else you'd like to see?"

"Not really. I plan on waiting for my brother."

"Okay, then can I set you up in a temporary office for as long as you're with us?"

"Sure."

The assistant extracted a key ring from her desk. "I'm

your mother's assistant. Since she's on sabbatical, I might as well put you in her office."

"Any other office available?" Taking her mother's office was eerie and would serve as a constant reminder of why Madeline had left.

"As you know, we've had quite a bit of shifting on our executive team. The only other office is Joel's old office. Don hasn't moved in yet, but I'm sure he will. It's the largest office in the building and has all the perks."

"Since the CEO's office is open, I might as well sit in there, at least until my brother officially claims it."

chapter 16

Tamara slowly took in the size of the office, soaking in the ambience of luxury. Her flat in England was about the size of two average bedrooms chopped into a kitchen, living room/bedroom combo, and bath. There hadn't been a real closet in the old apartment, which wasn't a problem given her amount of belongings. She hadn't complained. She'd learned to live with the minimum, especially once her funds began evaporating. Surprisingly, being in the presence of excess ignited a tiny glimmer of envy and a slight desire for more.

Tamara eased into the oversize, leather wingback chair and pulled into the desk. She clasped her hands together, letting her elbows rest on the desktop. She'd actually spent the past decade and a half staying far removed from the world that choked the life out of her family so many years ago, yet there she was, sitting in the building of deceit.

A knock on the door interrupted Tamara's thoughts. "Hello, hello, I'm Abigail Gerard," a brown-skinned woman said, wearing a skirt and tailored blue shirt. Abigail approached the desk and extended her hand. Tamara saw no reason to retreat. "The assistant told me you were here. I'm pleased to meet you, finally." Abigail was bubbly. Tamara smiled without responding. "I've heard so much about you."

"Oh really?" Tamara couldn't imagine from whom, or why she would get much attention at DMI. She'd spent a few summers working as an intern for her parents when she was a teenager, but that was years ago. She was certain most of the people working at DMI in those days were long gone.

"Your mother talks about you every chance she gets."

"Oh."

"Between Madeline and Don, I feel like I know you." Abigail oozed energy to the point that Tamara felt exhausted.

"Well, I guess I'm at a disadvantage, because I don't know you. Actually, I don't know anyone around here except for Don, and he's not here."

"That's right, it's been what, fourteen or fifteen years since you left." Tamara nodded. "Wow, that's a long time to be away from home."

"It is." Tamara's spirits dropped. She wasn't prepared for Abigail to touch upon the topic. She had to redirect the conversation. "Never know where life is going to take you," Tamara said. "What about you, is Detroit home for you?"

"No, I grew up in Maryland, went to college in Indiana, and now I'm here," Abigail said.

"Family?"

"Still in Maryland."

Tamara wasn't accustomed to interacting with strangers and engaging in small talk. Meeting a friendly face was refreshing but there wasn't much more to discuss without Tamara having to avoid divulging personal information. Her habit of staying guarded hadn't vanished when she landed in the U.S. "I'm glad you came by. I look forward to seeing you again," Tamara said, initiating the end of the conversation.

Abigail stayed in the office. Tamara wasn't sure what else to say, feeling crowded.

"I keep staring at you because it seems unreal. Your family has been special to me for a very long time. Your father was my mentor." Tamara scratched the back of her neck, turning away from Abigail. "Right now, I am so happy for your family."

"I can see that you're very happy, a lot happier than I am," Tamara told her.

"What makes you say that?" Abigail asked.

Tamara waved off the comment. "No big deal, consider it a brain quirk. I'm not really thinking straight these days. Must be the jet lag."

Abigail sat on the corner of the massive desk. "Your mother always talked about getting you here. Don too. It's ironic that when you finally get here, neither of them is here. How weird is that? With the way your mother values family, I would have expected Madeline to have a full parade prancing up and down Telegraph Road. I'm shocked that Madeline isn't here, especially after wanting this so badly."

Tamara could have let Abigail go on and on, but she thought Abigail might never leave. "I might as well tell you. Before I agreed to come back, my mother had to leave."

"Oh," Abigail said with eyes wide open and mouth too. "Oh, that had to hurt Madeline." Tamara could read Abigail's disdain. "I don't know what to say. Madeline mentioned the two of you had a few little disagreements but nothing that major." Abigail's disdain remained. Tamara could tell.

"My mother and I have had more than just a few disagreements."

"I know for a fact she loves you and her family."

Tamara didn't like how loosely Abigail tossed around the notion of family. Family was the key contributor in creating her personal prison. "My family isn't exactly what you would consider loving."

"No family is perfect."

"You got that right. I'm a child of Madeline and Dave Mitchell. That says it all. Anybody coming from those two is bound to have problems."

"We all have our challenges," Abigail commented.

Tamara laughed. "You said you're close to my family, but I'm not sure how much you've been told about me."

"Only that you were angry at the family and preferred to live abroad."

Tamara laughed more. "'Preferred to live abroad' is a nice way to put it. There's a lot more to it." Tamara shouldn't have cared what Abigail thought about her. Yet she felt compelled to defend her character, though she wasn't sure why. "Since you're so close to the Mitchell family, I would think you'd know everything."

Abigail shifted the weight from her left foot to her right one while continuing to sit on the corner of the desk. "I've heard bits and pieces but not the full story." Neither spoke for a moment. Then Abigail said, "Look, we don't have to talk about this. It's personal and I understand."

"No, it's okay. If we're going to be working closely together, I'd like to set the record straight. I was raped by my brother in my mother's house."

Abigail's eyes widened. "I really didn't know the details, seriously."

"So when you toss around the term 'loving family,' it doesn't mean the same to me as it might to somebody else. You won't see me at a family reunion any time soon."

"Well, I don't know what to say. 'Welcome back' is obviously inappropriate," Abigail said, standing. "I'll just say that I'm here. If there's anything you need, please let me know."

Tamara pocketed the offer, acknowledging that she had to learn the dynamics and pitfalls of DMI. She should have been second-guessing her decision to spill details into Abigail's lap, but Tamara was sure Abigail already knew. Yet there was something very trustworthy and endearing about Abigail that caused Tamara to be okay with the revelation. She was tired of running, hiding, and carrying her load of shame and disgust. Purging was good for the soul. She reclined in the CEO's seat, recognizing how natural it felt. She would make her mark on the company and prove she belonged, without needing Madeline's help to survive.

chapter

17

Pity was for punks, not for him. His DNA bred leadership. Joel wasn't willing to settle for less. He paced from his office to the library, grabbing at ideas as they bounced in and out of his mind. Orchestrating a takeover was out of the question. Don and Madeline would be on the alert. His move had to be smooth with an element of surprise. He kept pacing back and forth.

Zarah entered. "I've been looking for you," she said.

"What do you need?" he asked, focused on business and less on his personal obligations. Zarah wasn't going anywhere. She didn't require as much effort.

"I was hoping we could take a ride together for the afternoon."

Joel kept pacing. "No, uh, not right now. I have some business to handle."

"I thought you were finished with DMI."

He didn't need to be reminded. "I still have business to handle, Zarah," he said, raising his voice.

She must have interpreted the tone correctly, because Zarah shifted her glance toward the door and took on a timid disposition. "I'm sorry. I didn't mean to upset you. I'm sorry," she said, shrinking away.

She was fragile. He got that. "Look, I'm sorry too. I didn't mean to yell at you." He approached her, getting close without actually touching. "I have a lot on my mind."

"Can I help?"

"Not unless you have a company that I can have." He paused and then told her, "Actually you do, don't you?" The creative wheels were turning, almost getting ahead of him. "You own the West Coast division. Remember, the one your father bought from me for you?"

"Of course I do."

"Would you be willing to keep the division for me?"

"Oh yes," she said with excitement. She reached for his hand. "Yes, I will surely keep the division for you."

It's not like he hadn't considered the division a few days ago, but he'd dismissed the idea. He was sure Don was going to make a decent offer for the division and fold it back into DMI. Joel had already told Don he wouldn't stand in the way if he wanted to reclaim the division. Changing his mind could be a declaration of war. Joel was willing to take the chance since his wounds from the last battle were superficial, nothing major. A set of bruised feelings was the extent of them. If necessary, he could go another round, this time expecting to be the victor.

"I'm glad that you want to help me." Zarah was inspiring a train of ideas. His personal money was tapped out after mortgaging his house, taking out exorbitant loans, and spending the cash to buy Harmonious Energy. After the board of directors wouldn't approve the purchase and wouldn't release DMI funds, he had no choice. The bad news was that he'd commingled his personal funds with corporate ones. Technically, Harmonious Energy was his. He'd forked over most of the money, but legally he had no claim. The company belonged to DMI, for now. His creative genes were flowing freely like a transfusion of hope into his veins, charging him forward. He pulled her in for a hug and held her there, forgoing the typical quick-hug-and-release arrangement they'd developed. Joel held her tighter than usual. He could feel her respond.

The pieces were cloudy. Joel would need time and cash to put together the right deal. It was possible. With Zarah's help, he could resume his trek to greatness. She could convince Don to sell Harmonious Energy to her. Don appreciated family. Plus none of the board of directors wanted the company under the DMI umbrella anyway because of its Eastern religious focus. Zarah could probably get her family's company at a discounted price. His enthusiasm oozed.

Joel let Zarah go and rushed to his office to take a few notes. He couldn't lose the details. This was his chance to redeem his legacy. Failure was avoidable so long as he could maintain control of the West Coast division and pick up Harmonious Energy. Both were critical, especially the West Coast division. It would enable him to reestablish his presence in the U.S., the place where his failure had been most visible.

There was no way around his situation. Zarah held the keys to his future. He mulled over the plan for a while longer before scouting through the house looking for her. Spending the afternoon together wasn't a bad idea. The two needed to spend more time together, especially if they were going to be business partners. Well, not really partners. Zarah had no interest in business. Once she secured Harmonious Energy and held on to the West Coast division, Joel could step in and take on the burden of running the new company. He bounced through the house calling out her name, exhilarated. Names for the new venture skipped around his mind. So much to do and he was eager to get started, tomorrow. This afternoon belonged to Zarah. She'd earned it.

chapter

18

Don entered the DMI building rejuvenated, drenched with South Africa's refreshing appeal. He was poised to take on the challenges facing him in Detroit. A slew of well-wishers greeted him as he jaunted from the executive parking spot, sailed through the lobby into the elevator, and stepped onto his floor. He poked his head into Abigail's office, catching her on the phone. "Stop by my office when you finish," he whispered.

"Good morning, Mr. Mitchell. Welcome back," Joel's assistant, Kay, said. Since Don had been working part-time at DMI until now, he didn't have an assistant. Don decided to keep her in the position for consistency until he figured out what changes needed to be made. "After you get settled in, I'd like to go over your calendar for today. There are a couple of important calls you'll need to take." She handed him a folder filled with papers. "These are documents that require your immediate attention. The ones requiring your signature have the big yellow arrow pointing next to them," she said, opening the folder to show him.

Don set his satchel on the counter to peruse the folder. His PDA was vibrating at the same time. The flurry of responsibilities had begun. He took a peek at the phone. The number wasn't Naledi's or his mother's, so the caller could wait until he was settled into his office. He juggled a couple of papers, the folder, and his phone.

"I also have today's menu from the executive dining hall. Let me know what you'd like by eleven and I'll get it ordered for you."

"Oh my goodness, who can think about lunch? It's only eight o'clock Monday morning and you've just loaded me with a ton of work." He chuckled and she returned a contained grin, placing the menu on top of the folder he was holding. "Anything else you want to pile on?"

"Nothing for the moment." Don gathered his satchel and paperwork. "Oh, there is one other item," she said. He waited for her to finish. "Your sister has been here since last Tuesday. She's in your office."

Don heard the comment and went inside, excited like a kid going to a birthday party. He was eager to see Tamara, although having her there was bittersweet without Mother. He could have allowed grief to dominate the scene but chose to stay upbeat. "Big sis, look at you," Don said, finding Tamara sitting in the CEO's seat. "Look at you, taking over already." He laughed. "I can't believe it. You're actually here, wow," he said, bursting with contentment.

"Well, well, well, if it isn't my little brother."

Don embraced her quickly and loosely, remembering that she shied away from personal contact. "I'm sorry it has taken me so long to get here." He dropped the satchel onto the conference table along with the other things in his hand.

"No problem. I'm a big girl. I can take care of myself." Tamara came from around the desk.

"No doubt." She didn't have to convince him. She'd lived on her own for years without any family. That was proof positive. "I'm just glad to have you here. Is that okay?"

She nodded.

"Knock-knock," Abigail said, coming straight toward Don. Their embrace was easy, tight, natural. She hung on a little longer than normal. He didn't complain. It was Abigail; why would he? "I'm glad to see you," she told him.

"Ditto." The Mitchell war had casualties. Abigail could be considered one, Don thought. "I hope you're ready to roll up your sleeves and help me get this company on track. I need you."

"What about me? What have you planned for me to do?" Tamara asked.

"You tell me what your strength is and it's yours," Don told her.

"I don't know. Give me some ideas," Tamara said, leaning on the conference table.

"Madeline is a marketing genius. Don too. It must be in your genes," Abigail said.

"Great suggestion, how about marketing?" Don said. He knew she enjoyed art and had creative talent. Perhaps that talent would lend itself well to marketing. "Since Mother is gone, the department is suffering a huge gap in leadership. We need all the help in marketing that we can get. Interested?"

"Not really. I don't have any experience in marketing."

Not what Don wanted to hear. Everyone in the building had to contribute, heavily. "Let's sit down and discuss strategy." The ladies followed his lead. "With Mother and Joel gone, I need a lot of help, especially since I'll be juggling DMI and LTI."

"Don't worry. I have your back. You know you can count on me as usual," Abigail told him.

"Our first order of business is to sell off Harmonious Energy." Don opened the folder and leafed through the pages. "Joel asked me to consider selling it to his wife since it belonged to her family. I don't have a problem with selling the company to her so long as she's willing to give us the West Coast division in a fair deal."

"Think she'll do it?" Abigail asked.

"What's Harmonious Energy?" Tamara wasn't familiar with the list of events that had occurred over the past month, let alone the last three years.

"A leadership development company based on Eastern religious principles. Joel bought the company to build our international presence. It would have been a good idea if the company didn't have such conflicting core principles."

"Did Joel realize that the companies were so different?"

"Oh, he knew. Didn't matter, though. Joel had his mind set and nothing or nobody could stop him . . ." Abigail said, letting her voice trail off.

Don wondered if there would be a time when her reaction to Joel would change.

"We lost a boatload of clients because of Joel's personal choices," Don said as Tamara listened. His sister had to catch up with a train of activity that was steamrolling along. Don scratched his head. "You know, this is a nightmare."

"Yep, I do. We just have to work together like in the good old days. You and I were a powerful team before your father died. I'm ready to jump into the trenches with you again," Abigail said, patting his hand. Don felt the subdued passion. Too much had happened. He couldn't let his feelings be clouded. There wasn't time to effectively balance his personal and professional challenges simultaneously. One had to be sidelined.

Don sensed Tamara's stares at him and Abigail. His PDA vibrated on the table. "Excuse me," he said, scooping up the phone and rushing into the hallway.

Tamara had been lost during most of the discussion. "Must be important the way he's racing out of the room."

"Humph, it's probably that Naledi. She's a business partner in his company, LTI."

"Really? He seemed awfully excited to only be talking to a business partner."

"Tell me about it. I met her a few months ago when she came to see Don. She was kind of territorial if you ask me."

"Does that bother you?"

"We've been close friends for seven years." The affection was evident to Tamara. She wondered if Don reciprocated.

"What about Naledi?"

"What about her? As far as I'm concerned, Naledi met Don during the lowest point in his life. Your father had just given the company to Joel. So Don got as far away from Detroit as he could. He was on the other side of the world and felt abandoned. Naledi provided some kind of comfort. I wouldn't get it mixed up with love." Abigail was fixated on Tamara as she spoke.

"So where were you during his time of need if you were so close?"

Abigail's gaze shifted. "Everything was confusing during those days. I was here helping Joel."

"Ah, and Don was in South Africa. So you and Joel had a thing too? I thought he was married."

"He wasn't married when we were together. Actually, we weren't together, not exactly, but the bottom line is that he wasn't married to anybody. That came later as a surprise to everyone."

"Including you?"

"Especially me. I don't know what happened to Joel. He was on top of his game. Somehow he got caught up with women and ego-tripping to the point where he wasn't thinking clearly. The work and vision that your father put into this company went down the drain when Joel went off on his power trip."

"You sound like you had a lot of respect for my father."

"I loved Dave Mitchell. He was like a father to me."

"Really." Tamara was agitated. She suspected Dave had started off like a father figure to Sherry too. Attraction to a much younger woman had destroyed their family. There were plenty of single men. Married men were off-limits. "So let me get this straight. You have a thing for Joel, and for Don, and for my father?"

"Not your father. I loved him but not in a relationship kind of way. Don and Joel are different. I admit it. I used to have feelings for Joel. That's over. I think Don is my destiny. I was a fool to let him get away."

"Are you serious? Two brothers and my father?" Abigail looked stunned. "You know there are more men in the world than the Mitchell men."

"I know that," Abigail said, firing back at her.

Each woman's defensiveness was intensifying. Tamara didn't want to alienate Abigail after being on the job only a few days. There was too much to learn and she needed Abigail's help. Tamara worked to change the conversation's direction. "I'm not judging you, just making an observation. I've only been here a few days. Don't pay me any attention. What do I know?" Abigail tapped on the table between crossing and uncrossing her legs. Tamara could tell she'd hit a sensitive spot. Hopefully Tamara could find a way to diffuse the thick tension blanketing Abigail. Losing allies before making them wasn't the way Tamara wanted to go.

chapter

19

on returned. The ladies weren't talking. They were looking at each other like two complete strangers. "Everything okay?" he asked. Both said yes to some degree. He wasn't sure what the problem was but didn't dwell on it. He wasn't eager to create problems when his list of challenges was already extensive. Don laid his phone on the table. "I'm sorry about the interruption. It was a call I had to take," he said, still soaring on a high note, ready to take on the world.

"My goodness, what's with you?" Tamara asked. "If a business call can make you that happy, maybe I should have been in the company a long time ago—"

"Was that Naledi?" Abigail cut in to ask.

"It was."

"Figured as much. She wants you back already? Geez, you've only been here a few hours." Abigail appeared amused.

Don wasn't fooled. He sifted through her reaction and

pocketed the underlying message. They'd have to talk about it later, in private. His immediate goal was to lighten the intensity. "Can't get rid of me that easily. I plan to be here for a couple of weeks, maybe a month, depending on how much we get done." A month wasn't an issue. Several months weren't a problem. Naledi had his operation running smoothly. "Cape Town and LTI will survive without me for a while." Naledi was his anchor, rendering her irreplaceable, but he couldn't possibly tell Abigail. He'd set romance aside and push their impending confrontation to the bottom of the list until later.

Kay interrupted. "Mr. Mitchell, your nine o'clock meeting will be a few minutes late."

Don glanced at his watch. "Is it nine already?"

"No, it's only eight thirty. I'm just giving you a heads-up."

"Oh, good," he said, relieved.

Kay walked over and handed him a sheet of paper. "I've updated your schedule for today. I kept your hour open at lunch since you're booked solid from nine fifteen to six." She left.

Don buried his face in his hands and roared, "Let the games begin! We're going to need all hands on deck. Ms. Tamara, have you decided what role you feel comfortable taking on?"

"Not sure yet, I may need a few weeks to figure this out."

He didn't have a few weeks. "We're going to have to get you up to speed quicker than a few weeks. We have a major hole to fill with Mother gone. She ran the East Coast like clockwork, perfectly."

The weight of Madeline's absence was heavy. No one could battle like her. Don was glad to have his sister within arm's reach, safely at home, but the trade-off between a seasoned executive and a junior administrative assistant wasn't easily overcome, not so soon into the postwar cleanup process. He wanted to close his eyes and fly away. Destiny kept him planted. Don was 100 percent convinced this was his God-appointed calling, to restore the fragmented company. However, an easy path to success wasn't promised.

"Maybe I can spend a few hours with you to learn the ropes," his sister said.

Tamara squirmed. "Time is going to be tight over the next week," Don said. He didn't hide his frustration. She was sitting there sucking up space with no ideas to add. Helpless. She couldn't run off, not again. There was nowhere to go. Remo and her limited funds forced her to stay put. "Can you help Tamara get situated?" he asked Abigail.

"I guess so."

Tamara could tell Abigail hadn't gotten over their earlier conversation. The overwhelming sense of being a burden frazzled Tamara. She had to figure out a strategy; she was determined to add value and refused to be seen as a second-best option. "Thanks, Abigail, for the offer. I'm committed to learning as much as I can very quickly." Abigail didn't say much. Tamara wasn't discouraged. She was eager to get cracking and work her buns off learning the business. Her worth wouldn't be questioned in a few months. They'd see. The time would quickly come when Don wouldn't notice Madeline's absence, at least on the professional end. Tamara was motivated. Besides, she was the eldest living child of Dave Mitchell and technically the rightful heir to the company. Three Mitchell men had taken a shot at running the company. Each of them had struggled in some way. Perhaps it was her turn.

"I have about twenty minutes before my next meeting. Save me, Abigail. Dig down in your bag of tricks and help me figure out the best way to approach Joel's wife about the deal."

"That's the easiest proposition. The challenge will come with recovering the Southern division. We have no idea who actually owns it."

"You're right," he said. "The only clue Joel gave me was to check with Uncle Frank."

"Our father's brother? He's still working for the company?" Tamara asked. Abigail and Don stared at each other and roared with laughter. "What's so funny?"

Abigail's laugh softened as she looked over a few papers on the table. Don kept laughing and then spoke. "Uncle Frank hasn't worked here in close to four years. Joel fired him."

"Really?"

"He had to let him go after Uncle Frank embezzled hundreds of thousands of dollars. Dad was traumatized by Uncle Frank's scandal right before he died. The media featured the scandal for months."

"I remember too well," Abigail said. "Your dad was very hurt. He trusted Uncle Frank, and he was crushed."

Tamara felt like an outsider. Abigail knew more about the family than she did. "What's funny about him getting fired?"

"Let's just say Uncle Frank is a funny man," Don said.

"The fact that Joel partnered with him blows my mind. He's unbelievable. First Joel gets into an arranged marriage with Zarah and then he cuts a deal with your uncle," Abigail said, bending both index and middle fingers around the word "deal." Abigail pushed back in her seat, flipping her pen onto the table.

Tamara was at a disadvantage, not having witnessed events firsthand in the family. But that didn't keep her from noticing that Abigail's reaction was overly sensitive. There was more to her and Joel's story. In time Tamara hoped to uncover details.

"Ladies, we won't solve every problem this morning. Let's reconvene this evening after my six o'clock meeting ends." Don turned to Tamara. "Hopefully your evenings are free. We have a boatload of work. You can learn a lot by hanging out with me and Abigail these next couple of weeks. We'll be practically inseparable. You might as well join in too."

"I'm in." Tamara agreed without hesitation. If she had to work twenty-hour days until her worth was established, then she would.

"That's what I need to hear. It's time for me to get prepared for my next meeting. Abigail, if you have time, can you spend an hour or two going over the basics with Tamara? I'm just too busy to give her the time she needs. I'll catch up with both of you later." He got a pad of paper from the desk. Tamara hated being passed around like a child needing a babysitter. If Detroit was going to remain a viable option, her state of ignorance had to be short-lived.

chapter

20

Nine A.M. Tamara poked her head into Abigail's office and said hello. "Do you have a few minutes to chat? I have a ton of questions."

"I have to meet with Don first, but come on in. If you don't mind waiting a few minutes, I'll be right back."

"No problem, I'll wait here."

Abigail left for Don's office, reflecting along the way. She'd sat on the sidelines and watched her relationship with Joel reduce to ashes. He was Zarah's husband. If she remained on the sidelines without a voice, Don would be married off too. She bolstered her courage, entered his office, and spoke. "Do you have a few minutes? We need to talk."

"What's up?"

Abigail closed the door and took a seat at his table. "Are you avoiding me?"

"Why do you ask that?" he said, distracted.

"You and I haven't talked privately in a couple of months."

He locked his gaze on her. "I've been on the road, back and forth between Detroit and Cape Town, working my hardest to take care of both companies. I've never avoided you, and you know it." His gaze stayed fixed on her. The sincerity he radiated put her at ease. "You add the London trip in and I'm officially tapped out."

Listening to Don made her feel silly and selfish. He had been a true friend, unwavering. This was the time when he needed her support, and she wanted to offer it unconditionally. But adoration continued rising within her, and she was unwilling to drop the notion. Heart and mind were dueling for an edge in the moment. A big shove and her heart pushed forward. "You've been busy. I get that, but I don't want to sit back and let you discount my feelings."

Come on, Abigail. Don peered at his watch. Eight minutes after nine. His jam-packed marathon of a day was approaching the starting line. "This isn't the best time to get into a heavy personal conversation."

"When is the best time? You said yourself that your day is filled."

"We can talk tonight or tomorrow or the day after." Don couldn't understand why Abigail was pushing to talk at this precise moment. They'd already talked about what used to be. The love he had held for her got marred when he retreated to South Africa and she threw her allegiance and affection to Joel. He wasn't mad at her. He took responsibility for the breakdown in communication. He had never stepped up and told her how he felt until it was too late. When he was ready to tell her, Abigail's dedication had moved to Joel.

"Waiting has been our problem. You waited to tell me

how you felt four years ago. I waited to share my feelings with you. I'm sick of waiting. If I don't speak up, I will never have a chance at a serious relationship with you. I'm not going to sit back and miss my chance, not again," she told him.

Don continued peering at his watch every couple of minutes. "Where is this coming from? I'm right here in town. I'm not going anywhere for weeks. Let's get together tonight and talk, please, okay?"

"Tonight it is," she said.

Don was unprepared for Abigail's forcefulness; this wasn't her style. His tight schedule didn't afford time for pondering his smoldering fondness for Abigail or kindling a flame with Naledi. The tangled web that existed between Abigail, him, and Joel added an element of complexity that Don wanted to avoid. He mellowed thinking about Abigail. She had a special place in his heart. Naledi's image whisked into his thoughts, scooting Abigail out. The relationship with Naledi was safe, pure, uncomplicated, and unrelated to Joel, a compelling point impossible to overlook.

A knock on the door zapped him away from the romantic chaos choking the room. Don closed the folder chronicling the remnants of Joel's destruction. There was more fallout to repair, Don's relationship with Abigail included.

chapter

21

Abigail was encouraged. Naledi wasn't the only woman vying for Don. The route to a committed relationship had been rocky and lined with detours. Abigail's and Don's paths were intersecting and she would take full advantage of the encounter. She skipped into her office to find Tamara handling a few books from her shelf.

"Can I help you with something?"

"Actually, you can." Tamara returned the books to the shelf. "I have quite a few questions. After the meeting with Don, I realize how little I know about the family and about the company. You, on the other hand, are very familiar with many of the pieces I'm missing." Tamara plopped into a seat on the short sofa. "So maybe you could be like a mentor to me."

Abigail was amused. "If I can help, fine. Where do you want to start?"

"With Joel and his wife. What's her name again?"

There was a wealth of topics to tackle, and Tamara had

to bring up Joel. "Zarah—sounds like 'czar' with a short 'a' on the end, 'czar-a.'" Abigail had to concentrate on keeping her wounds hidden. Tamara was smart. If a glimmer was exposed, she was going to pounce on it. Abigail covered up.

"What's this business about an arranged marriage? Did he literally just show up at the altar and there was a woman waiting there for him, someone he didn't know or date beforehand?"

"I don't think it was quite that dramatic." There had to be at least one other person in the world more willing to share the details of Joel's wedding with Tamara than Abigail. She hadn't gone to the wedding. Her trampled love sat at home watching the media highlights along with the rest of the world. "I believe they'd only met a few times before the wedding."

"How intriguing. Traveling around the world, I've seen plenty of arranged marriages, but it's kind of shocking for someone in my family. Americans pick who they want and stay with them until they die, get tired of them, or dump them for someone better."

Abigail had to change the subject. Lingering on Joel's romantic escapades was certain to expose her healing wounds. "Do you have any questions about DMI?"

"I do, but Joel and Zarah seem a lot more interesting," Tamara said. Great, Abigail thought. She'd peel the skin off her wounds and let Tamara have at them. Tamara wasn't going to stop until they were exposed and raw again anyway. Abigail dropped her guard, not caring. The hiding was too much work. "Do they have any children?" Tamara asked.

"Nope."

"I wonder if they're going to have any. Do you think they'll stay together since the company fell apart?"

"You'd have to ask your brother that question."

"I guess he is my brother. I'm not accustomed to the label, that's for sure."

Abigail picked up on the uneasiness. "I'm sorry, did I say something wrong?" She thought her comment might have triggered a reminder of the rape. What else could it be?

"Can I squeeze in one more question?"

"Ask away," Abigail told her.

"Don is the new CEO. I understand his role. How does the rest of the family fit in? Who owns what?"

"In your father's will, Madeline and Sherry were each given twenty-five percent stock ownership. His three children got fifteen each."

After a brief pause, Tamara spoke. "That's ninety-five percent. Where's the other five percent, or did I add wrong?" Tamara asked.

"You're right. The last five percent went to me."

"You. Oh, my dad must have really liked you."

Abigail didn't comment. The discussion of the Mitchell men hadn't gone so well the last time Tamara broached the subject. She'd tread lightly this round. "I'm surprised Madeline or Don didn't tell you the details about the stock ownership split."

"Don told me about mine and his, but honestly, he didn't have much chance to tell me the rest. He probably tried, but I haven't made it easy for people to talk with me."

chapter

22

Pooped, Don leaned on his assistant's workstation. "I'm ready for lunch."

"Already on the way. I'll bring your lunch in as soon as it arrives." Don slapped his palm lightly against the workstation counter and went into his office. "Oh, Mr. Mitchell, I have another change to your schedule. Your four P.M. meeting with the Association of Ministers is being swapped with your five o'clock. Also, the president of the Mid-Atlantic Federation of Free Churches is in town. Since Mrs. Mitchell isn't here, he wants to meet with you, but your schedule is booked solid."

Don was concerned.

"I told him there's no way we can squeeze them in today. He wasn't happy," Kay said.

"Guess not, he's one of our largest clients in the East Coast division. They've always had hands-on attention from my mother. What am I going to do? I can't ignore him, but I can't cancel the other clients. This is awkward.

Can you get Abigail for me, please? Thanks." Don trudged into the office. He missed Madeline. She was well versed in the East Coast division. She owned that part of the country. If she were there, it would have been a cinch to convince the Mid-Atlantic Federation of Free Churches that DMI was stable and thriving. He was a poor substitute but had to get ready for the meeting. He'd review the history and prepare to dance around topics he wasn't familiar with. As CEO he had no choice.

A few minutes later Abigail was coming through the doorway, with Tamara following. The executive waiter pulled up the cart carrying a linen-covered tray with several covered dishes.

"I heard you're looking for me?" Abigail said.

"I'm double-booked this afternoon. One of Mother's clients from the East Coast is here and I have to meet with him."

"Who is it?"

"Mid-Atlantic Federation of Free Churches."

"Oh, definitely you have to meet with them. They're like the fourth- or fifth-largest account in that division. How can I help?"

"I wish there was a way to give me an injection of Mother's knowledge about the Federation. Since that's not going to happen, can you take a meeting or two for me?"

"I can move a few things around and free up time this afternoon. Sure, no problem."

Tamara stood around. She couldn't take a meeting and there wasn't time to teach her much today. He'd make time for her when his calendar lightened, sometime in the next three months. He knew her return was critical to the long-term healing of his family, but swirling in a litany of meetings, none of which she could help run, clouded the significance of her being there. The trade-off with her for Madeline was tough to measure as he sank into the mire of getting through the day.

"I have to prep for my next meeting." Don raised the lid off the salad and forked a few bites.

"We'll leave you alone," Tamara said. She and Abigail left.

Don forked more salad and gulped a glass of ice water. He ate a small portion of the sandwich and put the lid back on top. He jotted notes after thumbing through documents. Work was piling up. He scrolled down his list of numbers in the PDA. Madeline hadn't returned his calls since leaving. He'd left a message about Tamara, but there were no responses. He prayed she'd answer. Four rings and there she was.

"Mother, it's about time. Where are you? I haven't heard a word from you in a week." Don's voice was elevated.

"Calm down, young man. I'm in Hawaii. I was going to stay at my place in Kauai but it won't be ready for a week, and I didn't want to wait. So I'm staying in a hotel suite. I had every intention of calling you once I got settled in, but my calls would have put more pressure on you. I can only imagine how busy you are."

"You have no idea how swamped I am. That's why I'm calling. I need your physical help here in the office. I mean it, Mother. I'm swamped. I have zero transition plans from Joel."

"I hate that you're struggling. Honestly, I wish there was a way for me to help you, but my options are limited. Tamara needs distance from me, and I promised to give it to her."

"I can appreciate your commitment to stay away, but this is the worst possible time for you to be away from

DMI. I'm serious. This is a bear. Today I'm booked from nine to six, solid, double-booked. After six, I can switch to LTI business and put in another three to four hours."

"I'm sorry, Son. I hate disappointing you, but this is one time when I must stick to my guns."

Don was more disappointed than Madeline realized. His rise to power in DMI was hard fought. This should have been his time of euphoria. Instead it was clouded with mayhem.

"Come on, let me talk to Tamara. I want to see if she'll reconsider the arrangement. If you come back for a few months during this initial transition phase, it will be exactly what I need."

"Absolutely not, Don, you can't pressure her. If you do, she might run and run far. No way, I can't take the chance. She stays put."

"At my expense."

"That's not fair. I would never intentionally sacrifice one of my children for another. Tamara is the lost sheep. She needs to be there with you. She trusts you. I suspect you might be the only person she trusts in the world. I can't dare compromise her return. I'm sorry, Son. I truly am. This isn't the way I wanted this to be, but my hands are tied. Please understand."

"If you can't help me here at DMI, then can you at least drop into my LTI office and give Naledi a hand with my business there? I'm going to be sucked into the bowels of this place for a long while. I can focus here if I know Naledi has extra support there. Can you please do that for me?"

"Now, that might be doable. Give me a few more days here in Hawaii, and I'll give you an answer."

"Just so you know, I'm meeting with the Mid-Atlantic Federation of Free Churches this afternoon."

"Give Kimball my regards."

"This meeting came out of left field. I'm not prepared. Any tips?"

"He's an easy one. Remind him of how many discounts and freebies we've given him over the years. Last year alone we trained fifty of his people for free and, on top of that, gave him three months of courtesy follow-ups. That was close to a hundred and seventy-five thousand dollars. We had to do that with most of our top customers to keep them from opting out of their contracts. Joel put all of us over a barrel." Madeline's passion was raging. "Tell him the freebies are over. You're in charge. DMI is on track and we expect to be compensated for our services. If he doesn't like it, tough, he can take a hike."

"Mother, I'm not sure what his angle is, but I'll keep what you've said in mind."

"Don't let anybody take advantage of you."

"Don't plan to."

"Good. See, you don't need me after all. You'll do just fine."

Don wasn't worried about failing, confident in his God-given abilities. However, having Madeline around would make the heavy load of reviving DMI much lighter.

chapter

23

The day stretched into the early evening. Tamara was tired, with little to show for her efforts. She decided to pack up and head out for the day. Abigail had given her a quarterly report to review. She shoved it into her bag, dreading the read. The shiny marketing portfolio was more intriguing.

"Tamara," Don called out from the other end of the walkway. "Are you heading out?"

"Yes, I am," she said, punctuating it with a long sigh. She didn't want to recap the highlights, or really low points, of the day. She'd toss away today and start fresh tomorrow.

"We haven't spent any time together since you've been here. Let's grab dinner."

"I don't know about dinner. I'm pretty wiped out. This corporate-America stuff is already draining, and I've been here less than a week."

Don chuckled. "Don't worry. You'll catch on." He extended his arm to tap her shoulder and withdrew it quickly just as she pulled away. "Come to dinner with me. It will give us a chance to catch up. Hold on a minute, let me grab my wallet." He went into his office.

Tamara wanted to make up an excuse—any schedule conflict would suffice to get her out of this awkward situation.

Don emerged. "Let's go."

Abigail stopped them on the way to the elevator. "Are you leaving?"

"I think so, if I can convince my sister to join me for dinner. You're welcome to join us," Don said.

"I would love to, but I have a ton of work to get done. It's going to be a long night."

"For me too. I'll be right there with you," Don told her.

Abigail and Don didn't explicitly call out Tamara's name as the weak link. They didn't have to; the message had been conveyed to her in four or five different ways throughout the day. Her pride rose up. "We'll have to make dinner short," Tamara said, giving in. "I have a lot of reading and documents to review tonight."

"Fair, whatever works for you," Don said.

Abigail eased to the other side of Don and whispered, but Tamara could hear: "Are you coming back?"

"I think so, unless I work from home. Why?"

"Because, remember, we need to talk." Abigail drew closer to Don but Tamara could still hear.

"No problem. I'll check in with you later." Abigail agreed and returned to her office. Tamara got on the elevator with Don. "Where are you staying?"

Tamara was careful not to divulge alarming details about her situation. She was at the Hilton Garden but would need to move to the motel with the $29.99 nightly rate she'd seen from the bus. She was determined not to tell Don. "I'm staying at a hotel downtown."

"Which one?"

"Hilton Garden."

"How long are you going to stay there?" he asked. Not long, that was for sure, she thought, not with her money troubles. "You know Mother's mansion is empty."

A gust of jumbled hysteria tackled her. Tamara's knees wanted to buckle. She had no intention of ever stepping into the mansion again, determined to keep her terror and despair buried. "No, thank you," she squeaked out.

Don showed an expression of embarrassment. "Tamara, I wasn't thinking. I'm sorry. I shouldn't have suggested the mansion, my mistake." She didn't respond. They stepped off the elevator and walked toward the door leading outside. "I have a better idea. Come stay with me. I have my condo downtown. It's four bedrooms, three baths, plenty of room for you."

She was broke and the answer should have been immediate. But the pressure of losing her anonymity made her put up resistance. "I'm not sure. I've lived on my own for so long."

Tamara's world was a simple one, consisting of two bags. She was wired to operate solo, to roll out on a whim when necessary, without lingering attachments. She had to remain nimble in order to stay sane. Remo was a contributor to her constant movement but not the sole source. Others, especially family, had deposited the seeds of fear, doubt, and isolation long before he entered her life. Remo just happened to be the one who watered those seeds and brought them to full maturity. She couldn't let her guard down, not even with Don. Closeness and bonding were too dangerous. She wanted to retreat to the hotel and reexamine what was going on around her. Maybe the Detroit endeavor was more than she could handle.

"My guest room has its own bathroom, den, and kitchenette. You could have your own suite."

Torn between maintaining emotional distance and keeping a place to stay, Tamara was reminded of the nine-hundred-dollar balance in her account, prompting her to be somewhat amenable to a temporary arrangement, until she could legitimately earn money from her new job. Rational thinking said to take the offer. The part of her that savored the notion of privacy said no, although another part of her didn't want to be alone knowing her crazed ex was roaming around somewhere in the world.

"Let's get some dinner, and I'll worry about my accommodations later." They approached Don's car. "Besides, I've already paid tonight's rate at the hotel. If I move out, it won't be before checkout time tomorrow," she said, sprinkling humor to lighten the mood. Tamara didn't tell Don, but most likely, the cheap motel would be home until she could afford a better place. Besides, the motel was safer, made it more difficult for someone to track her down. She was pretty certain Remo didn't know where she was. Her survival instincts told her she couldn't be too careful.

"What do you have a taste for?" Don turned to look out the rear window as he backed out of the parking spot.

"Doesn't matter." Tamara typically ate fresh fruit, rice, and a small portion of protein. Meals were for survival, nothing fancy. For the past couple of years, she couldn't afford fancy. "Don, I'm not sure if this is the best time to broach the topic, but I need to discuss a salary."

He stopped the car and turned to face her. "Do you need money?"

"No, no, not like I need money to pay bills," she said,

seeming poised but feeling nowhere near it. "I think it will be symbolic of me carrying my weight, earning my keep."

"Oh, all right, because if you need money, all you have to do is claim your inheritance. Dad left a pocket of cash and the beach house in California for you." Don put the car in motion.

Tamara was intrigued. She hadn't been concerned with the details of her father's will and as a result didn't know her worth. Independence had been on her terms. Broke and needing cash, Tamara had to consider outlets she'd previously smashed in the past. "I'm not asking for handouts."

"Your inheritance isn't a handout. It belongs to you. Twenty million isn't a handout. It's a gift from your father."

Twenty million versus nine hundred, she thought. The temptation to accept was alarming.

"Just so you know, when I left town, I didn't want Dad's money either," Don told her. "I was determined to make it on my own. I didn't want him to get any credit for my hard work, especially after he slighted me for Joel. So I definitely understand how you feel. But after I allowed myself time to begin thinking clearly again, Mother convinced me that I should take the money and make good use of it. I did, and I offer the same advice to you."

Made sense, but she'd wait before getting in too quickly with the family rites of passage. She couldn't be blinded by the money. "For now, let's start with a salary."

"Fine, name your price."

"No favoritism. Pay me what a new employee would get."

"Come on, Tamara, you're not the typical new employee. You are a Mitchell heir. You have a fifteen percent stock ownership in the company. You can't expect me to start you on a forty-thousand-dollar salary."

"Is that what people make at my level?"

"Pretty much."

"Then there it is, forty thousand."

"If that's what you want, I'll go along with it."

Tamara was thrilled to get the forty thousand. Having money coming in instead of constantly pouring out allowed her stress to lessen. In the short term, she might still have to relocate to the discounted motel until cash was in hand. "Couple more questions: how soon will I get paid, and can it be in cash?"

Don cut his gaze her way and let silence speak. She knew that he knew and kept silent too.

chapter

24

Abigail waited for Don in her office. He'd called around seven o'clock after finishing dinner with Tamara. She was reading a contract when Don walked in. "How was dinner?"

"Weird. I mean it's great having my sister here, but it's an adjustment for both of us. I'm not sure what to say around her."

"You kept in touch while she was away. I'd think the two of you wouldn't have a problem talking. Maybe she would with Madeline, but not with you. Everybody gets along with you."

"Is that right?" he said.

"That's the way it looks from my vantage point. As a matter of fact, there are those who get along better with you than they do with anybody else."

"Anyone in particular?" he said, sitting on the edge of her desk, facing Abigail.

"I plead guilty as charged, Mr. Mitchell. What are you going to do about it?"

"So, the heck with small talk, you're jumping right into the conversation," he said.

Sitting back and keeping quiet hadn't worked. "You got it, time to put our feelings out there and decide where this is headed."

"Abigail, it's no secret that I care about you. You are and always have been a special friend to me. What's wrong with letting our friendship stay strong and letting the rest come as it will? Why add the extra pressure of forcing a relationship?"

"There was a time, and it wasn't too long ago, when you wouldn't have labeled us as a forced relationship." Perhaps she could let time dictate if there wasn't an immediate threat on the horizon. Abigail saw each call to Naledi as something that enticed him further away from what could be and should have been between them long ago. Abigail felt like she was at a disadvantage. Naledi had his full attention when he was in Africa. She didn't have to share him with a floundering company, or an unpredictable brother, or a protective mother. When he was with Naledi, she had all of him. Abigail didn't have the same opportunity to win his affection. Four years ago, he was completely hers. If he'd let her know then, perhaps their relationship would be fully formed. Instead Don hadn't shared his feelings with her, and she ended up with Joel. "When your father was alive, you and I were linked," she said, locking the fingers on both hands tightly. "Your feelings were a lot stronger than just caring about me. We worked. You know it. I'm asking you to give those two people a chance to find each other again."

Don stood and meandered to the window, leaning his

back against the frame. "Many changes have happened since my father died. I've changed, you've changed, DMI has changed, and your feelings have changed."

"They haven't," she said.

"So, are we going to ignore the elephant in the room, my brother? You admitted to being in love with him less than six months ago."

Her gaze sank. "Joel is history. To be honest, we never had more than a close friendship. We were never sexually involved. I guess I got our commitment to achieve a common goal mixed up with love." Her affection for Joel was packed and tucked away. Joel's priorities and needs didn't match hers, and it didn't appear they ever would. Don was her destiny. She wholeheartedly believed he was. Her adoration for Joel was a youthful aberration built on mutual validation.

After Dave Mitchell passed, Abigail was consumed with helping Joel fulfill his father's legacy. The fact that they were constantly together and respected each other had translated to love for her. It wasn't until a couple of years later that she found out Joel didn't reciprocate her feelings. The rejection was piercing, but after six months, the hurt had dissolved. Except for a residual faint ache, Joel was out of her system.

"But you chose him, that's a fact."

"Joel wasn't the man for me. Forgive me for my lapse in judgment. I made a critical error in letting you go. I'm hoping it's not too late to correct my mistake," she said, swinging the chair around, letting their gazes connect. Don grinned. "I know Naledi is in the picture, but that's not going to stop me. She's there and you're here with me," she said, crossing her legs and volleying a grin into Don's court.

"Ms. Abigail Gerard, what has gotten into you? You were not this direct back in the day."

"And look where it got me. Let's just say I'm smarter." Abigail acknowledged the uphill battle she was undertaking. Glancing at Don, she decided he was worth the effort.

chapter

25

Today wasn't going to resemble yesterday. Tamara was braced for Don and Abigail. She'd studied last night like a college student cramming for an exam. Tamara wasn't naïve in believing her contribution could be on a par with her mother's. She was committed to learning the business quickly and finding an area that she could master. If the Mitchell genes were as dominant as those around her believed, then she was guaranteed success at DMI. Maybe more than people were expecting or prepared to see.

Tamara knocked on Don's door. The clock above the administrative workstation read seven forty-five. Kay wasn't out front. Most people weren't in the office yet. Don told her to come in. "Good morning, everyone," she said, seeing Don and Abigail already meeting at his conference table. She thought seven forty-five was early. Tomorrow, it would be six forty-five. Whatever gave her the edge, she'd have to do it.

"Good morning to you," Abigail said. "You seem awfully cheery for a Tuesday morning."

Tamara pulled a seat from the table. She plucked the marketing portfolio and quarterly finance report from her bag and plopped them onto the table. Yellow mini stickies were protruding from every angle. "I'm starting to get a better understanding of the business," she said, sitting.

"Are you telling me you went through both reports last night?"

"Yes, and you can see I have a slew of questions."

"Fire away," Don said. She couldn't tell if he was impressed. Bringing questions instead of answers might be perceived as a burden but she accepted the positive perspective, for now. "On page fifteen, the income statement shows the company is worth half as much this quarter as it was at this same time last year?" She put her finger on page fifteen, which was heavily colored with highlights, and flipped a few more pages. "The number of clients is a little less than half compared to the list from last year."

Don and Abigail peered at each other, then centered their gazes on Tamara, almost in precise unison.

"Do you want to take the question or should I?" Abigail asked Don.

His PDA buzzed. "It's on you. Excuse me," he said, and walked toward the door to take his call.

"You've summed up our problem. I have to tell you that I'm impressed with your questions," Abigail told her. Tamara was pleased with the comment but not deceived into false security. "I don't know exactly where to begin." As Abigail spoke, Tamara noticed her constantly looking toward the door where Don had gone.

"I've heard you and Don talking about the trouble DMI is in. Exactly how bad is it?"

"Let me put the answer this way. We're not going out of business tomorrow."

"That's good to hear."

"But if we don't flip the current tide, we will be out of business in six months or less. This is like stage-two cancer. The problem has been detected, and with the right treatment our prognosis is good. If we do nothing, we're done. That's as plain as I can put this."

"I don't remember much about the company, but what I do recall is that DMI was running better when my parents were here. What happened?"

"That's a long story. How much time do you have?"

Don returned as Abigail was speaking. "Sorry about that," he said.

"Who was it, Naledi?" Abigail asked with a smirk. Don grinned.

Tamara detected the unspoken language between them and changed the topic. "I have as much time as you can give me," Tamara told Abigail.

"What did I miss?" Don asked.

"I was filling Tamara in on how the customer list got cut in half and DMI's value plummeted over fifty percent in the past year."

"So you see why we have a sense of urgency at this critical moment in the company. Everyone has to contribute. No free rides around here," he said.

Tamara could have slumped in her seat and retreated to some undiscovered corner of the world to escape the scrutiny. He didn't put her name on the comment, but she felt it was expressly for her. Wasn't much she could do, not yet. She hadn't been around to be mentored by the founders. Joel had. Don had, but the company's current state didn't reflect the benefits coming from the extra dose of hands-on support they'd received. Seeing the quarterly reports, she was confident she could do as good a job or better running the company. Maybe she'd have to take her chance. Dave Mitchell's other children had. She was the oldest. There had to be a slot for her.

"Is there a plan to fix this?" Tamara asked.

"Remember, yesterday we talked about getting rid of Harmonious Energy and recouping the two divisions Joel sold off. We can start with the West Coast division, which his wife owns," Don said.

"How soon is that going to happen?"

"Funny you should ask. I'm having my assistant schedule a meeting with Joel, hopefully today."

"Today?" Abigail said, alarmed.

Tamara wasn't sure why Abigail reacted the way she had. Of all people, Abigail should have understood the urgency. Tamara had been in the building less than a week and she got the message.

26

Joel paced around the library, not convinced he should have agreed to the meeting with Don. Meeting at the house instead of having to face the DMI staff was the only decision Joel wasn't regretting. He'd handed the keys over to Don less than two weeks ago, but it felt like a millennium. Joel should have taken his mother's advice and held off overnight before making a fatal decision. He was pretty sure the outcome would have been different. DMI was struggling but not doomed, as the press pretended. As smart as he was, the recovery would have been rapid. As quickly as DMI rose in his first three years, the bottom had fallen out in a short three months. There were no barriers to building the dynasty again. Joel pounded his fist into the palm of his hand, repeatedly feeling strength multiplying in his bones. The yearning to return to the corporate grind wasn't to be denied.

The doorbell rang. Joel didn't wait for the staff to answer. He went to the door, prepared for a short meeting with Don. Zarah came into the foyer. He opened the door and his heartbeat sped up. Don he was expecting, Abigail he was not. The term "awkward" was too minuscule for the gravity of their moment. She avoided eye contact and he did too. Zarah locked her arm into his as they backed from the door and invited the team in.

"Thanks for fitting us into your schedule," Don said.

Joel couldn't stop staring at the other woman with them. "Yeah, no problem, come in," he said, waving in the entourage. He and the other woman peered at each other; it had to be his sister. "Tamara?" Joel asked with reservation.

"In the flesh."

It was Tamara. Joel wasn't sure how to react. The reunion was emotionless, which wasn't surprising. They didn't know each other, given the nine-year age difference. She'd left town when he was twelve. Constant fighting between their mothers didn't foster or necessitate a loving relationship among Dave Mitchell's two sets of children. Last time he'd seen her was several months ago as she ran past him, tearing out of the DMI lobby. He hadn't recognized her then and not much had changed. Standing in his foyer, she was no more than a stranger.

"Welcome to my house. This is my wife." Sterile greetings ensued.

Zarah clung to him. Joel had to look away from Abigail. He didn't thrive on cruelty. He realized how painful it must have been for Abigail to stand in the house she designed and watch him hold another woman. He got that and didn't intentionally flaunt his marriage in front of her. Joel wanted to pull away from his wife but couldn't jeopardize the security and trust Zarah was building in their relationship. He needed her to fulfill his budding plan. Casualties were inevitable.

"Is this where we're going to meet?" Don asked.

"No, let's go to my office. We'll have more privacy there." Joel considered letting Zarah join the group. Most of the conversation would center on her family's company. Quick thinking brought him down on the side of caution. She was showing significant progress in her recovery. Adding stress in an area where she wasn't equipped to handle it didn't make sense. "Excuse me," Joel said, stepping to the side with Zarah. "Why don't you get a cup of tea and take a rest in the library?" Zarah didn't loosen her grip. He had to gently peel her fingers from his arm.

"I'd like to stay with you and meet more of your family."

Joel turned to the group. "If you don't mind, you can follow the walkway to my office, which is in the rear of the house. I'll be there shortly." Abigail led the way. Joel wouldn't have asked her to go first. It was her choice. Since she understood the layout better than anyone, it freed him to talk privately with Zarah. Shifting his attention to his wife, he said, "We'll be talking about business matters. You won't be interested."

"I don't mind. If you're going to be there, I'd like to be with you." She couldn't be in the meeting. Joel had no idea exactly what was going to be discussed. He wasn't dictating the agenda. Better to keep Zarah out.

"Please, for me, I don't want you to be uncomfortable." She began to speak, but he talked over her. "And I will not be able to focus if you're in the room. You will have my attention and not the group who has come to take care of important business. Can I count on your help in letting me go into the meeting alone?"

"You can."

Joel got her situated and proceeded to his office. When he arrived, Don, Abigail, and Tamara were seated and waiting. He closed the door and braced for the discussion. "How can I help you?" he asked, carving a path to his desk chair.

"I figured we'd jump right into the reason we came, Harmonious Energy and the West Coast division. Is your wife joining us?" Don said.

"No, she's not feeling well. We thought it best that she rest."

"Oh, how unfortunate. I was hoping to strike up a deal where she can take control of her father's company and DMI can regain ownership of the West Coast division, just like you and I discussed a few weeks ago."

"I can have the discussion with you."

"But she's the sole owner of the division. At some point she has to be the one who accepts or declines the offer," Don said.

"Let me worry about the details. Why don't you just present the offer and let me take care of the rest?"

"If you say so, as long as we agree that any deal established here is contingent upon final sign-off from Zarah," Don stated for the record.

"Are you speaking for the board of directors?" Joel asked. He hated being discounted. Don was sitting there smug, dictating the state of Joel's world. Zarah was sequestered in the kitchen or the library, holding the keys to his future. He wasn't going to let either bend him until he broke. Regaining control was his top priority.

"I don't need the board of directors to tell me the contract basics. The owner of the company has to sign off on the deal, plain and simple."

Joel had no power. Don was right, but Joel refused to be treated as powerless.

"I don't know what to tell you. If you want Zarah's

approval, you'll need to sell the idea to me first. My wife trusts me." As soon as the words were airborne Joel took a quick glance at Abigail and looked away. "I'll speak on her behalf for now. If we reach a deal, and that's an awful big 'if,' she'll be more than willing to sign the papers." Joel wasn't relinquishing power over the negotiations with Don and DMI. He'd almost let the division slip through his hands once before when Madeline tried to secretly cut a deal with Zarah. Thank goodness he found out in time to halt the transaction. He was more resolute about controlling the process now than he was then. Zarah's money and holdings were the primary assets that could get him back into the corporate game. They were his ticket to freedom. If she came with the assets as a package, fair enough. Sacrifices were to be expected.

"Let's table the discussion about Harmonious Energy and the West Coast division. What can you tell me about the Southern division?" Don asked.

Joel winced. The topic was expected but not welcome. "I told you Uncle Frank is the one you need to see about the division. I'm not involved and can't offer any details."

"Come on, Joel, you must know how that sounds," Abigail said, finally opening her mouth. He was beginning to wonder why Abigail and Tamara had come. Don was doing all the talking.

"Like I said, if you want information about the Southern division, Uncle Frank is your man."

"That's all you're going to tell us?" Don said, clearly agitated.

"You got it."

Don slammed his portfolio shut. "Let's go," he told the ladies. "This was a waste of time."

If tension hadn't been so prevalent, he would have

chuckled thinking about Madeline. She would have never sat in his office and remained as calm as the three sitting in front of him. She probably would have lunged over the table, grabbed him by the throat, and demanded answers. He wouldn't have told her what she wanted to know but the image was electrifying. There was an undeniable charge that came with battling the alpha lioness. She wasn't at the meeting, but he was certain they'd cross paths again and secretly looked forward to it.

The three were ready to leave. Joel stopped Abigail at the front door, breaking her away from the pack. "Abigail, do you have some time? I'd like to speak with you." Don and Tamara stopped too. "Privately."

She wriggled from his psychological grip. Her gaze danced from Don to Joel, back to Don. "I can't stay. I rode over with Don, and I don't have my car."

"I'll make sure you get a ride back."

"I don't think so. My schedule is packed today, and I just don't see squeezing another meeting in."

Joel could have pushed but opted not to. He understood, although her rejection sliced at him. He recalled the time when there wasn't another commitment on earth that would have kept her from rushing to his side. Her support had been constant. Realizing she was no longer his Abigail felt surreal, a fact he hadn't fully digested or anticipated. He opened the door and leaned against it. "I will see the three of you around," he said, not having much more to offer.

Joel continued leaning against the open door. He wasn't lingering there to extend sweet good-byes to his sister, brother, and close friend. Relations were strained before they arrived with no sizable change after they left.

"Did your family go already?" Zarah emerged from the

kitchen and asked. "I was looking forward to chatting with your sister. I've not met her before today." Join the club, Joel thought. Zarah had as much knowledge about Tamara as he did. She was a wild card in the Mitchell game. He'd have to figure out her agenda. Certainly she had one. Why else would she be in Detroit? She hadn't lived in town for ten or twenty years.

"We finished our business sooner than we expected." He didn't need to elaborate on the details. She wasn't a businesswoman.

"Will they return soon?"

"Doubt it," he said, easing the door shut, leaving the two of them standing in the foyer.

"How would you like to spend the day?"

He couldn't truthfully tell her where he wanted to be. She wouldn't understand his insatiable hunger for Chicago, and not just the city, although it was a cool place to be. His favorite five-letter word, Sheba, was the source of his hunger. He had stayed away; it wasn't easy, but he had. One day at a time was the most he could promise.

"Let's go for a ride," she said.

Fine with him. A break was going to be refreshing and allow him to clear the cobwebs lurking in his takeover plan. His edge hadn't dissipated. His naysayers would soon be marveling at his miraculous comeback. He ushered Zarah toward the garage. He was intent on keeping her happy. His return to glory hinged on her, a fact she wasn't aware of. Best to keep her unaware.

Don careened the BMW 7 series down I-94 going from Joel's home in the southwest suburbs to the office downtown. "Come on!" he yelled, zipping the car around a driver who must have been going forty miles an hour or less.

Abigail sat in the front seat. "This is why you should use the company driver instead of taking your own car."

"You know me. I'm not into the prestigious perks. There's no reason I can't drive my own car. I have a license. Come on!" he yelled again, encountering another slow driver.

"You're not usually this riled. Joel got to you, didn't he?" Abigail asked.

"Maybe I did let him get to me. I'm sorry."

"No need to be sorry. He ticked me off too. I can't believe how much he's changed. I don't recognize him."

There was no denying Don's frustration. Joel wasn't to be trusted. What had made him think Joel had changed?

The five minutes of weakness Joel exhibited a few weeks ago, when he resigned, were a distant memory. Abigail might have seen his behavior as a recent change. Don saw the behavior as Joel's norm.

"We have to figure out how to recoup the West Coast division," Abigail said.

"The reality is that we might not be able to get the division from Joel," Don said.

"I thought you said it belongs to his wife," Tamara said, chiming in from the backseat.

"Joel is calling the shots in their house, make no mistake about it. If we get the division, Joel will be the one making the final decision, not Zarah."

"Is it worth talking to her directly?" Tamara asked.

"How? Joel is like a watchdog over her."

"But it sounds like she has the power, not him," Tamara commented.

"Don't count on it."

Don drove with newfound calm, purging his anger, refusing to let frustration take root. He'd worked too hard to forgive Joel, his father, and God. One day lined with undesirable results wasn't strong enough to push him out of the space of grace he'd carved. Joel was a handful, but God had a big hand. Don had to trudge along. To think he had dreamed of assuming leadership in his father's company nearly four years ago. Now that he had it, the role didn't feel much like a dream.

"Then we have to be prepared to move DMI forward without the West Coast," Abigail said.

"It's not ideal, but you're right. We only need to recover one division to stabilize our income base. We might have to focus on recovering the Southern division alone, but Joel was awfully vague about the details."

"Your uncle holds the key."

"He might be easier to deal with than Joel," Don said.

"Maybe, but you know we'll need Madeline to deal with your uncle," Abigail said, and then erupted in laughter.

Don had spent the last two days being overly sensitive to conversations about his mother, respecting Tamara's insecurities. There were going to be times when he didn't feel like completely burying his mother. Laughing about her antics with Abigail was good.

"We certainly have our work cut out for us," Don said, rolling into the parking lot. "I'll have to call Naledi and tell her I'm going to be here longer than expected, unless I can work out a way to get Mother here for a temporary stretch." Don let his gaze search out Tamara in the rearview mirror for a favorable response. He needed her to make room in Detroit for Madeline; even a short while would work. She returned the gaze and then looked in the other direction. That was his answer. Car parked, he turned off the engine. "Go on up. I'll catch up with you both when I get upstairs."

Abigail and Tamara got out. He longed for a safe haven from the fray. He called Naledi. She calmed his stormy seas. "I am glad you answered the phone," he said without hesitating when she got on the line.

"Your timing is spot-on. I have a bit of good news." Don was eager to hear something good. His soul was calming. "The proposal for our expansion in London has been accepted at the full value."

"You're kidding." Don was amazed at how Naledi had assumed responsibility for the deal and had taken it to completion without requiring his hands-on input. She was a true partner.

"We're very elated here," she said with the French twist

in her accent dominating. "Can you return straightaway to complete the sign-offs?"

Don was grieved, unprepared to answer. He couldn't let LTI flop while scrambling to restore DMI. The debacle earlier with Joel was disappointing and a setback. Naledi needed him and he was going to have to say no—or should he? How many times was he going to let his family put a chokehold on his personal path to success?

28

Yesterday's fiasco with Joel had passed. Don was on to step number two in the DMI recovery plan. He had to link a chain of calls to get his uncle's telephone number. Uncle Frank had been a regular visitor to their home during Don's childhood. He used to be the chief financial officer in the company when Dave Mitchell was in charge; he had the role from the beginning. Dave Mitchell had relied heavily on his brother, trusted him with full financial responsibility. Don dialed the phone resting on the sofa in his condo.

"Uncle Frank, it's your nephew Don."

"The good son. Hello there, Nephew. I haven't spoken to you since your father's funeral. What's going on?"

"I'm calling about DMI business."

"I don't have any business with DMI."

"If it's all right with you, I'd prefer to meet in person," Don said.

"About what?"

"I don't need more than a half hour."

"Well now, Nephew, my time isn't free."

Don hated having to rely on his uncle for information. Joel had created a situation that left him no choice. "Let's meet and then we can talk about your fee."

"Normally I agree to terms up front, but since you're my brother's son, I'm going to give you a pass, for the first half hour. The clock will be ticking after that."

"Fair enough, Uncle. Where do you want to meet? I'm at my condo downtown."

"Oh, I try to stay out of the downtown area, too busy. I prefer discretion with my meetings."

"Name the spot."

"Meet me at the Westin, near the airport."

Uncle Frank lived in the northeastern suburbs, the opposite direction from the airport and close to forty miles away.

"You want to meet way out there?" Don asked.

"That's the spot. It's my personal office for initial negotiations. Depending on where this leads, we may have to move to one of my other offices."

Don wondered how Joel had sunk to the depths of needing Uncle Frank's help. The ball of deception was going to take time to unravel. With Uncle Frank involved, there would be money required too. Money Don had, but time was in short supply. "I'll see you in an hour."

"Ten fifteen, don't be late. I charge by the minute."

Don got his keys off the kitchen countertop, pausing to reflect. He understood his challenges with Joel. They were wedged into a family that didn't want to be related. Frank and Dave were born to the same parents. Yet they had little in common. Father and Uncle Frank tolerated each other longer than most would have, longer than most *could* have.

Don shut the door, locking it from the outside, still thinking about his uncle and father. His dad had to cut ties when Uncle Frank started robbing clients by overcharging them and then siphoning the extra money into his private account. In spite of his brother's repeated betrayals, Dad wasn't the one to fire him. He let Joel do it.

Don stepped into the elevator, clinging to his remaining shred of forgiveness for Joel, and prayed he could maintain the kind of grace his father had. He had seen his father as weak, letting people take advantage. Sitting in the seat of maturity, the landscape looked different. Forgiving he could do. Forgetting the sting of betrayal, hurt, and animosity was a larger undertaking, but it was required for him to continue progressing. Don exited the elevator, picking up his pace. Uncle Frank wasn't joking about the per-minute charge. Don intended to pay the minimum amount for information that should have freely been provided by Uncle Frank and Joel.

A forty-minute ride along I-94 deposited Don at the Westin hotel. He crept along, looking for a glimpse of Uncle Frank. Not finding him outside, Don parked and went inside with ten minutes to spare. Uncle Frank walked in precisely at ten fifteen. Don hadn't had any personal run-ins with his uncle. They locked hands, pulled in for the manly shake-bump, held for a split second, and released.

"So you're back from big old Africa, bush man."

Don used to love his uncle's sense of humor. Had his character not become so questionable, Uncle Frank would have been a decent guy to befriend. "What can I say, South Africa has been very, very good to me . . ." he said, trailing off with a chuckle. Uncle Frank joined in.

"Let's grab a seat in the bar area. They have my special seat in the rear corner, nice and quiet."

"Why the bar area?"

"Best place at ten o'clock in the morning on a weekday. Anybody with a job is at work. Anybody without a job in the city doesn't have gas money for this long ride, and anybody else here this early in the morning has a drinking problem. We don't have to worry about those poor slobs. Their attention will be on that line of bottles," he said, drawing a line in the air that pointed toward the bar. "They won't know we're here," he said, laughing a little and tapping his hand across the small table. "Enough with the small talk, let's get to business. A half hour will click by quickly," Uncle Frank said, snapping his fingers.

The clandestine meeting humbled Don. The notion of running DMI without scandal constantly pranced in his thoughts. What was he thinking? Out with it, and he could get out of there before anyone caught him carousing with the fired executive. "What can you tell me about the Southern division?"

Uncle Frank rubbed his fingers along his chin, resting his elbow on the other folded arm. The waiter approached and Uncle Frank waved him off. "What can I tell you about the Southern division," Uncle Frank responded.

Don prepared for a long, meaningless conversation, replicating the one he'd had with Joel yesterday. "Joel sold the division to somebody. He sent me to you, because he's not talking."

"I don't know why he sent you to me. Joel was the CEO. He ought to have the information you want," Uncle Frank said as he toyed with the drink coasters situated in the center of the table.

"Between the two of you, somebody knows something. Just give me a name. I can go from there."

"Nephew, you're a pretty decent guy. I've never had any

trouble with you. That other brother of yours is another story. But you, you're all right. I like you. So let me give you this little piece of advice for free, no charge," he said, swiping his hands in the air like an umpire calling a base runner safe. It was difficult for Don to see a single aspect of his father in Uncle Frank. "Your brother found himself in a jam. He needed money, lots of it." Uncle Frank leaned over the table, lowering his voice. "I introduced him to some people in the lending business, people you may want to avoid. That's what I know," he said, leaning back.

"Are you going to give me a name?"

"Nope, I'm not. I like you, Nephew, but I don't like you that much. As a consultant, my customers pay dearly for discretion, and that's what I give them," he said, leaning in again. "Take my advice and move on without the Southern division unless you're interested in paying twice the value. I doubt if they would let you in the door for less."

"You're crazy. I'm not paying twice the value for any division," Don said, getting worked up.

Uncle Frank raised and lowered his hand for Don to keep the volume down. "You're getting mad at the wrong person. I'm not the one who set this train in motion. You can thank Dave's baby boy for his business acumen," he said, chuckling to the point of taunting. He kept laughing, pausing to say, "Ironic, isn't it? Joel fired me for questionable decisions and turns out he's no different than I am." He resumed chuckling. "I guess the streak runs in the family." Don was beyond pleasantries. Anger, humility, and sheer shock meshed, leaving him in awe. "Of course if you want to disregard my advice and go ahead with this Southern division business, then I can offer my consulting services, for a one percent fee of course." Don remained speechless. Uncle Frank pulled a calculator from his pocket and a set of reading glasses from his top inside jacket pocket. "Since the original sale was close to three hundred million . . ." Don wanted to bellow, *What?* That was ludicrous. It was a struggle, but Don contained his outrage. Uncle Frank was correct. Don's anger had to be directed at Joel. Uncle Frank punched keys on the calculator. "Double the price and you're at six hundred million. Take one percent and you're looking at my fee of . . . ," he said, and held the calculator for Don to read. "Actually, I didn't need a calculator for that."

"No way, I'm not paying you six million. I'm not paying them six hundred million for a division either. The company's worth far less than a billion with two divisions gone. And until I get rid of Harmonious Energy we're bleeding clients and value. No way am I paying that kind of money. Who are these investors anyway?"

Uncle Frank plucked off his reading glasses, slowly returned them to his pocket, and casually said, "Let's just say these investors and the devil are tight."

Don concluded the meeting with three minutes to spare, completely convinced Uncle Frank intended to charge for any overage. A barrage of thoughts bombarded Don. The extent of Joel's failure was mounting, and it was far-reaching. Don had to vent. He wasn't going to lay his challenges onto Naledi. He dialed the one person who would understand and possibly assist. Please answer the phone, he thought. The phone rang and rang with no answer. He sighed in disappointment, tossed the phone onto the passenger seat, and pulled the seat belt across his chest. As he was about to slide the buckle into the hook, the phone buzzed. He glanced at it and snatched the phone quickly. "Mother, where are you? I just called you."

"Well, hello to you too. I was half-asleep. Remember I am in Hawaii. It's not quite six A.M."

"Oops, I'm sorry, Mother. I did forget."

"So, what's so urgent?"

"You won't believe my morning. I had a very strange meeting with your brother-in-law."

"Who, Frank? What in the world were you doing with him?"

"Trying to regain the Southern division."

"How did it go?"

Don recalled the outrageous price tag on his services. "He is expecting to make a small fortune with this deal. There's no way I'm paying him six million dollars and his investor buddies six hundred million for the Southern division."

"Is that what he's asking?"

"Can you believe him? Even if I wanted to entertain his offer, DMI doesn't have the cash." Don let his neck hang down with his head following. "If we paid Uncle Frank and the investors what they want, DMI would be bankrupt. We're close as it is, but those two transactions would push the company over the edge."

"Why don't you let me talk to Frank? We've had dealings in the past and I kind of understand his language."

"I don't want to pursue discussions with Uncle Frank. I have a bad feeling in my gut about making a deal with him or his people. I can't get caught up in a scandal, and you know Uncle Frank breeds scandals."

"I can't argue with you there. He dragged your father's name down. Frank is not for lightweights. Sounds like Joel got in over his head. I'm proud of you, Son. You're more like your dad every day. Dave had his shortcomings, but professionally he was a smart man. I'm not going to speak about his lapse in judgment and morals when it came to that home-wrecker of his."

"Mother, I agree. We're not going to get sidetracked

with Sherry. I have too much to accomplish today with zero time for slashing Sherry."

"I've gotten better, you have to admit."

"Perhaps; only time will tell."

"Let's get back to your situation. How can I help you without coming to Detroit?"

"Go to Cape Town and give Naledi a hand for me. That will free me up to get submerged in unraveling this fiasco without feeling guilty about leaving Naledi completely alone."

"I'm not sure."

"What's holding you back? You've always told me you will support me when I need you. Well, I need you." She'd done the unthinkable for Tamara. His request wasn't nearly as extreme. "I need your help, Mother, seriously."

"You are not going to let me out of this, are you?"

"The only other alternative is for you to come here and work with Abigail. Then I can go handle LTI."

"I told you that's not an option." He knew her answer was no, but it forced Madeline to give more consideration to his request. "If my going to LTI means this much to you, then I have no choice. I'll have to go."

"Don't make it sound like the kiss of death."

"I'm sorry, Don. I didn't mean to seem begrudging. Actually, I'm glad to help, honored to be asked. At least one of my children has use for me. So I should be thanking you for allowing me to be relevant."

"Relevant and a whole lot more," he said, feeling lighter. Having Madeline on board was a priceless asset. She could take care of her business and his. Naledi was covered. He was relieved and rejuvenated.

"One more question before you go: how's Tamara doing?"

She's doing very little, he wanted to say, but opted to paint a rosier picture for his mother. With the price Tamara made her pay, he wanted Madeline to realize a return on the investment. "She's coming along, jumping into the fray. There's plenty of work for everyone to get a healthy share."

"Good to hear; then my decision to go was the right one." Don didn't think so. Three to six months from now would have been better. Immediately following changes in the executive team was the worst possible time. The timing wasn't fair to Tamara, to Don, or to Madeline. But wallowing in faulty acts of reality was pointless. He would shun the thoughts and press on.

"When are you heading to Cape Town?"

"Next week," she replied.

"Fair enough. Now that you're going to Cape Town next week, I can concentrate on selling off Harmonious Energy first and then worry about regaining the fractured divisions." There was plenty to do without adding Uncle Frank's extortion to the list. That was Joel's style, not his. Don was going to have to rely on his faith in God's favor to move the boulders piling up in his path to victory. Relying on his own skills hadn't worked for Joel, and Don was resolute that he would not travel the same path.

They were ending the call when Madeline yelled, "Don, wait!"

"Yes?"

"Tamara didn't take the money I offered. Do you know if she has any?"

"I'm not sure but I don't think so. She asked for a salary the other night, and I gave it to her."

"Where is she staying, at our house?"

"She was totally against staying there." Don understood

and was sure Madeline did too. "I offered to let her stay with me. She said no. As far as I know she's staying at the Hilton Garden downtown."

"This is ridiculous. I'm in Hawaii and my daughter is in Detroit, broke."

"We don't know that she's broke for sure."

"Something is going on. I need to check into this."

"No, Mother, don't. You can't cross the line. Now that Tamara is here, we can't spook her into running away again." He didn't have to dig deep to find compassion for Tamara. She wasn't helping his cause professionally but work didn't trump family or love.

"I'm not trying to drive her away, just the opposite. It's hard to stay at arm's length when the two of you need me, maybe more than you ever have. I'm doing the best I can not to intervene. That's why I haven't jumped at your invitation to join Naledi at LTI. I'm like an addict. Giving me a taste of the family business and interaction with my children and then shutting down full access is a recipe for failure. I don't know how to do less than a hundred and ten percent. I'm trying to maintain distance. I'm trying, and it's the hardest feat I've tackled in my sixty-five years. So when you tell me my daughter is broke or you suspect that she is, my millions don't mean a hill of paint if they can't support the people I love."

Don's heart ached for his mother. Her pain was sharp. He could feel it in every fiber of silence choking the call.

chapter

30

Joel flipped through the pages of his marital contract, letting the strangled rays of sunlight pierce the partially closed blinds. The paragraph radiated like neon lights. Funds were to be held in escrow with a minuscule one million dollars paid to Zarah each year until the fifth year, when the entire Bengali estate transferred to her. Divorce provided the only exception. If Joel left her, she'd immediately assume ownership of the entire estate.

He kept reading, searching for a glitch. Several rounds of scrutiny netted the same outcome. Sole ownership of DMI's West Coast division and the money belonged to Zarah. He estimated her net worth to be one and a half billion. Joel pumped his fist lightly against his lips. He was certain Zarah could be talked into purchasing Harmonious Energy. She was eager to please, giving him the leeway necessary to take risks. If they were going to stay together, she had to understand his need to be stimulated professionally. The rest of life was lumped into a huge secondary category. How far up the list their marriage ranked was going to be up to her.

Joel pondered his options. The three noticeable gaps in his plan made his head hurt. They were not insurmountable, more like a few notches short of impossible. First he had to figure out how to convince Zarah's executor to release her inheritance early. Assuming the first feat was accomplished, the second hurdle was waiting patiently. Zarah had to assign ownership of her family's company to him. He had to be secure in the leadership position in order to make bold and uncompromised decisions. He didn't have the ultimate authority at DMI and it cost him. The board of directors kept cuffs on his vision, neutralizing his abilities. His reign at Harmonious Energy wouldn't start off flawed. Ownership was mandatory. Without the transfer from Zarah, their marriage would have no merit. Hopefully she could understand.

Joel hated being reduced to this level of dependence. He reflected on his predator. Madeline led the pack of wolves who'd sought his demise. Don trailed in the rear, nipping at his heels every now and then. They weren't alone. Zarah's father had taken a few bites too.

Musar Bengali had the stipulations locked down. His dying wish was to ensure that his daughter, his sole heir, was secure in a marriage with a strong man of means. He'd handpicked Joel and sought him out for Zarah. Joel acknowledged that he still possessed half the qualities of a suitable husband, though the decline of DMI had eliminated the "means" component.

Musar was shielding his daughter from the grave. Joel wasn't sure if the gods of Zarah's father could help. He didn't know much about them but desperation made options he'd once ignored suddenly interesting. He wasn't about to go to the God of his father. They'd parted ways a few years ago. Joel wasn't ready to make amends. Circumstances hadn't gotten quite so desperate. He acknowledged that his faith fell pitifully short compared to what was needed.

Joel dove deep into strategizing. If he got the cash to buy Harmonious Energy and Zarah signed over ownership, his plan would hinge on taking ownership of the West Coast division too, beating out Don. The move was critical in establishing a U.S. presence, enabling him to keep a toe in the DMI world. This was going to be tricky. Zarah couldn't sell or transfer ownership to her husband until three years into the marriage. If there were no children in the marriage after three years, Joel could divorce Zarah and have the right to purchase the West Coast division at fair market value. Three years might as well have been a thousand. His funds were depleted. He owed everybody for everything. Joel was operating in the red but his mother's offer to help wasn't to be considered.

Betrayal reeked and his anger fumed as he paraphrased the next clause in the marital agreement. There were no restrictions on Zarah selling or transferring ownership to another person or entity. His anger heated. Vultures were hovering. He had to keep Don and Madeline at a standoff until the pieces of his puzzle were secure. Letting any of them take possession would be the final blow in his demise. His recovery would be officially terminated. Joel closed the contract and returned the document to the top drawer in his desk. He turned the key in the lock and went to find his partner. They had a bond. She needed security and a husband. He needed a company and cash. The arrangement was suitable so long as each was getting what they needed.

He turned around, going back to his office. Sheba was due a call. He'd refrained for weeks. No logic in dragging the communication ban any further when he knew their reunion was inevitable. He rushed to his office, closing and locking the door behind him, dialing rapidly. Like a kid headed to Disney World, he never tired of the thrill.

chapter

31

Tamara scrambled to collect papers spread across the modest-sized table. She emerged from the cramped conference room, excited. Abigail was standing in the doorway of Don's office, across the hallway. "Good night," Tamara said to Abigail.

"You're leaving?"

Tamara didn't feel obligated to justify her time. A quarter to five represented a full day, especially when she started before seven. Her eight and a half hours were more than satisfied.

"I'll see you tomorrow."

Don came to the doorway. Abigail stepped to the side. "I've been meaning to ask if you're still at the Hilton Garden," he said.

"I am, but not for much longer." She was staying there until cash from her first paycheck was received; she had to in order to be able to cover the bill at checkout. The bill was larger than the money she had left. "I'm looking at three apartments this evening."

"Sounds like you're going to stay around."

"I'm looking at short-term leases until I can see what my future holds. The apartments close at six thirty."

"You need a ride?" Don asked.

She wanted to decline but didn't want to miss her appointments. A taxi was too much. "Actually I would like a ride. Are you leaving now?"

Don took a quick glance at his watch. "I intended to stay here until eight or nine, since we're preparing a presentation for the board of directors. But don't worry about it. We can take a break. I can zip you to the apartment and come back later to finish up."

"You're too busy, don't worry about the ride. I'll take the bus or get a taxi, no big deal."

"No, it's not a problem. I want to take you."

"But I don't want to pull you away." Tamara's excitement faded. The duo expected her to work late too, she thought. Yet, the apartment held her attention. The building offered the first month free, which was too compelling. She had to go. She had to stay.

"Seriously, it's okay. I can finish tonight," Don said.

"How about this?" Abigail interjected. "Go with Tamara. I'll keep working. By the time you get back we can knock out what's left. You can take a final review in the morning, mark it up. I can make your changes and have the final version on your desk by noon."

"We could shoot for an early afternoon meeting with the board," Don added. Abigail gave a thumbs-up.

Tamara was growing antsy. Each tick of the clock seemed like an hour. Four fifty already. Stay. Go. She needed the apartment. Equally she needed Don and Abigail to believe in her genuine commitment to learning the business. "Oh what the heck, I might as well stay."

"Don't change your plans," Abigail said. "Don and I can get this done. We've burned the late-night oil together many times." Tamara noticed the lift in Abigail's voice when she spoke about Don.

"Tamara, she's right. Between the two of us, we can do this. I don't want you to put a hold on your apartment hunting. Finding a home is your top priority, and I don't want to interfere. We can handle this round for the directors, but you keep reading and jump in when you feel ready."

They weren't taking her seriously. Tamara hated being viewed as a burden and constantly being marginalized. She wasn't a child waiting for her babysitter to let her stay up late or to give her a larger slice of pie. She had as much right as Don to be engrossed in DMI, definitely more than Abigail. The "M" in "DMI" stood for "Mitchell." Tamara wanted to be included in the big meetings. That's how she was going to learn the business. "I definitely want to be involved with the presentation. I may not understand every detail, not yet, but I'll get there."

"Let's get to work then," Don said. Abigail didn't seem too bothered.

"What time is the meeting with the board of directors? I want to block off the time on my schedule," Tamara said.

"We don't have a time yet, but the meeting is only for board members. We can fill you in afterward," Don told her.

"Who are the members?"

Don shifted his weight from one leg to the other. She could tell he wasn't prepared for the question. "Let's see, there are nine in total. Mother and I are the last of the Mitchell clan." He named four other people. Abigail filled in the two he missed; they finished each other's sentences.

"The ninth seat is open since Joel stepped down. I want to nominate Abigail for membership at the next regularly scheduled meeting. She's earned the role."

"Thank you," she said, appearing demure. Tamara didn't believe the reaction to be totally sincere. Any woman who'd worked her way to the boardroom couldn't possibly be as meek as Abigail appeared. There had to be a pit bull personality hidden just below the surface.

Don beckoned for them to come inside his office and close the door as the conversation continued. Tamara didn't worry about the apartment search. There was a little more time.

"Tomorrow is an emergency meeting. Total focus is on getting the members to endorse our recovery concept. On a high level, I'm proposing we sell Harmonious Energy to the highest bidder."

"I thought the company belonged to the family of Joel's wife," Tamara said.

"Correction, the company belongs to DMI," Abigail stated.

"I wanted to give Joel and Zarah first crack at the sale, but you see how he reacted when we met. I have very little confidence about cutting a deal with Joel on the company," Don said.

"But Zarah is the one who has to make the decision."

"If you believe that, Tamara, then I have a patch of swampland to sell you in Louisiana as a prime resort property," Don said, tickled. "Don't be fooled for a second. Joel is running the program. Any deals will go through him."

"Unless she begins to understand her worth," Tamara added.

"Good luck with that," Don said, still amused.

"So what do we do?"

"Sell to the highest bidder. Use the cash to stabilize our cash flow and to shore up operations on the East Coast and in the Midwest."

"What about the two missing divisions?" Tamara asked.

"Let them go. That way Joel can't use the West Coast division as leverage to run up the price tag on Harmonious Energy. I'm not going to be strong-armed into a deal that makes DMI worse off. We can shut down the loopholes up front by removing those two divisions as pawns."

"Sounds like the way we need to go. Will the board members buy it?" Tamara asked.

"We'll see. I have at least one vote in my favor," Don said, glancing at Abigail. "I'm going to have her temporarily occupy the vacant seat."

"Why couldn't I?" Tamara asked.

"What?" Don said.

"Temporarily fill the seat." Don and Abigail wore dumbfounded expressions. "I figured Mother would want me to fill the seat. You know how she is about her children being in charge. I might as well dive in if this is where I'm going to end up." Don had to be wondering how an employee making forty thousand a year could be on the board of directors; it didn't make sense. But her last name was Mitchell; it didn't have to.

Tamara did feel bad for Abigail and for Don. Tamara could boast about being self-made, having taken care of herself for years without the help or wealth of the Mitchell family, but the claim wouldn't be completely accurate. Truth be told, Don had always stayed in contact. She always had him. Feelings of endearment for him resonated in her, while she loathed the rest of their family. They didn't require or deserve special consideration. He did.

chapter

32

Three hours had screeched past in Don's office. Tamara was ready to grab a pillow, lights out. "I'm pooped. I'm going to cut out on you," she said. Her determination voted to stay longer but conceded to fatigue.

"We'll be wrapping up in an hour, tops. You want me to arrange a car? Or if you can hang around, I'll give you a ride to the hotel," Don told her.

"Thanks for the offer, but I really am exhausted. I'm going to leave now." Sleepless nights were commonplace since she arrived in Detroit. She hoped her sheer exhaustion meant the night had been productive. Tomorrow represented her debut as a seated board member. She had to be well rested.

"I can't let you leave alone."

"Then I'll take a taxi instead of the bus." Might as well splurge on a taxi ride home to celebrate her progress, she thought.

"Okay, that works for me," Don said.

Tamara left Don's office. She waited in the lobby as the security guard called her a taxi. Fifteen minutes later, her ride was out front.

"Where to, miss?"

"Hilton Garden downtown, please." She eased into the backseat, peering into the night. "Excuse me, sir, can you change that to Rochester Hills?" she said, rattling off the address and not sure why. Drips of fear trickled in. For a few nights, she'd forgotten how rampant fear felt. She hadn't dwelled on Remo in days. Thirty-five minutes deposited Tamara in front of her mother's mansion, the prison of her childhood innocence. "Can we please sit here?"

"Sure, miss. I'll have to keep the meter running."

"Fine." She wanted to speak as little as possible. Tamara stared at the house. She got out of the car to get a closer look, protected by the twelve-foot gates separating her from the grounds of despair. She was numb. So much of her life was tied up in the skeletons of the past. Tamara was weary from lugging the emotional anchors, broken beyond immediate repair. She yearned to be whole again, to be free from her shattered existence, but fear kept her crippled. Letting go meant facing the pain head-on, anguish that had been strategically suppressed. She'd mastered running. It was her sedating drug of choice. Tamara gripped the iron fence, and her emotions crested and broke into a steady flow of warm tears streaming down her cheeks. She remained silent in the dark, and not for the first time. She clutched the fence tighter, clinging to the fragments of her broken soul.

She could grab her suitcase from the hotel and vanish into the world, returning to a life she understood and controlled. The urge was there, undeniable. But the feeling that she had a right to be there was greater. Had her world been uninterrupted, maybe she could have learned the family business and been the savvy marketing executive her mother and brothers were known to be. She never got the chance to craft her future. It was savagely forced upon her. Zeal burned inside her, fueling her tenacity. She wasn't going anywhere, not until she was ready. No more running. She was tired of instability. She slapped away the tears, building courage. She was a Mitchell, born and raised, and it was time to assume the benefits. Strength and resilience were her birthright.

Tamara declared that this was her moment. She'd paid the price; now it was time for the retribution. No one and nothing was going to stand in her way. Tomorrow, she'd move out of this tiny space and into an office befitting a board member. The salary was also open for discussion. She'd ask Don for more money—much more.

The administrative area seemed super-quiet, or maybe she was too tired to hear anything. Abigail was sleepy but rest wasn't on the schedule. She could pause tomorrow, on the weekend. She was buried in the presentation they'd drafted last night and was determined to deliver a stellar finished product. Tamara wasn't in a position to fully produce. Don needed her support and she was eager to help. Naledi wasn't the only one who could deliver big for him in his time of crisis.

Rushing from the ladies' room to her office, Abigail wasn't paying much attention when she heard her name called. She looked up. "What are you doing here?" she asked Joel. He hadn't been to the building since resigning. Abigail had to focus. Having Joel standing a foot away wasn't going to work.

"I'm taking my mom to lunch. Want to join us?"

"I'm too busy," she said, curt.

"Too busy for everybody or for me?" His honey-laced

aura spilled over her, sticking her feet in place. She wanted to run away and ignore him but couldn't move. The heat of his presence caused a meltdown. He was too close and getting closer. "Too busy for me?" he asked again, lowering his voice while shrinking the distance between them.

Tamara entered the administrative area. Abigail stepped away from Joel, not wanting to give Tamara the wrong impression.

"Joel, we meet again."

"Tamara, I expected you'd be gone by now. I hope this works out for you," Joel told her. Then he redirected his attention to Abigail. "Can I talk to you for a minute?" She said no. "I will be quick, come on, just a few minutes."

"Five minutes is the most I have to spare."

"I'll take it."

She ignored his manipulation and they went into her office. Joel closed the door behind him. "What do you want, Joel? I'm serious. This is a very busy morning."

Big coincidence having him show up unannounced on the day of an emergency board of directors meeting. Abigail was restless. Joel had to get out of there before Don found him hanging around. A wave of memories poured over Abigail, especially the feuding between Joel and Madeline. Board meetings were brutal with those two. Abigail missed working with both of them but not the relentless fighting.

"Can I trust you?" he asked.

"What do you think?"

"Forget about my personal life. I'm talking about my business experience. Do you trust me?"

"Joel, how can you ask me that? You resigned because the company is practically bankrupt. You drove off half the clients, sold two of our four divisions. Are you really asking me that question?" Her lips were tight and jaws locking.

"I had a few setbacks, but come on. Abigail, you know me."

"I thought I did."

Joel came closer. There was nowhere to retreat to. She stood her ground. "Abigail," he said, grabbing her hand. She pulled it away. "I hurt you. I get that. I was wrong. I won't apologize for my business decisions. I'm not going to do that, but I can honestly say that I never meant for you to get hurt in the process. You have to admit, though, I never misled you." He was telling the truth, as much as she disliked hearing the words coming from him. "At first I was driven to fulfill my father's vision. Once I felt comfortable as CEO, my vision took over. It consumed me. Like I said, I won't apologize for handling business. But I will apologize for how I handled our situation. You didn't deserve that."

"You don't need to apologize. Like you said, you never made promises to me. I can't blame you for not reciprocating my feelings." Abigail had to be careful not to be drawn into his web. She was helpless there, squirming like a bug to get loose from his clutches. None survived. Zarah was the target in his web and it nearly killed her several weeks ago, literally. In a bizarre way, Abigail thought, she should thank Zarah for saving her from Joel.

"Abigail, I'm going right to the bottom line. I need your help, and there's no one else who can help me."

"What can I possibly do for you?" She had nothing left to give him.

"I want to be back in the game. I'm a leader. I have to lead."

"Are you staging a takeover at the board meeting?"

Abigail's heart pounded to the point that she needed to gasp for air.

"Are you okay?" he asked. "You don't look so good."

She was fine before he arrived. "Depends on what you have on your mind."

"I don't know anything about a board meeting." Abigail may have been accommodating in the past when it came to Joel, but he would be making a mistake thinking she was flat-out stupid. "Staging takeovers and theatrics at board meetings is Madeline's style of doing business, not mine. I'm here because I need your help."

"Joel, what do you want? I can't keep this going. I have work to do." She took her seat behind the desk. The clock was ticking, and Abigail was running out of time. She had to complete the edits on the presentation and get the final draft to Don before he and Tamara went to the meeting at two o'clock. She was determined to help Don. Joel had to step aside.

"I want Zarah to buy Harmonious Energy."

"Good for you. Don will be glad to hear your news. He'll sell the company to you at a fair price, but he's not willing to let you inflate the price by holding the West Coast division over his head."

"I can guarantee you my plan doesn't include using the division as bait."

"I'm relieved."

"Maybe not, once you realize I'm keeping it."

"I knew it. You have a trick up your sleeve. Aren't you tired of this constant manipulation?" she shot back at him, voice slightly raised but controlled. "I am. You resigned. Why don't you do the right thing one more time by selling the West Coast division to DMI and buying Harmonious Energy? Why can't you leave well enough alone?"

"I can't. Running a company is my passion. You know who I am."

"Why are you telling me this?"

"I need your help." She was afraid to guess what he was thinking. Joel's rational meter wasn't functioning. "The terms of our marriage won't allow Zarah to sell the division to me. However, she can sell the division to someone else at any time." Abigail was waiting for Joel to explain why this should matter to her. "I want Zarah to sell the division to you."

"Are you kidding? No way."

"Wait, hear me out before you give me an answer. You don't have to do anything except sign a few papers. She'll sell it to you. No money will be exchanged. You will then immediately transfer ownership to me."

Abigail couldn't get her brain to settle down. Besides the obvious questions, such as who was going to handle the tax ramifications and legal fees, her major concern was how Joel could think she would be willing to betray Don. "I can't believe you're seriously considering this craziness, let alone asking me to get involved. I can't do it."

"Why not? This won't cost you a dime. I really need you to do this for me."

"I can't betray Don. I simply can't do it."

Joel came to her, placed his hands on her shoulders. "I wouldn't ask if this wasn't very important for me. Abigail, I mean it. I need this deal to save my life. I'm drowning in complacency in the house with Zarah. I need to be in the game. You have to help me get on my feet. I'm not asking for a lot, just a small favor from a dear friend."

She realized love didn't shut off like a faucet. Joel had a portion of her heart, though it was a tiny part and shriveling daily. She didn't have the same loyalty to him as in the days of old. "I can't do it."

"You can't or you won't?"

She pulled from his grip. "I won't. Is there anything else you wanted to discuss?"

Joel stood, stared at her for several seconds. She pretended not to watch as he turned to leave the office. Before opening the door he said, "Are you absolutely sure?"

"Positive."

"I know money won't change your mind. I know you, but I have to ask anyway." She shook her head no. Money didn't supersede integrity. Her priorities weren't distorted. "One more request?" he asked.

"I can't imagine," she said.

"Don't tell anyone about this conversation. It never happened."

"Honestly, Joel, why would I want to share this foolishness with anyone?" She waved him out the door. "Go, your secret is safe with me." Joel left, taking her anxiety with him. She couldn't believe him. Abigail wanted to tell Don about Joel's antics. He would want to know, but she decided against telling. Better to let calamity rest without stirring up new trouble. The old dose was plenty. She plopped down in her seat and began reviewing the presentation again. Much work had to be done; pointless distractions were banned.

Preparation was complete for the board of directors. A half hour before the meeting, Abigail was dropping off the final version of the presentation. "We did it," Don said, taking the document and flipping past a few pages. "We do good work together."

"I know," she said, holding back a grin that wanted to explode. "You're the one who seems to be forgetting these days."

"Abigail, what am I going to do with you?"

Friendship and dedication were synonymous with Abigail. Their relationship was simple when she allowed the natural ebbs and flows to happen, not forcing more, he thought.

"I've been asking the same question. I'd love to hear your answer."

"You're quite a character, Ms. Abigail Gerard. Let me get to the board meeting."

"No answer, huh? What's it going to be, Mr. Mitchell?

Are you going to give our relationship another chance?"

Abigail was somehow different. Perhaps the fallout with Joel had changed her. Don had to wonder if he was also a contributor. The evolving Abigail wasn't waiting for an opportunity. She was creating one. He appreciated the gesture. Had he done the same years ago, they'd already be together. Don shook his mind clear. Pining over what could have been was pointless. He took a peek at his watch. "I do have to get going," he said, walking to his conference table to grab a pen and portfolio.

"That's it, no answer at all?"

Don paused near Abigail, tucking the presentation inside his portfolio. "Abigail, let's not do this. You know where I am."

"No, I really don't. Seriously, I need to know if there's any hope for us."

"You know I adore you."

"But you don't love me?"

"You know I have love for you."

"Having love for me and being in love with me aren't the same, and you know it. You sound so callous." Abigail shied away.

Don couldn't believe they were having this kind of conversation right before a critical meeting. This wasn't the Abigail he knew. That she would push at such an awkward moment told him this topic was extremely important. He had never discounted her feelings. The meeting would have to hold a few minutes. "I don't mean to sound callous. Please forgive me," he said, pulling her to him and embracing her for an extended hug. When she was ready, Abigail pulled away, which was the signal he needed that she was feeling better. "I never meant to hurt you, not now, not ever." She nodded in affirmation. "But I have to be honest with you."

"I know."

"Then you have to accept the fact that I'm not available for a serious relationship with you right now."

"Is it because you're with Naledi, or is it because I used to have feelings for Joel?"

"Both."

There was a knock on the door, followed by Tamara sticking her head inside. "Ready for the meeting? Starts in five minutes. Oh, excuse me," she said, seeing Abigail standing near Don.

"Give me a few more minutes and we can go together," Don told her.

"Better yet, I'll wait for you outside the boardroom." Tamara closed the door.

"Let me get out of here," Abigail quickly responded. "Go to the meeting. Kay will be there with copies for the other board members. She will also take notes for you. Let me know if there's anything else you need during the meeting. I'll be in my office." Her chill permeated the room.

"Abigail, I'm sorry."

"For what, pursuing a relationship with Naledi? For Joel being a total jerk and trampling on my heart? What exactly are you sorry about? What?"

"All of it; whatever makes you unhappy bothers me. I care about you and that's not going to change."

"Thanks a lot, can't wait to lay those sweet lullabies on my pillow tonight. I'm sure they will help me sleep very well."

Don remained reserved. He understood that Abigail had to release and he happened to be the closest person to receive the brunt of her fury. He was her listening ear when needed. She'd been there for him many times. Reciprocating was an honor. "I'll see you after the meeting. We can talk more if you'd like," he said, letting his hand slide slowly down her shoulder.

"We're done. Go, go, the board members are waiting."

"I wish you were going with me to this meeting."

"Me too, but I'm not a Mitchell and it doesn't look like I will ever be."

No response was best, Don thought. Abigail walked out. He waited a minute, giving her space. He'd go to the meeting, present the recovery proposal, and work hard not to let personal issues compromise his ability to lead. The pitfalls Joel encountered weren't going to be his.

Don arrived at the boardroom slightly winded. He'd jaunted down the executive corridor. Tamara was waiting outside the door. "Ready?" he asked.

"Certainly am."

They went inside. The other six members were seated with a copy of the presentation in front of them. "Good afternoon. I apologize for being a few minutes late, got tied up in a meeting right before this one." Don took his seat and Tamara took one, too. "Before we get started I'd like to introduce you to my sister, Tamara Mitchell." Muffled chatter erupted. Each member had heard about Tamara. None had met her previously. "She's going to sit as a proxy in the vacant seat."

"Where's Madeline?" a member asked.

Don was intent on tact, disclosing the minimal amount required. His family was slowly recovering; extra speculation and misguided rumors were to be avoided.

"My mother is on sabbatical. Since this is an emergency meeting with short notice, she'll be absent." Don balanced on a delicate tightrope, careful not to slip into a willful lie. The truth was, she was too far away to make the meeting. The sabbatical story would last for only a meeting or two. They'd need a better excuse soon. "This meeting is primarily to get you up to speed on our financial status and to propose a recovery path. We can proceed with the members present."

His best strategy was to take command up front and hold the reins. Images of out-of-control meetings were too raw, the ones where Joel and Madeline initiated heated disagreements with each other, consistently derailing the agenda. Remembering those confrontational times under Joel's command, Don was inspired to grab hold of the meeting and maintain order. He asked Kay to take roll, documenting each member present for the record. "Let's turn to page two." The group followed his direction. "As you can see, the numbers haven't changed much since our last quarterly meeting. We're bleeding profits in each division." He turned to the next page. "We need to take action in order to stop the hemorrhaging."

"Drastic cuts," someone said with endorsement from others.

"Cuts are going to help in the short term. For our long-term strategy, we need to create a leaner company, which brings us to section two of the presentation. We're proposing that DMI move forward without recovering the West Coast or Southern divisions."

Papers rustled and there were low groans. "We'd be changing the core strategy of the company. Your father intended for DMI to operate with all four divisions, in order to impact all regions of the country. We can't do that with only the East Coast and Midwest," a member said.

"If we don't move forward with just the two, we'll be out

of business and won't be able to impact anyone. Take your pick." Don appreciated their passion to maintain Dave Mitchell's wish. As founder he'd never wanted the company to be sold off in parts. But it was too late for those sentiments; Joel had shattered that wish. Don didn't create the situation. His job was to salvage the most he could and help DMI emerge from the doorway of bankruptcy as a viable company.

"I thought you were going to merge DMI with your offshore company."

The merger was a possibility, but Don wasn't about to incorporate the disease-ridden DMI into his healthy LTI. "Once DMI is on the mend, we can tackle other scenarios."

The crowd seemed to accept his rationale.

"What about the East Coast? At the last meeting, Madeline recommended an approach for retaining key accounts. How's it working for us?" a member asked.

He gave a general response. The board wasn't satisfied and pressed for specific details.

Don didn't have the answer readily available. He thumbed through the report, finding no answers. Madeline could have answered in a split second. But she wasn't there. Abigail was the next-best option. She wasn't there either. He glanced at Tamara to see if she might have something to add. Nothing was offered. "I'll note your question as a takeaway and get back to you with an answer." He jotted a note to Kay as a reminder.

"What about results from the marketing test performed last month?"

Two questions in a row that he couldn't readily answer aggravated him. He wasn't adequately prepared. After only a week on the job, he didn't expect to be. But he knew the board didn't agree. He was the company head. Whether his tenure had been a day or a decade, he had to know the answers or have the people with him who did.

Don felt like the U.S. president calling a press conference to give an update on a specific topic and being bombarded by the media with a series of unrelated questions. Once the press conference was under way, no topics were truly off-limits.

"I've been in the CEO role for two weeks." One week of it had been spent at LTI, but they didn't care. The board of directors' business was DMI. "But that's no excuse. Rest assured I will be better prepared in our next meeting." He took a quick glance at Tamara. He could tell she was uncomfortable, which didn't help their cause. He did what had to be done. "Excuse me for a second," he told the group, then whispered to Kay. She left immediately. "I've asked my assistant to get Ms. Gerard. She will be joining us for the rest of the meeting. You all know her." Don saw Tamara fidgeting in his peripheral vision. "She's on the executive team. She's been in the trenches for the past two quarters and is intimately familiar with the lay of the land." Don's rising frustration weakened. "She's not a board member yet, but she can add vital input into this meeting. Any objections to her joining?" No objections were raised. All were in favor. "Good, then let's continue with the proposal in the interim. There's a lot of ground we need to cover." His resolve was restored.

The meeting ended after an hour and a half. Tamara bolted from the room, ignoring a few members who wanted to meet her in person. To call the meeting a disaster would be a drastic understatement. Humiliated, Tamara bypassed the crowd. She had to stay steps ahead of Don, Abigail, and the rest of the group with their stares reinforcing her incompetence. Six flights of stairs dumped her into the lobby. Her purse and few belongings were being held hostage upstairs, with the exception of her hotel room key card and the eight dollars she had in her pocket for lunch. Her things were safe until later, when she could return undetected. She paced along the sidewalk. Where she went was insignificant as long as she was moving away from the building.

She couldn't appear inadequate again, not if the goal was to stay on board. Tamara pondered how to fix her problem. She needed more time. That's all. She'd been at the company only two weeks. Another two months and concerns about her worth would vanish. Based on Don's reaction in the meeting, he wasn't going to give her the time she needed. He could be asking Madeline to return at this very second. Now that she had been lured into coming back, Tamara wasn't interested in bailing. Figuring out a plan of action was her priority.

Tamara's walk slowed four blocks from the DMI building. When she initially arrived in Detroit, every man had looked like Remo, creating constant bouts of subdued hysteria. The two weeks since then had converted into dog years. Europe and Remo felt like fourteen weeks ago, at least. The bouts of fear were faint, a low-grade pain she could feel only when her mind was completely idle. Establishing a presence in DMI was the healing drug she'd come to crave. Getting smarter was the foremost objective, and she had to do it quickly. She'd walk until either the sidewalk ran out or her confidence started rising. She stepped into a local café. "May I please have a large latte with a splash of cinnamon, to go?"

"Will there be anything else with your order?"

Tamara completed her order and waited for the drink, thinking hard. The latte was handed to her. "Thanks."

"If your drink isn't exactly the way you want it, please don't hesitate to bring the empty cup back. We'll give you a new cup or fully refund your money," the worker standing behind the counter said.

"What great customer service," Tamara said. "How refreshing."

"That's our policy. I make sure every one of my employees understands how valuable each customer is. Every cup we sell has to be perfect."

"Are you the manager?"

"Worse, I'm the owner. The cup stops with me."

Tamara laughed. "Well, I'm impressed." She extended another thank-you and exited the café with her enthusiasm soaring. The café owner inspired her to think broader. Ideas were flying around as she strode down the sidewalk, sipping the latte. Two blocks' worth of thinking and *bam*, her answer was clear. She had to create her own company. That was it. Taking direction wasn't her preference. She had to be in charge of her business, no matter how small. She radiated excitement, dumping her cup in the nearest garbage can, eliminating even the tiniest distraction. Focusing was critical. Time was short and getting shorter as Don grew more disappointed with her menial contributions.

Despite Tamara's allegiance to Don, she decided she deserved to have her own piece of DMI.

Bolstered by hope, Tamara considered walking to her hotel, ten miles away. The distance was great. Her tenacity was greater. She picked up the pace, letting the possibilities catapult her forward. Today was ending much better than it had started. The Mitchell name was fitting better and better. This weekend she'd secure a furnished apartment, move in, and lay the foundation for stability, for the first time in her adult life. Good times were ahead.

36

Saturday was winding down and Tamara was chomping through her short list of potential apartments, standing in the last place she'd selected. Getting the right unit was taking longer than she'd hoped, but there wasn't room for compromise. Her criteria had to be strictly enforced, with the most important component being security. She didn't mind having to pay for two or three extra deadbolt locks, but the unit needed at least two for starters. A doorman or some form of building security, like locks on the entrance doors or a coded entry system, was critical. She couldn't budge on that requirement. The apartment also had to be under $500 a month, be on or near the bus route, and offer a short-term lease. As of today, she was set on staying in Detroit for a while. Several factors would determine exactly for how long.

Tamara was anxious waiting for the rental agent to unlock the door leading into the model apartment. "This is our one-bedroom," the agent said, finally getting the door open and handing a brochure to Tamara. "It has the standard bedroom, a small eat-in kitchen, living space, and a nice-sized bathroom. Each unit has a small balcony too." They walked inside. The layout was fine. After a few of her last flats, size wasn't as important as other things. They finished the mini tour and the agent asked, "Well, what do you think? Any questions?"

She had plenty. "How many locks come standard on the door?"

The agent appeared perplexed. "That's an unusual question. I don't generally get asked that one." Tamara wasn't surprised. Most people didn't have someone chasing them down. "Each unit comes standard with one deadbolt lock."

"Oh." Tamara groaned, afraid this last complex wasn't going to be suitable either, adding to a long list of rejects for the day. She was irritated, because every item on her list was mandatory, except maybe the term of the lease. She could always sign a long-term contract. If an unexpected situation required her to bolt without warning, the contract would be the least of her problems and wouldn't hinder her from going. With further consideration, Tamara couldn't turn the unit down yet. Each of the other choices had been eliminated. She was tired of looking. This had to be it. "Can you add another lock?"

"I suppose we can easily add a basic lock into the doorknob if that will make a difference for you."

"That would be great."

"Good, and since security seems to be an important factor for you, I want to point out the security keypad at each of our buildings. Our tenants use their keys to get into the front and rear doors. Visitors have to ring your unit from the keypad and be buzzed in for entry."

"That's good to hear." The place didn't have a doorman,

but the security pad, the two basic locks on her apartment, and one or two more added could work.

Tamara felt better; the most important criterion was checked off. A few more to go and this could possibly be the one. She preferred a unit without a balcony. It added an extra safety risk. In order for her to be comfortable, she'd have to be on the seventh floor or higher. Any fool willing to climb that high wouldn't be deterred by anything, but the seven stories could possibly give her the lifesaving time she needed to escape. "Do I get to choose a floor?"

"Depends on what's available. When are you looking to move in?"

"Today, if I find the right place. Tomorrow would work also."

"Move-ins are only allowed on the first of the month and on Saturdays. Each moving van is given a time slot. It's very organized."

"I won't have a moving van."

"We treat carloads the same as a moving van."

"No carload either, just one suitcase."

"I see," the agent said, sounding bewildered but seeming reluctant to ask details. Tamara didn't care so long as it didn't hinder her ability to get an apartment. "Then you can move in as soon as the credit check clears and the paperwork, deposit, and first month's rent are settled."

"How much is the one-bedroom?"

"It's $595, utilities and cable included."

"When I was online, the ad said, 'Starting at $465 per month.' I need to be in that range."

"I'm not sure what they had online. You know, corporate runs ads and doesn't tell us the details."

No, Tamara didn't know. She needed this place and was counting on the price being right. She'd planned to ask for a raise and didn't anticipate a problem getting the increase, but today's lease had to be based on her current salary. For every dollar she spent in a month, she had to save two. Being home hadn't altered her world much, not yet. She still had to keep sufficient funds to hop a plane and get a room in an undisclosed location without notice.

Her enthusiasm was dashed. She couldn't afford the extra hundred dollars. "That's going to be too much."

"I see," the agent said, scooping her clipboard from the kitchen counter along with Tamara's hope. "Have you considered a studio? It's about the same size as this one, minus the wall separating the bedroom from the rest of the unit." The agent had Tamara's full attention. She preferred studios anyway, allowing her to see every inch of the place at any time. "Those run four ninety-five a month."

"That's great, any on an upper floor?" She contained her glee. She was getting close to finalizing a deal and was thrilled; there were just a few more requirements to be satisfied.

The agent scanned the set of papers on the clipboard, pointing to several highlighted lines; there was nothing on page two, so she flipped on to three with Tamara's anxiety steadily increasing. "I'm trying to find a studio that's available this weekend. I'm not finding any," she said, and flipped to the last page, letting her finger run down the list. "Ah-ha, wait, I found one, bingo. We have one on the eleventh floor. It was a corporate rental and the company terminated early. The only catch is that we won't get the furniture out until midweek for garbage pickup."

"But is the unit clean?"

"Absolutely, it's clean."

"Then is it possible to keep the furniture, since you're going to throw it out?"

The agent hesitated. "I don't see why not. Actually, you'll save us the hassle of having to empty the unit."

"Okay, just so that I'm clear, this is a furnished studio on the eleventh floor for four ninety-five per month, and I can move in today?"

The agent checked a few more pages. "Yes, looks that way."

One last hurdle. "How much is the deposit?"

"Normally it's half the first month's rent. Since you're saving us the cost of emptying the unit, we can knock it down to one hundred dollars. How does that sound?"

"Where do I sign?"

The agent chuckled. "Follow me to the office. We'll do a quick credit check, get the papers signed, and have the keys in your hand this afternoon. You can move in this evening."

"Great." Tamara would move in tomorrow or Monday, right after the locksmith added a couple more locks. She wasn't certain of the building policy with regard to adding locks and wouldn't ask to avoid a problem. No one was going to have unapproved access to her unit, not Remo or the handyman, not even the building's owners. They just didn't know it.

Tamara was pleased, except for the reality that a credit check and lease were going to make her more vulnerable and possibly easier to locate. Doubt tried to push past her and the agent and beat them to the office. Tamara shoved doubt from her thoughts, refusing to be deterred. She was finished running. She had to take a break and establish a new normal. Restless nights were sure to get better once she was settled into her new apartment.

chapter

37

The plan could work if Joel could get cash. He closed his office door to avoid being interrupted. It was eleven fifteen in the morning. Zarah and her assistant had gone to pick up a few things from the store, allowing him time alone, a rare commodity lately. He added the ten-and-a-half-hour time difference to get nine forty-five P.M., the time in India. Hopefully Zarah's family attorney would be available today. Tomorrow was too far away.

He made the call. As he'd hoped, Kumar answered.

"I'm sorry for calling you this late."

"It is no problem. How can I help you?"

Joel couldn't come straight out and tell Kumar he needed cash, and millions of it. He'd have to slither into the conversation, minimizing suspicion, fully aware that he might be Zarah's husband but that Kumar held the purse strings as the Bengali estate's executor. "DMI is going through a rocky transition with integrating Harmonious Energy. You can imagine how difficult it is to blend two robust companies together with little support from the board of directors." True, except Joel left out the part about his resigning as CEO and no longer being in charge. There was no integration path. Don planned to divest DMI of Harmonious Energy as soon as a suitable buyer surfaced. Kumar didn't need to know.

"Merging with your company is very important to Musar. He wants to make sure Zarah is provided for now that he's in the next stage of life."

Joel had tried, a little, to live with their religion and failed. He recalled Musar describing life as a burst of energy that changes forms as a person moved from life to what Joel knew as death. Hearing Kumar speak in the present tense, as though Musar were around the corner, was spooky, but not spookier than being broke and without a company to run. He could go along with the energy theory if it deposited a bucket of money on his doorstep. Leprechaun, tooth fairy, or burst of energy would work if it was delivering the goods. The notion of Joel reaching out to his God attempted to squeeze into his mind, but he bashed it down and kept talking. "We're several months into the merger, and it's clear this is a much larger effort than realized. I'm wondering, if we need additional funds to assist with the merger, is there any way we can count on your help? Like you said, I know Musar would want Zarah to be secure."

"We don't have much leverage now that you own Harmonious Energy."

"Is there anything you can do?"

"How much money are you seeking?"

No way was Joel going to give the real number of four hundred million and raise the alarm before he had an opportunity to mitigate it. A fraction of the total was best. "One hundred million." It wasn't enough, but the goal was to see if Kumar would release some of Zarah's inheritance early. If he could get Kumar to agree on one hundred, two or four wouldn't be so difficult.

"It is a great deal of money."

Joel waited for Kumar to continue. After a pregnant pause, he couldn't take the waiting any longer and broke the silence. "What do you think? Can you help?"

"We don't have many funds available for you, but I could connect you with our bankers again. They could secure you a loan."

Joel cringed; it was a good thing Kumar couldn't see his face. The nightmare that had ensued three months ago was still raw. He'd borrowed money from Kumar's bankers to pay Uncle Frank's investors. The payment had to be wired into the investors' account by midnight. Joel was dependent upon the bank. As fate would have it, a computer glitch at the bank, mixed with the time difference, had been the cornerstones in his demise. Painfully, the bank didn't complete the transaction until twelve twenty A.M. The twenty minutes cost Joel the Southern division since it was used as collateral on the loan. No one at DMI knew about the deal, and he'd resigned before they could find out. His anger still brewed thinking about how the investors had stiffed him on the deal. Taking out a loan from anyone wasn't his preferred choice. He wanted money from the Bengali trust and felt entitled to it. His entire world was destroyed the moment he acquired Harmonious Energy and married Zarah. Musar transitioned, died, or whatever, as a happy man knowing his daughter was safe. Joel craved the same joy in seeing his dreams come to pass, one of which was being a key player on the international stage. His strategy in merging the companies wasn't wrong. It was his execution. He'd do a better job managing this time around. "We don't want to take on more debt at this stage. What about accessing Zarah's inheritance just to get us through the tough transition period?" There, he'd said it; what a relief.

"That is not possible."

"Why not?"

"Musar incorporated firm rules for the inheritance."

He didn't have to be reminded of the terms. Joel had read each line repeatedly. There had to be a loophole. Getting Kumar to agree was his best shot. Dragging Zarah's family to court in a foreign country, for access to his wife's money, wasn't viable, although he would have considered the option if there was any chance of succeeding. He didn't think there was and let the notion of filing a lawsuit drop. The option of asking for the funds directly wasn't dead yet, though it was crippled.

"I would think Musar would be okay with us using funds if it meant protecting Zarah."

"I would like to help you, but it's not possible. She can get her full inheritance in five years." Joel couldn't process five years. His body wouldn't allow it.

"No exception?"

"Well, there is the one exception," Kumar said. Joel knew where he was headed but let him finish anyway. "If your marriage is terminated, she receives the full inheritance immediately."

"You know that's not what I want to hear."

"No, I would hope not."

"No other provisional clause to help me at this critical point?"

"I'm most sorry, Joel. We can do nothing. Musar was very certain of your abilities. So much that he made no provisions for failure."

Thanks for the vote of confidence, Joel thought; a lot of good the gesture was doing.

The call died along with Joel's hope. Without the funds he had no leverage with Don on purchasing Harmonious Energy. The only hope remaining was to get Zarah to sign over the West Coast division. It wasn't much, but it was a start.

His mind was overloaded. He had to take a break, preferably before Zarah returned. There wasn't enough of him left to share today. He had to get recharged. There was only one place to make that happen. A month ago he would have hopped on the corporate jet and been in Chicago within a few hours. No longer having the luxury, he had to take a commercial flight or make the five-hour drive— actually four, if he took the Lamborghini. He grabbed his keys from the desk. He'd dash upstairs, pack an overnight bag, and hit the road. Detroit would be in his rearview mirror and the Chicago skyline on the horizon.

Then he remembered that he'd better call Sheba to make sure she was in town. Otherwise there'd be no cause to go. They'd spoken a few days ago and she hadn't mentioned traveling, but he'd confirm. He got her on the phone. "Sheba, my girl, what are you doing the next couple of days?"

"Working hard on this expansion. Fifteen new boutiques in four countries is exciting and consuming. You know how it goes with expansions."

Actually, he didn't know how it went but longed to. "Sounds like you're pretty busy."

"I am, but I always am. You know that."

"Too busy for me?"

She laughed out loud. "What do you think?"

"That's what I needed to hear. I'm on my way."

"Okay, but I have to ask. What about your wife? I know how concerned you've been about her recovery. Are you sure this is a good time to take flight?"

The timing wasn't right. But the reality was that it was never going to be with Zarah. He didn't have to worry about the future and solve every problem in the marriage at this very moment. This time was about his sanity. He had to take this break. He needed his muse. "She's much stronger and doing much better. As a matter of fact, she's out shopping as we speak. The staff will look after her for a few days. Between her assistant, our housekeeper, and our cook, she's in good hands. I'm not worried." He shook off his guilt, rationalizing that he was a husband, a business mogul, and a man with real needs, not a babysitter.

"Your decision."

"Done, I'm on my way. Now, how long can I stay?"

"Oh come on, you know we don't put our time together in a box. Stay for as long as it makes sense, one day, ten days—we'll go with the flow, no strings attached. You know how we do," she told him.

He knew exactly, and that's why they worked.

chapter

38

Abigail walked down the street reading signs overhead in search of a café nearby. Tamara had asked to meet with her at eight thirty. Interactions between the two had gone well when Tamara initially arrived at DMI. Their rapport became strained when Tamara pushed past Abigail to fill the vacant seat on the board of directors. The fact was, Tamara was a Mitchell. Abigail understood why Tamara would be a candidate for the board of directors. What she didn't get was Tamara's eagerness to take the position at a time when her brother desperately needed to be surrounded with knowledge and experience. Of all the occasions to assert her Mitchell clout, Tamara picked the worst. Abigail set her personal opinion aside in support of Don.

Ten minutes early, Abigail entered the café, peering through the crowd, looking for Tamara. In the corner farthest from the door, she spotted her. Tamara saw Abigail at the same time and beckoned for her to come over.

"I've worked in the building eight years and never knew

this café was here. It's cute. I like it," Abigail said, sitting at the two-person table.

"I stumbled across the café last week. I've been here every day since."

They were silent. An awkward moment lingered. The silence was broken when Tamara asked, "What would you like to drink?"

Both ladies went to the counter. One ordered tea and the other a latte. They chatted as they returned to the table.

Abigail had a heavy day starting late in the morning. She had to get into the office. "I have a busy day. So I won't be able to stay more than a half hour with you."

"Then I'll get right to the point," Tamara said. Abigail had been curious about the purpose of Tamara's meeting ever since she got the call last night. "I'm sure you've been wondering why I asked to meet."

"I have been."

"I've given a lot of thought to the current structure of the company and to my role," Tamara told her. "I'm thinking about breaking out on my own."

"Really? Doing what?" Abigail said, taking a sip of tea while listening intently, wondering where Tamara was headed in the conversation.

"Running DMI."

"What do you mean? Don's running DMI." Abigail's words were tripping over one another.

"I understand, but please hear me out before you make a judgment."

Abigail was speechless. She couldn't possibly be sitting across the table from another Mitchell trying to undercut their own brother in his CEO role. She'd listen, but unless Tamara cleared up some major misunderstanding, the conversation was going to be short.

"I'll need you to explain exactly what you mean when you talk about running DMI. I hope it's not what I think you're talking about." She stirred her drink. "I have to be straight with you. Don is a dear friend and longtime business colleague. I won't betray him." Abigail doubted that Tamara was aware of Joel's brewing plan to take over a portion of the company. Sadly, Don was unaware of both. She'd kept quiet about Joel's plan, unwilling to share unsubstantiated threats with Don. He was knee-deep in recovery efforts and didn't need the extra drama.

"I understand your loyalty to Don. I admire it, but when are you going to step out of the shadows of the Mitchell men?"

Abigail set the cup down and her gaze burned into Tamara. "We've had this conversation and I'm not having it with you again," she said, grabbing her purse, which was hanging across the chair.

"Wait, please don't leave until you hear my proposition."

"I really don't have much time," Abigail said.

"Then I'll talk fast. My father ran the company, then Joel, and now Don. Every Mitchell man alive and over the age of twenty has run the company, and what's the state of DMI?"

"The company is in its current state because of Joel. Your father and Don had nothing to do with what's going on with DMI."

"My father was the one who put Joel in charge."

Abigail couldn't dispute that fact. Telling Tamara that Dave felt led by the Lord to make the decision would bear no fruit. Regardless of the reasons, Joel had bungled DMI, making it difficult for anyone to see merit in his appointment. "What does this have to do with how Don is running the company today?"

"The men have run the company for forty years and done a terrible job, including my father. My mother was just as loyal to him as you have been, and how did my father repay her? By leaving us for a younger woman. That's not going to happen to me. I believe it's time for the women to take charge."

"What women are you speaking of exactly?"

"Me, you, and possibly Sherry."

Abigail burst into laughter. She roared on for a short while. Tamara wasn't amused. "You can't be serious. Even if there ever was a takeover orchestrated by the women, I can't see the scenario making sense without Madeline. She is a fixture in DMI."

"My mother is a part of the old, failed administration. I'm looking at adding a new perspective, fresh blood, new ideas."

"You actually believe Madeline is going to let you take over the company along with Sherry?" Abigail wanted to laugh again, but Tamara's serious disposition forced her to hold off on the humor.

"I'm not talking about a takeover. Joel hasn't left much to take over. I'm talking about pooling our stock ownership. We'd have twenty percent between the two of us. If we decide to add Sherry that takes us to forty-five percent. We'd have to be taken seriously. We'd have a legitimate voice wielding serious power."

"I would never go against Don."

"Nothing else has proved successful long-term. Why not let us take a shot at being in control? We'd have a solid voice, and I'd expect to have my say."

"And who exactly do you see leading this posse?"

"Me, of course. As a direct member of the Mitchell family, I see the lead spot as rightfully mine. After all, I'm the oldest living heir of Dave and Madeline Mitchell. I deserve a chance to run the company without having to take orders from people who haven't been able to get DMI on track. It's simply my time."

Abigail remained in awe of the words coming across Tamara's lips. She couldn't process them. Pure common sense wouldn't let the words enter her mind. "This is crazy. I can't sit here any longer."

She stood with one hand resting on the table. Tamara pressed Abigail's hand down gently, causing her to pause. "Abigail, think about this. You could finally have a voice. I wouldn't just talk about getting you a seat on the board of directors. I would make it happen, day one, not one day. Can either of my brothers say that?" Abigail didn't respond. Tamara kept on talking. "Don has been in charge for weeks. Why hasn't he officially made your recommendation to the board? He let me take the spot instead, right off the street. I know my experience doesn't warrant the title, but I'm not going to sit around waiting for my shot to come knocking at my door. Sometimes you have to claim it. I wanted the seat. I asked for it. I got it, straightaway."

"Because you begged for it."

"No, I didn't beg. I asked and he gave it to me. There wasn't an ounce of resistance. He didn't stage a big protest on your behalf. He didn't fight me at all."

"You're a Mitchell. You were more entitled to fill the temporary position than I was."

"Precisely my point. There's always going to be one or two Mitchells ahead of you. If it's not Don, it's Joel, or Sherry, or my mother. I've been gone for a very long time and within a week of being in town I have an office on the executive floor and a seat on the board of directors. How long has it taken you and your loyalty to get both?"

Abigail had heard enough and was ready to leave, though not because Tamara was lying. It was the truth shoving her from the café. "You might be right, but I'm not going to backstab Don for anyone. He's been a good friend to me. I won't betray his trust."

"Suit yourself."

Her attempt to leave wouldn't be delayed. Abigail hustled to the door, almost gasping for air once she made it outside. She was fueled by uneasiness. Listening to Tamara lay out the scenes of her DMI life so casually, but accurately, made her sick. She walked aimlessly for several blocks, consumed by Tamara's comments. Abigail contemplated her place in the Mitchell family and didn't like how she felt. Changes had to be made. She still wasn't willing to undercut Don but was no longer willing to let her success depend on what happened with the Mitchell clan. Her walk slowed to a comfortable pace. She could see DMI about three blocks away. The building seemed dwarfed by the massive city skyline. There was so much more to the downtown landscape, more than she'd noticed before today. Thanks to Tamara, she was seeing from a new vantage point and the view looked promising.

39

Betraying Don was heavier than Tamara had antici-pated. She ordered a cup of tea for this round, some-thing different, and a raspberry scone. Don had been her constant source of support during her time alone in the wilderness. He hadn't abandoned her when it would have been easy to do. She pondered their relationship and contemplated changing her plan, but the urge to run a portion of the company, whereby she could prove her worth, wasn't to be ignored. The memory of last week's board meeting disaster was the impetus she needed to ven-ture out on her own. She suppressed her guilt and decided to move forward. It wasn't difficult; she'd become an expert at suppressing unpleasant feelings and memories. That was one area where she didn't require mentoring.

Tamara finished her snack at the café. She might not have had Abigail's endorsement, but that wasn't going to deter her. She was going to plan B: buying the West Coast division from Zarah. The division was small, a great place to start her corporate career. She hailed a taxi and slid inside.

"Where would you like to go?" the taxi driver asked.

It dawned on her that she didn't know. Tamara had gone to Joel's house once several weeks ago. Don had driven and she had ridden in the backseat with no intention of returning, not then. The situation had changed. Joel's estate was the only place she wanted to be. "One minute, please." She used her phone to search for his name and address on Google, WhitePages, and Yahoo! with no luck.

"I'll need an address or I'll have to go on," the taxi driver said.

"I'm definitely taking a taxi. Give me another minute or two to find the information. You can start the meter while we sit here." The gesture seemed to appease the driver. He turned on the meter. She searched a few other sites until "Joel Mitchell" came up on some obscure page, with his address and wife's name and background, more information than Tamara could process. She rattled the address off to the driver and read a few more pages linked to Joel.

Given ample time, Tamara was convinced a person could find out every minuscule detail about someone. There were no secrets, which reminded her to be careful. She couldn't let her guard down. Remo hadn't found her. Hopefully he wouldn't, but she'd had the same thought the last four times he'd chased her from one country to the next. She dreamed that one day he would vanish, leaving her alone for good. No more looking over her shoulder or scrutinizing each person in a crowd. She could sleep the entire night under the protection of one deadbolt lock, not three. Reality set in. Unless she killed him, her dream was not to be. She couldn't waste energy dwelling on impossibilities. Better to focus on more plausible feats, such as working with Zarah.

Thirty-five minutes set the taxi in Joel's circular drive. Tamara paid the driver using her remaining cash. She'd have to get a ride back to town, a tiny problem to be handled later. She knocked on the massive door and waited. Pretty quickly a woman came to the door. "Can I help you?"

"I'm Tamara Mitchell, Joel's sister."

The woman appeared stunned. "Please, come in. I didn't recognize you. Please accept my apology."

"No need for an apology. Most people don't recognize me. I've been away for many years."

"Was Mr. Mitchell expecting you? Because he isn't here at the moment. I'll have to call him and find out what time he's returning."

"That's okay. I just dropped by. They weren't expecting me." She was elated but refrained from displaying her thrill at not having to deal with the watchdog. "Is Zarah home? I can visit with her."

"Mrs. Mitchell is here. I'll get her for you. Are you sure you don't want me to call Mr. Mitchell?"

"Positive." She followed the lady to the study and took a seat. A few minutes later Zarah entered. Her countenance seemed to brighten when she saw Tamara.

"What an honor to have you here," Zarah said, pressing her palms together and bending her neck until her nose touched her hands lightly. Tamara hadn't noticed exactly how captivating Zarah was. Her deep brown eyes framed by her thick, dark eyebrows were perfectly placed against her naturally tan skin. She was simply beautiful. Zarah took the seat closest to Tamara with only a small table holding a stained glass lamp between them.

"I'm sorry for not calling ahead of time. I got an urge to come by, and so I just came over."

"It is no worry. I am pleased to have company. I haven't

met many of my husband's family, only his mother. I am very pleased to have you here." Tamara was caught off guard by Zarah's reaction. She was too elated. "My husband will be disappointed that he missed your visit."

Tamara wasn't disappointed. "When is he coming back?" Hopefully not for hours, Tamara thought. She didn't want to be rushed. Winning Zarah's trust was going to take several uninterrupted visits. Whatever time there was, she was going to maximize the opportunity.

"I'm not sure. He went to Chicago this morning for very important matters. I'm not exactly sure when he will return. I hope he will be home for dinner."

Tamara breathed easier. She had most of the day to lay her foundation without the watchful eye of Joel Mitchell.

Another Indian lady entered the room.

"Tamara, this is Ana, my personal assistant." Tamara's ease diminished as the assistant walked to them, extending a greeting. "Ana, this is Tamara, my husband's sister."

"Pleasure to meet you," Ana said. "Can I join you?"

Tamara spoke out before Zarah had a chance. "If you don't mind, I'm looking forward to this time alone with my sister-in-law." Zarah exhibited a shy, girlish disposition and giggled softly. "This is our first visit."

"Absolutely, I will let the two of you chat. Please let me know if I can be of assistance," Ana said, backing from the room.

Tamara was relieved, having dodged three bullets targeted at shooting a hole in her plans: the woman at the door, probably the housekeeper; Joel; and Ana. Luck was on her side, finally. Time was precious; there wasn't a millisecond to waste. "Tell me about your family. How did you end up in Detroit, Michigan?" Tamara asked Zarah.

"I'm from a small town outside Jaipur, India. My father

was Musar Bengali and my mother, Neepa. They have both transitioned to the next stage of their lives."

Tamara didn't ask what she meant to avoid seeming ignorant about Zarah's beliefs. There was much to learn in time. "Do you have any siblings?"

"Sorry?"

"Brothers and sisters, do you have any other family in the States?"

"No, I don't have any family in the States, only my husband." It was easy for Tamara to tell how Zarah felt about Joel. She even said the words "my husband" with passion. "He is my family. One day I pray I can give him children and make my family here." The volume of her voice dipped. "So far, the gods have not blessed me with children."

Tamara was intrigued by her sister-in-law's mind-set. She spoke as though becoming pregnant depended exclusively on her efforts, with no input from Joel. Odd. "I didn't realize you wanted a family so soon."

"Oh yes, very much."

"I thought I heard someone say you wanted to buy your father's company and work in the business. How are you going to start a family and run a business?"

"I don't want to be in business. My husband wants to be in business. I want to be a good wife and a good mother. That's my dream."

"I'm a little surprised you don't have any interest in the company." Tamara felt a genuine connection to Zarah. Her story was familiar: being alone in a foreign country, with no family, and living with a man who didn't appreciate her worth. "My father was a very successful businessman. I didn't set out to get involved in our family business but, as a Mitchell, it has come naturally to me."

"My father wasn't blessed with a son. He showed me

many elements of Harmonious Energy. Many people don't believe I know much about my father's business matters. They would be wrong. I choose not to be involved. Taking care of a family is much more fulfilling."

Tamara was pleased with the visit. Building trust and a friendship was going to be effortless. Her optimism escalated. Building a company seemed like a real possibility. Tamara would need to claim her inheritance to get the cash necessary for a deal. One step at a time, she was closing in on her goal and feeling pretty inspired.

"Let's go for an early lunch." She believed Zarah would eagerly accept, putty in her hands. Tamara could already envision a corner office in her new company, overlooking the city with a humongous sign out front. Coming home was the best decision she'd made in years.

"I don't feel up for lunch. I have a bit of a virus." Tamara was disappointed. She needed Zarah away from the house and possibly Joel's unexpected return. "Is there somewhere else we can go?"

"Sure, how about the art museum to see the new exhibit?" Tamara suggested.

"Sounds lovely."

Tamara was rejuvenated. She wasn't about to let a little stomach virus derail her visit.

Zarah was grateful for Tamara, eager to be included in the Mitchell family. "I'm ready to go," Zarah said, walking to the front door. "Are we taking your auto?"

"No, I took a taxi, and I've already let him go. Can we take your car?" Tamara asked.

"I haven't driven since I've been here in the States. I don't have a license."

"What, you don't have a license? We have to correct that."

Zarah hadn't given driving much consideration. Between Joel, her assistant, and the housekeeper, they took her wherever she needed to go.

"Stick with me," Tamara said. "We'll get you a license. That way, you can go wherever you want whenever you want and you won't have to depend on anybody."

"Yes, I think I will." They continued chatting. "Can you drive one of our cars for our trip today?" Zarah asked.

"I don't have my license either. I have to fill out a bunch of extra forms since I've lived abroad for many years. I have to confirm my residency, citizenship, and all that business. Rest assured, I will have mine in a matter of weeks. Even though I don't have a car, I'll have a license, and you too," she told Zarah as they went outside.

Tamara called the taxi service.

Zarah was pleased to wait outside with her new family member and friend.

chapter

40

Zarah was delighted to spend most of the day with Tamara and was saddened when she left. Zarah was eager to share her joy with Joel. Dinner with Ana came and went.

"Do you want me to stay with you?" Ana asked.

"You can go. I'm going to wait up for Joel."

Alone, Zarah went to her favorite room in the house, the library. She would let the quiet soothe her restless soul. Forty minutes later, the phone rang. The housekeeper came to find her.

"Mr. Mitchell is on the line."

She leapt to her feet, running to the closest phone, located in the den next door. "Joel, my darling, where are you? I missed dinner with you."

"I'm going to be delayed in Chicago. My business here deserves more time, and I'm too involved to leave. I haven't felt so charged up since I left DMI."

Zarah didn't want to dampen Joel's happiness. She bottled her disappointment. Spending the night without her husband was awful. He'd gone to Chicago and stayed there many nights right before she got sick. She didn't want to experience the harsh loneliness again for a moment longer than necessary. "Will you be home tomorrow?"

"I should be able to tear myself away from my business here and come home." Zarah struggled to conceal her regret. She needed to support her husband without exception. A good wife had to. It was her duty. "Why don't you choose a restaurant for tomorrow night? You can get dressed up extra special for me and we'll spend the evening together."

She perked up. Maybe tomorrow they could be together as husband and wife. She yearned for intimacy with Joel again, cherishing each of the five times they'd had. The time they'd spent together two weeks and five weeks ago rested in her memory, driving her to yearn for number six.

"I have very good news. Your sister came for a visit. She's quite delightful. We had a very nice visit."

"What sister?"

"Your sister, Tamara."

"What did she want? You didn't sign any papers with her, did you? Don't sign anything without me." She could tell he was angry. "Be careful. Don't believe what she tells you without talking to me first."

"I won't sign any papers." She remembered what happened the last time, when Madeline wanted to buy the division from her without asking Joel. He was furious. The heat of his anger still singed her spirit. She wouldn't make the same mistake again.

"I mean it, don't sign anything."

"I won't." Her bliss faded when she heard Joel's displeasure. "I look forward to our dinner tomorrow night," she said.

"We'll see how tomorrow goes," he told her. Her hope of intimacy faded too. She longed to please him but wasn't convinced she could. She was terrified. The birth of her children depended upon her ability to change their father's heart. She would work on it until her soul gave out.

chapter

41

Don was still reeling from the board of directors meeting. Nearly a week had elapsed and the sting hadn't diminished. If Abigail hadn't come in when she did, his leadership and vision for the recovery would have been undermined. Thank God the proposal was well received; Don was relishing the taste of accomplishment. He languished in the executive dining hall, opting to savor the mini-break. There had been few. He requested the *Wall Street Journal* and ordered another cup of coffee.

Suddenly Tamara popped into his thoughts. He'd forgotten the message she'd left yesterday asking for an increase in her salary. He typed a reminder into his PDA, which was sitting on the table.

"Can I get you anything else, Mr. Mitchell?" the waiter asked.

"I'm good," he said, attempting to continue reading the newspaper. Tamara's request wouldn't go away. He debated for several minutes about whether he should call Mother.

On several occasions, she'd asked about Tamara's financial situation. Don honored his mother's place in their lives and made the phone call. She would want to know, and as far as Don was concerned, she deserved to know.

A sensible person would have accounted for the time difference before calling. It was eight twenty A.M. in Detroit. If she was in Hawaii it was three in the morning. In Cape Town it was three in the afternoon. Don could wait four or five hours for a more sensible time, regardless of her location. On second thought, he didn't want to take a chance and forget as the day kicked into high gear. He dialed. The call connected and his mother was on the line. "Hello, Mother. Where are you these days?"

"I'm sitting at the airport in Japan. I have a three-hour layover."

His excitement shot up. "Tell me you're on your way to South Africa."

"I'm on my way to South Africa."

"Excellent, I knew I could count on you." His stress sank to an undetectable level. "Have you spoken with Naledi? Does she know you're coming?"

"I didn't call. In a quick second, I was at the airport in Hawaii yesterday. I intended to call you later today, after I got closer to South Africa."

"Why, in case you changed your mind?"

"You know your mother."

"I still can't understand why you are apprehensive about helping me out with LTI."

"I always want to help my children. That much you can be certain about. I already told you, I don't like being partially involved in anything. When I get involved it's one hundred and ten percent. You know how I am."

He did. She'd take the most ferocious adversary down

in the blink of an eye and meander away in her high heels, without a scratch.

"Nobody is putting the reins on you at LTI. Just the opposite; I'm thrilled to have you there. Naledi is doing well, exceptionally well. She's been a rock for me, and I don't want to wear her down."

"You're telling me to run free when I get there. What happens when I get there and get too involved? I've been known to take over. Not saying I'm proud of it, but that's apparently who I am."

So far Don was in agreement with what she said and didn't see her strengths as flaws. "I know how you operate, Mother. Remember, I worked with you here at DMI for years. You're totally right, and that's why I'm thrilled to have you on board."

"Okay, I'll go along with your arrangement. If my presence at LTI creates a problem in any way," she said, letting her promise resonate, "I'm begging you to be direct and tell me. That's my stipulation. One thing is for sure: you and Tamara are the most important elements in my life. In my zealous effort—sometimes overly zealous—to help you, I may get a bit pushy and take over. I don't want to do that with you. I will walk away first."

"I'm not worried."

"Well, good. I'm glad to help. Now that you're set, what about your sister? Is she adjusting? Did she get a place?"

"I think so. She was looking at apartments last week."

"That's a good sign. Maybe she's planning to stay for a while."

"I hope so. She's actually the reason I'm calling. She's asked for a raise."

"I can't believe she agreed to such a pitiful salary from the beginning—simply ridiculous. I have millions of dollars at my disposal and it irks me to have my daughter living paycheck to paycheck. I have to get some money to her. This is absurd." Madeline's anxiety was escalating. He had to curtail her discontent before she overheated.

"Don't worry. I'll make sure the raise is significant. She'll have more than enough to get any apartment in the city."

"But she's entitled to so much more."

"We can start there and see how much further she wants to go." Increasing her salary was simple. Keeping Tamara from being overwhelmed with the Mitchell way of life wasn't as straightforward. He had to be careful not to drive her away. There were going to be frustrating situations but nothing could surpass his commitment to her adjustment. That's what family did.

"You think she'd take a financial gift from me?" Mother asked.

Don didn't think so. He tempered his response to protect Madeline's feelings. "I don't think she's ready to fully reconcile."

"I'm not talking about a warm, fuzzy reunion. I just want to dump some cash into her account. I accept the message that she doesn't want to be near me. I don't understand why, but I respect her wishes. In the meantime, she doesn't have to live like a pauper."

"Tell you what. Let me talk to her about accepting her inheritance."

"Fantastic idea, you think she'll go for it?" Madeline asked.

"I can try. What steps will she need to take?"

"Call Attorney Ryan. Tell him I said to expedite the process. If he has any questions, have him call me. I don't want this to drag out."

Madeline was doing what she did best: taking charge.

"Okay, Mother. I can handle making the call to our family attorney."

"See, that's what I told you. I take over without realizing that I'm taking over. Are you absolutely sure you want me at LTI?"

"Absolutely."

"Okay, but don't say I didn't give you fair warning," she said with humor, soothing Don's soul. He thanked God in the moment, grateful to have Madeline as a mother. She was one of a kind, not to be replaced. Hopefully, one day Tamara would have the same appreciation.

chapter

42

Abigail didn't want to rush into the office. She'd linger at home for a while and go in later. Tamara's razor-sharp honesty repeatedly sliced at Abigail. *There's always going to be one or two Mitchells ahead of you.* A decade of loyalty had earned her a nice office on the executive floor, a quarter-of-a-million-dollar annual salary plus bonuses, and a corporate car allowance. Yet she had to face facts. Without the Mitchell name, her perceived value would always have a limit.

She'd spent countless nights working side by side with Joel during his early days as CEO, and actually throughout his entire three and a half years as the leader. She'd set aside the desire to have a personal life outside of DMI. Joel needed her and she'd been there for him. When he spent those months frolicking with a slew of women, she didn't bail on him. Instead, she dug in deeper and carried more than her share of executive responsibility. Swirling thoughts moved like a tornado in her mind. The house, she couldn't forget the house. She'd designed every inch of the place, supervised the entire construction when she and Joel were tight. The love was there—or at least she had thought it was, only to find out he had other plans.

Sitting on the bed, she closed her eyes, attempting to calm her racing emotions. The thoughts continued flooding in. She poured her devotion into Joel, and what did he do? Married a complete stranger. She held back the tears, got up, and paced the room, letting her feelings have their way. It hadn't mattered that she was in love with him at the time. Joel was about Joel, achieving his goals, fulfilling his vision, with no regard for her. Somehow he believed that if he let her know his marriage was purely a business arrangement, Abigail would feel better. But forget about what he was thinking. What was she thinking to let him get two syllables of nonsense into her ear?

She paced, but not aimlessly. With 20/20 vision, she wasn't stumbling over uncertainty anymore. Denial had sliced away her common sense. As much as she dreaded saying it, Don wasn't much better. The harsh reality was difficult to escape. Tamara's truth rang in her ears repeatedly. She could see why Joel never got around to recommending her for the board of directors, but Don was steady, supposedly more dependable. In the end, the results were the same: no Mitchell name, no extra benefits.

As soon as Tamara hit town, Don elevated her to the top spot. Abigail had slaved to achieve a spot on the board and would have appreciated the acknowledgment. But if she stayed at DMI, under the Mitchell spell, she could work twenty-four hours a day, seven days a week, supporting Mitchell men, women, boys, and girls, and still end up exactly where she was, at home wondering what happened. No tears. Her Mitchell ducts were empty. She was done crying and fretting. She grabbed her keys and briefcase, along with her laptop. As of this very moment, Abigail was looking out for Abigail; to heck with the others.

Twenty-five minutes later she was in her office. She took another five minutes to boot up her laptop and type out a three-line letter. She retrieved the page from her printer, quickly glanced over it for errors, and signed across the bottom. She pulled an envelope from her drawer, tucked the letter inside, and zipped to Don's office. Kay gave the okay for her to go in.

"Good morning, Ms. Gerard," Don said. "I stopped by your office a little while ago. I was shocked when you weren't there. You're usually in here by what, seven? And out by seven?"

"Not today. I decided to take time for me," she said, walking to his desk and handing him the envelope.

"What's this?"

"Open it and see."

Don extracted the letter and read it. He rapidly shifted his stare from the letter to her, back and forth, for seconds, which felt like an hour. She was prepared for his reaction.

"Is this a joke? You can't be serious."

"I'm serious," she said, offering no further explanation. Maybe she wasn't the only one who'd been operating under cloudy assumptions.

"You're resigning?"

"I am."

"Please sit down, clearly we have to talk." The time to talk would have been last week, last month, last year, any time before today. She took a seat out of courtesy; she wasn't going to change her mind. "Where is this coming from?"

"I've decided it's time for me to move on. I've had a great run here and it's time to venture out on my own."

Don pushed back in his chair, letting his elbow rest on the chair's arm and his chin rest against his fist. She perceived the distressed look choking him but could offer no help. To rescue him was to deny her freedom.

"I am absolutely speechless. This can't be happening. You belong here. You're as much a Mitchell as I am."

"That's definitely not true, and apparently never will be."

"Wait, is this about Naledi, because you think I'm going to marry her down the line?"

She resented Don for reducing her decision to the ranting of a jealous schoolgirl. "My professional future is not contingent upon who you marry. This decision is about me, not about you, or Naledi, or Joel, or Zarah. This is about Abigail Gerard and what I want."

Her tone must have come across harsher than she intended because Don said, "Okay, I apologize. I didn't mean to offend you." She let the tension release. "You realize I'm shocked. You're my wingman, without a doubt. It will be difficult getting this place on track without your help during this volatile time." He tucked her letter back into the envelope and slid it to her. "I can't accept your resignation. You are too valuable to this company. We owe you more than we can pay."

Money wasn't the issue. Respect and tangible appreciation was the bottom line. Her worth was overshadowed at DMI, completely taken for granted, had been for years. Consolation coming now was inadequate. Her mind was set. She was like a caged bird set free; there was no turning around. "I'm resigning, that's certain."

"Do you have another job lined up?"

"Not yet, haven't even started looking," she said, watching Don's gaze sink to the floor. "Since I'm in a senior-level position, it's only fair for me to give you three months to fill my position." He perked up. "But rest assured, I'm leaving in three months. Please take me seriously."

Don didn't try to beg her to stay. Maybe he was stunned by her boldness and impulsivity. Maybe it was the shock of her setting DMI to the side in pursuit of her own dreams. She didn't know which had him speechless. Maybe he needed time alone. Abigail got up to leave. Her compassion for him tugged at her. He was a good guy. Being caught up in the Mitchells' perpetual drama was a burdensome cross thrust upon him at birth. Her love and respect wouldn't vanish overnight. No need to force it. "One more thing," she said.

"What else could there possibly be? Nothing can be any worse than this."

His despair wasn't concealed. She couldn't be deterred and fall prey to a nostalgic moment. Her path was clear.

"I debated whether to tell you this or not. I realized that if it were me, I'd want to know." Don sat up in his seat with a bewildered expression. "Tamara approached me a few days ago about taking over the company."

"Say that again, I didn't hear you correctly."

"Tamara is working on a scheme that allows her, Sherry, and me to rally together in DMI. She didn't call it a takeover. That's really my term, but she wanted to pool our stock ownership in order to have a strong position in the company. 'Having a voice' is what she kept saying. Just so you know, I want no part of it."

Silence took a seat and rested. Abigail left the office, allowing Don and his troubles to be alone.

chapter

43

Don couldn't move. He had to organize his thoughts, which were mangled by deceit, shock, anger, and simple sorrow. What was wrong with his father's offspring? Each sibling born to his father had blindsided him, each time with an unimaginable element of selfishness. He tried his best to be a loyal, loving, and supportive brother. Of his siblings, Tamara had truly received the best of him. He had traveled from one end of the earth to the other on countless occasions to check on her welfare, to make sure she didn't feel abandoned even though it was her choice to be estranged. He hadn't ever judged Tamara or made her feel unworthy. He had a hard time digesting Abigail's story. She had always been honest with him. He knew she was telling the truth.

He went into the hallway in search of Tamara. She had some explaining to do, and a lot of it.

"I'm sorry, did you say Banray?" Kay asked a caller as Don approached her workstation. "Tamray?" She covered the mouthpiece, signaling to Don that she would be available in a minute.

He wasn't in a hurry. Worry had slowed him down. Standing there waiting, he kept thinking about the Lord and his purpose for Don. Each step forward seemed to be two backward. Yet he was reminded that each person who tried to overtake him was defeated. Not only did Joel lose the war, he surrendered to Don. He was certain God still had His hand in the matter; faith would be required until the dust cleared. If history was an indicator of the future, then as soon as he got past this dust storm and got into the clearing, another storm would be waiting. So, no hurry.

"Sir, are you asking for Tamara? Tamara Mitchell?" The caller must have said yes, because Kay looked relieved, as if she'd solved a major mystery. "Okay, yes, this is the correct place for Ms. Mitchell. She's not in right now, but I'll gladly take a message. Who's calling?" Kay held the phone away from her ear and told Don, "He hung up." She placed the receiver on the base. "That was weird."

"What do you mean?" Don asked.

"I could barely understand him. His accent was so heavy, Italian, I think. Anyway, he asked for Tamara. He was very hyper. When I asked for his name, he hung up. Weird. Anyway, did you need me?"

Don leaned against the workstation. "Where is Tamara?" He wasn't going to rage out of control in front of the staff. He'd save his response exclusively for Tamara.

"She's working from home today."

Don was pretty sure she had moved into an apartment but wasn't sure where. He had more insight into her address when she was living abroad than he did having her home. "What is her address?"

Kay looked up the address in the corporate database and rattled it to Don as he scratched it onto a sticky note.

"You want me to let her know you're on the way?"

Don responded quickly. "No, let it be my surprise." He'd return a tiny portion of the surprise she'd given him.

The high-rise apartment building was right outside downtown, in a decent section of the near east side. Exiting off the Lodge Freeway, he combed the street slowly, reading each number. Finally he arrived at Tamara's block and spotted the building. He went farther down the street in search of a parking space and whipped the BMW into the closest one. Don paused to say a quick prayer. The way he was feeling, barging in was bound to lead to a fruitless confrontation. He was determined not to let the predicament get out of hand. He counted to ten, then twenty, then thirty. By the time he got to fifty, he was ready to go inside.

As Don approached the building's entrance, a group of ladies was coming out. He held the door for them as they exited and eased into the building, allowing him to bypass the security keypad. In a flash he was off the elevator and walking down the hallway looking for her apartment number. There it was, a few doors from the end. He knocked, holding back, breathing slowly and deeply. His knocks grew louder each time. Tamara finally came to the door. "Who is it?"

"It's me, Don, open up," he said, restrained.

He heard the first, second, and third lock. The door opened. "Come on in," she said. "Welcome to my new place." Don entered and closed the door. "You must have thought I was sick since I'm working from home today."

"More like crazy," he said.

"Excuse me?"

"Tamara, have you lost your mind? What in the world would make you want to undercut me and go for DMI?"

She heaved a sigh. "So dearest Abigail told you about our conversation? I shouldn't be surprised. She's die-hard loyal to you and Joel, and look where it's gotten her."

"Honestly, what is wrong with you? Haven't I consistently supported you?" Don scratched his head. "Why are you doing this? Did Joel get to you?"

"No, why does this have to be Joel's idea? I don't have to rely on a man to think for me, Don. I came up with this on my own, little old me. As far as I'm concerned, there's nothing wrong with the women in the company having a voice. You men have pulled the strings for so long. We deserve a chance. Abigail didn't go for it; her loss."

Tamara held firm, but she did feel guilty about hurting Don, the only person she trusted and who had supported her unconditionally.

"Losing two brothers to murder and suicide was bad. Fighting Joel year after year was horrible. And now you. You're the last person I would have expected to do this to me," Don told her.

"Stop being so melodramatic. This isn't about you."

"Then tell me what it is about, Tamara, because I'm not getting it."

There was no way to escape her yearning to be in charge and to be counted. Her response wanted to rush out, crammed together, ahead of her thoughts. "I want to run my own company."

"Go ahead, nobody's stopping you. Do something in the art arena. That's where your passion has been for twenty years, but leave DMI to me. Let me spend my time and energy on getting it fixed so we can all benefit in the long run."

Art would always be a passion for her, but maneuvering in the corporate arena was in her DNA. "I've wasted so many years on the run. I can't start a company from scratch at my age, not if I want to achieve a reasonable level of success." If there was a way to grab a piece of the company without crossing Don, then she was willing to listen. "Let me go after the West Coast division. I think I can get it from Zarah. Let me take the division, move to California, and be out of your hair." Don didn't react. Hopefully he was becoming more receptive to her request. "Once I'm on the coast, you can have Madeline come back to help you fix the company. It's a win for everyone."

"Tamara, this isn't about the division. It's how you're going about this, behind my back, like an enemy. I expected more from you."

"I love you and I really do care, but I don't need your approval, Don. I'm getting my piece of the pie and heading west."

"You're really going to trample on our father's legacy? If you proceed with this, all of the Mitchell children will be at war. Is that what you want?"

"Exactly what father are you talking about? I can't speak for you, but I didn't have a father growing up. He was with Sherry and their child. He threw me away. If it hadn't been for him, Andre wouldn't have become so jaded, and Sam wouldn't have died for me. So save the sympathy for our father. He got to enjoy his happiness at our expense. Now I have a chance at contentment, and I'm taking it!" she screamed.

"Tamara, please, I'm begging you, work with me and together we'll figure this out."

She pursed her lips and let her eyes do the communicating. Don must have gotten the message. He trudged to the door. "Oh, I almost forgot. Some guy called the office for you."

Tamara tensed in an instant. Her heart was pounding hard, her blood flowing fast. "Who w-was it?" she stammered, struggling to speak.

Don turned the knob and opened the door. "He didn't leave a name, but he had a heavy accent. Italian, I think." Tamara buried her face in her hands. "What's wrong with you?" Don asked. She wondered if there was time to pack up and get out. She was scattered, not sure what to do next, instantly terrified. "Tamara," Don called out.

"Yes?"

"Didn't you hear me? I called your name three times. What's wrong with you?"

"You have to go, right now, go," she said, anxious to get an escape route under way.

"Tamara, I'm not going. What's the big deal? Why are you so frantic all of a sudden? Does this have something to do with the guy?"

"No, I need you to go, please. I'm in a hurry," she said, grabbing the doorknob.

"Fine, I'll go, so long as you tell me what's up with this guy. You know who it is, don't you? Is he a boyfriend?"

"Please go!" she yelled at him, feeling her temples begin to throb. "Go, go, go," she said, swinging the door forward and backward.

"Calm down, I'm leaving."

Don was finally gone. She knew he wasn't satisfied with her response and she would have to deal with him later. Her focus was on a bigger problem. Two years ago, Remo had threatened to kill her if she left him. She had and he'd been chasing her ever since. She was still scared, but she was tired of running. That was for certain. It was time to face her fears. Perhaps she should get the police involved, but what proof did she have that he was a threat? There weren't any taped messages or threatening notes, but she knew how volatile he could be. No more moving. She had to regroup, maybe get a gun. Survival was paramount and extreme measures had to be considered.

chapter

44

Don left Tamara reluctantly, not sure how she had managed to pull a scheme on him, igniting a fresh battle for DMI. He stayed put in the car, letting events of the day fully digest, first Abigail and then Tamara. Tamara was entitled to the emotional damage resulting from her rape, but what made her think she had exclusive rights on disappointment, heartache, and rejection? It certainly didn't give her the right to wreak havoc on others. He had his portion and so did every other Mitchell family member. He wasn't going to minimize her former trauma, but to carry it for eighteen years, long after the perpetrator had died, was a waste of life.

Don wanted to go back to Tamara's apartment and plead with her to change her mind. He knew it probably wouldn't do any good, but he preferred diplomacy over war, especially when there wasn't a viable exit strategy. He was willing to try Tamara again, especially since he wasn't sure how many rounds of warfare he had left in him.

A quick flight to South Africa and the drama could be over. Who needed the company now? The fight didn't seem worthwhile any longer. He had LTI. Madeline was gone. Joel was defeated. Abigail had given notice. Sherry would be okay. Tamara was left, but she would be fine without DMI, having never cared about the company previously. Maybe that was the answer, finally: to let the source of the family strife collapse. Let DMI die a natural death and be done, leaving nothing to fight about. Don started the car's engine. The thought was compelling.

On second thought, why delay the inevitable? Don turned off the engine. He called Madeline, prepared for the hurricane of the century. Somehow she'd blame the entire business on Joel or Sherry; it was easier to blame the bogeyman than her own misguided child. He was prepared. He dialed her number and the call went into voice mail. The recorded voice played, followed by the beep, signaling it was time to leave the message. Don held the phone and disconnected. He'd try to reach Madeline by calling the LTI office. Halfway through dialing the string of international numbers, his PDA buzzed. He answered.

"Don, I saw your number come up. I was finishing an introductory meeting with marketing." Madeline was in her element. He was pleased to have her at his company and allowed himself to be rescued for a brief period, focusing on the positive. "How are you doing?" she asked.

"I've been better."

"I don't like the sound of that. What's going on?" Don was reluctant to share the details. "Come on, out with it. I know you're trying to figure out how to protect me, aren't you?" He couldn't deny it. "Well, I'm a big girl. I have my war wounds. I'll survive. Lay it out."

Madeline thought she wanted to know. Don was certain

she didn't. "Tamara wants to start a business," he blurted.

"Okay, it's not what I want to hear. I'd like to see the two of you work together at DMI, but if you don't it's not the end of the world."

"Mother, she wants to use the West Coast division as the cornerstone of her company."

"What are you talking about? Why would she want to do something like that? How is she going to get the division?"

Don had a similar question, one of many. "Some craziness about talking Zarah into selling it to her."

"Oh my goodness, that's not going to work. Did you tell her I tried that once and it backfired? The poor woman tried to commit suicide when Joel found out what she'd done behind his back. Please tell her not to go there. I haven't lost any sleep over Joel, but I certainly don't want any permanent casualties. It's not that serious."

"Mother, I talked to Tamara until I was blue in the face. She is not budging." Madeline gave an "umph." "She's as stubborn as you are," he told her.

"She is my only daughter; not many ways for her to get around the genes."

Don normally would have appreciated her humor. Today he was somber. "I just got a reprieve from Joel and now it's Tamara nipping at my heels. I'm not ready for the next battle. I thought the war was already over. I blink for a second, let my guard down, and my ally attacks."

"I'm sorry, Son. I know this hurts coming from Tamara. I know she's mad at me, but I didn't dream she'd shun you, too. If you want, I can come home tomorrow and talk to her. It's okay if she cuts me out of her life. Well, it's not okay, but there's not much I can do. But it's definitely not acceptable for her to do this to you. You've gone out of your way to help her. This kind of crap has Joel's name all over it. I bet he has something to do with it." Don knew Joel or Sherry would be blamed sooner or later. "Joel is a snake. I should have known he was up to something. I will gladly come home if you think it will help."

Don didn't believe Tamara was interested in listening to anyone. "Thanks for the offer, but based on where Tamara is, I think your being here will only make matters worse."

"I agree. Then what can I do for you from here?"

"You're already doing it by being where you are."

"I have to admit, the time here has been therapeutic. I love it," she said. "I can see why you hibernated in Cape Town. The place is amazing, the weather, the people, and the food. I'm having a ball. The air has done me good."

Don was pleased and told her so. At least one member of his family was content. "Mother, one more note before I go. Tamara was on edge when I was with her."

"I would be on edge, too, if I was backstabbing my devoted brother."

"No, this was different. Some guy called the office looking for her. The call was odd. He hung up, refusing to give his name. When I told Tamara about the call, she seemed distressed."

"Who is he?"

He heard the roar rising in the lioness. When the den was threatened she was known for leaping into action, going for the kill. He'd try to contain her concern until more information was available.

chapter

45

Zarah's alarm was fitting. She'd had the same problem two months ago. Zarah was stronger and was feeling much better up until the last few weeks. She emerged from the restroom, hoping a spot of tea could calm her restless stomach. She yearned for Joel. Whatever the ailment, it was better when he was at home with her. She went to the kitchen, finding the cook there. Getting something to eat was simple. Getting Joel wasn't. She took a rest, hoping her husband was coming home today. His business required him to be in Chicago a couple of days this week; his trips to Chicago seemed to get longer each time he went. Maybe one day he would let her come with him. Then it wouldn't matter how long he had to travel. They could be together.

The phone rang. Zarah grabbed the call before the housekeeper had a chance to answer from another room. "Zarah, it's me. I'm calling to let you know I need to stay another day."

"But it's Friday. Will you be home for the weekend?" She desperately wanted a yes.

"I should be in town tomorrow."

"Joel, is there something I've done to displease you?"

"No, what made you ask?"

She wouldn't soon forget the despair, a deep, deep cut that only his love could heal. She was willing to do anything he wanted to be the wife he desired. She'd tried repeatedly with the same outcome: they spent many days apart. Zarah wanted to cry out. She couldn't. Her father would be disgraced along with her entire family in India if she was set aside in marriage. She had to work harder.

The ringing doorbell permeated the house. Zarah was still a bit squeamish and didn't rush to the door. It couldn't be Joel; she'd just spoken to him. There was no one else who could spark her troubled soul. Within a few minutes, Zarah saw Tamara walking into the kitchen. She was a pleasant surprise. Her day was brightened by a visit from a member of Joel's family. Tamara was very nice to her and made her feel not as alone in the United States. "I'm very glad to have you here."

"Figured I'd stop by. I really enjoyed my visit a few days ago and thought I'd see if you're up for another outing."

"Yes, I would be honored."

"Do you want to go to lunch, since we didn't make it last time?"

Zarah squinted as she rubbed her belly. "I'm not good for lunch."

"You still have that virus?" Zarah nodded. "Maybe you should go get some medication before it gets worse."

The possibility of being really ill without Joel shot a chill through Zarah's body. She remembered dehydration had had her in bed, near death. The doctors said her problem was dehydration and an emotional overload, but a broken heart was her diagnosis. The sickness was bad; being without Joel's love was unbearable. "I will see the doctor soon, but not today. I want to get out."

"Let's go, then."

"Ana is coming to meet me, but I'll give her the day off. I'd very much like to get a breath of fresh air. Our last visit was lovely."

Zarah made the call, telling her personal assistant to take the day off.

Tamara pulled the taxi receipt from her pocket and called the driver back. If Tamara had known they were going to leave so soon, Zarah suspected she probably would have held the taxi.

"Since the driver just left, he isn't far away. He's turning around and coming back. Should be a short wait," Tamara said.

Zarah didn't mind the wait. She was pleased to have a companion.

"We still have to get our license," Tamara said.

"Yes, we must. I will have my husband teach me how to drive here in the U.S."

"You rely on Joel a lot, don't you?" Tamara asked.

Zarah was uncomfortable, not knowing the right answer. In her family, dependence on one's husband was honorable. She was being obedient, but the way Tamara asked made it seem wrong. She didn't want to lose her new friend, the only person who spent time with her.

"He is my husband and I respect his wishes."

Tamara couldn't imagine total submission. "Is it working out for you?" she asked Zarah, keeping watch for the taxi. Processing the concept was difficult, let alone applying it to her own life. She actually liked Zarah, and would like her more once the shroud of Joel's dominance was ripped away. "You know men like gutsy women who can stand on their own."

"My culture has roles for women and for men."

"Mine too, but I decide how I'm going to be treated, not my culture." The response was automatic. Had Tamara taken an extra second, she would have refrained, not wanting to offend Zarah. Culture, like family sins, was heaped on a person without their say. Zarah wasn't any different from Tamara when it came to where they were, clawing their way out of a ditch created by the men in their lives. The taxi hadn't arrived. They kept talking. Tamara wasn't wasting a moment with Zarah. Tamara needed to gain her trust as quickly as possible. "If you want my advice, take charge. Show Joel you're exciting and full of spunk. Show him another side of you."

"What shall I do?"

Tamara decided to go for it, putting the notion out there and getting a read on Zarah's reaction. "Buy your father's company and run it. Not Joel; you do it." Zarah listened as Tamara continued. "Sell me the West Coast division. I'll take the tiny group and turn it into my own large company. All I need is a seed to get started."

Zarah was processing the suggestion but didn't pounce as enthusiastically as Tamara would have liked. "I don't want to run a company. I want to take care of a family."

"Fine, then hire a strong team of people you can trust and who can run your company."

"I trust my husband; let him do it."

Trust and men were incompatible, never to exist together. Whether she sold the division to Tamara or not, Zarah had to get real and take charge. Tamara would settle for no less. Women couldn't be totally dependent upon men. Watching Zarah cling to Joel nauseated her. "Where do you think Joel is right now?"

"In Chicago for business," Zarah said with an element of certainty.

"With whom?"

Zarah couldn't answer.

"For how long?"

No answer.

"Has he ever offered to take you with him?"

"No," Zarah said, sounding downtrodden.

No cause to fret, Tamara thought. The solution was to take charge and regain power. She was gladly willing to offer an encouraging push.

"Do you really believe he's there for business? Think about it. Why would he go so often, stay so long, when he doesn't have a job or a company there? I can only think of one answer: another woman." Tamara didn't want to be cruel but Zarah had to know. This wasn't about coercing her into selling the division. This was one woman encouraging another to regain the power a man had snatched from her and was keeping in a stranglehold.

"I can't bear the thought of another woman. He's my-y husband."

"Then make him act like it."

"How do you mean?"

"Make him treat you right. There's no justification for you sitting in this big house by yourself half the time and socializing with the housekeeper, the cook, and your assistant the rest of the time." Tamara couldn't quite relax. Joel was a wild card who could return home without notice and would be quite upset with Tamara. Until he surfaced, she would continue destroying his yoke of bondage over Zarah. "What did your father leave you in his will?"

"I don't know."

"You better find out. He probably left you everything as his only child." Tamara was fueled by the suspicion that Joel was manipulating Zarah's money and independence.

"I don't care about the money. It doesn't bring me happiness."

Wake up, Zarah, Tamara almost screamed. "Don't you understand? If you have the money, for men like Joel, you have him too."

She could tell the cobwebs were finally being cleared away and Zarah was thinking.

"I never had to worry about business with my father. Maybe I can find out about my father's will from his attorney."

"Joel isn't your father." He didn't appear to be a husband either. "He's not supposed to take your worries away. He's supposed to love, respect, and protect you. He should make you feel like the most important person on earth." Zarah's eyes watered but not a drop fell.

The taxi pulled into their driveway, moving slowly. It was about time. If Tamara hadn't been talking with Zarah all this while, she would have been upset about the wait.

"Excuse me, I have to go inside," Zarah said, covering her mouth and holding her stomach.

That pesky virus was disrupting Tamara's afternoon again. Zarah had to hurry up and get over the bug. Distractions weren't welcome. Two meetings down and she had no idea how many more to go before Zarah would consider selling her the division. Tamara stood near the taxi waiting patiently for Zarah. Time was short but there were a few minutes to spare. Joel was most likely far enough away to pose no threat.

chapter
46

Sunday morning ushered in another day of reflection. Days and nights had blended since Don's meeting with Tamara and Abigail midweek. He had to shed the distress, not allowing seeds of resentment or excessive disappointment to take hold. Forgiveness was his weapon to defeat the emotional and spiritual attacks. Reconciliation was his path to recovery. His pride made him want to stand up and retaliate against those who wronged him, but God's word had been deposited in his spirit, saturating his conscience, and wouldn't be silenced. The time of his greatest despair was the precise moment to forgive and let go. It was a mandatory step in the journey to healing and restoration. Depleted and struggling, Don decided to go where he'd get answers and a surge of hope.

He gave Abigail a call.

"Don, this is a surprise. I don't think you've called me on a Sunday morning since we went to church together earlier this year."

"That's why I'm calling. You feel like going to Greater Faith Chapel with me? I need a dose of inspiration."

"I don't know, Don. You're not going to use this as an opportunity to talk me into staying on board, are you?"

"No, not at all, this is about church, nothing more." He could easily go alone and wouldn't hesitate if she said no, but hopefully she wasn't going to.

"I'll go. Do you want me to meet you there?" she asked.

"I'll pick you up around a quarter after nine."

Don would dress right after calling Tamara. He wasn't pleased with her actions, but she was his sister, flaws included.

"Tamara, I'm calling to see if you're interested in going to church with me. I figured we could shake off our disagreement and start over today. What do you think?"

"I think it's early, Don, and I'm sleepy."

"Come on, Tamara, you're coming up with excuses. Give us a chance to work out the issue. Church is neutral territory. You'll be safe."

"Thanks for the offer, but I'm passing. Sleep is more appealing. You have fun."

Don wasn't going to push. They ended the call and he got dressed. An hour and a half from the time he called Abigail, he was sitting in front of her town house. She got into his car. "I'm glad you're coming with me."

"Why not? If I wasn't going to Greater Faith Chapel, I'd be going to my church anyway," she said.

Don didn't let awkwardness prevail. This was Abigail, his beloved friend. They had to work beyond her discontent with him and the Mitchell family. He would do his part. "We haven't talked much since you submitted your resignation."

"I haven't been avoiding you if that's what you mean. I've been busy at the office."

"Actually, I didn't mean anything," he said. Personally, Don wanted to see Abigail fulfilled, but professionally he needed her to stay on board for at least six months. He knew what would have taken precedence with Joel. The company would have come first. Maybe it was to his detriment, Don thought, but the bonds of love had a tighter grip on him than selfish desires. He had to support Abigail, and what a difficult feat that was going to be with DMI in its current state. "I want you to know directly from me: I admire you. I appreciate what you've done for me, for the company, for my family—you name it, you've been there, and I want to say thank you."

"Don't get mushy on me. I have absolutely loved my time at DMI. It has been a dream job."

"Why not let the dream continue?" he said, filled with lightheartedness.

"Let's not go there. We're going to church, and let's pray that the Lord helps all of us, because Lord knows we all need help."

She was right. Don had watched his family implode, not so much financially or physically, but certainly emotionally and spiritually. It wasn't too long ago when he'd battled his relationship with the Lord, calling into question why God continually allowed Joel to get the best of everything set before them. For a long time Don saw himself as the second son, not with top billing in their father's presence, as Joel had. He hadn't realized the depth of the loss he felt when his father moved out, creating another family and replacing him with Joel. Because of Sherry and her son, Don grew up without a father in the house.

Without any conscious knowledge or warning, the grief had transformed into resentment and bitterness, spreading like a virus. Once he discovered his true feelings, the blame was squarely directed at God, Dave Mitchell, and Sherry. South Africa had given him the distance and solitude to search his heart, find out what really mattered, cleanse his spirit, and heal his soul. God met him where he was. His faith said that if God could deliver him from the ravaged remains of his childhood, He could do the same for Tamara, Mother, and even Joel. Discord wasn't going to be the Mitchell legacy. He was certain.

chapter

47

Don exited the highway and traveled a few blocks off Outer Drive to Greater Faith Chapel. "Ready?"

"Always," Abigail responded as they got out of the car and went inside the church.

"I hope we get a chance to see Mother Emma Walker again. She had a strong message of direction and encouragement for me. I could use one today." Last time he was at the church, she'd shared a prophecy that basically told him some battles were destined if they led a person to fulfilling the purpose for which God created them. There was no way around challenges and adversity if a person was to fulfill their destiny. She didn't say it in quite the same way as Don recalled, but where her phrasing fell short, her wisdom more than compensated. He hoped to see her today.

"Greetings in the name of Jesus," a young lady said, approaching them. "Are you visitors?"

"Yes we are," Abigail said.

"Well, double welcome to you."

"We've been here before, though," Don said as a man approached. He looked familiar.

"Then welcome back. We're glad to have you. We pray you enjoy the service and leave here stuffed with the spirit. We call it the hallelujah buffet. Eat as much as your soul can hold," the man said, roaring with laughter, and the small group around them erupted into laughter as well.

Another gentleman interjected. "I remember meeting you several months ago—Mr. Mitchell and Ms. Gerard? Am I right?"

"You are right," Don said, pausing because he didn't know the man's name. He extended his hand to shake anyway.

"I'm Pastor Clyde Daniels. It's a pleasure seeing you again."

"Likewise," Don said, totally embarrassed to realize that he was speaking to the pastor. Even though he'd only met him briefly five months ago, during a tumultuous time in his life, Don should have remembered the head guy.

"I know Mother Walker will want to see you."

"Is she here?" Don asked, sounding more eager than he wanted to.

"She's here, all right. Mother Walker doesn't miss a day in the house of the Lord." The crowd around Don, Abigail, and the pastor was growing. They erupted in laughter again.

Someone else chimed in: "I know you're right."

"She's here at times when I have to miss. Yes, indeed," Pastor Daniels said, rolling back on his heels. "She's a true godly woman." A series of people echoed his sentiment.

Like the Red Sea parting before Moses, the crowd began to fan out in slow motion. There she was, a petite woman no taller than five feet, moving slowly toward him. Don shortened the distance and went to her. He extended his hand.

"Oh, son, Big Mama doesn't shake no hands. I'm going to give you a great big old hug, that's what I'm going to do." Don bent down without hesitation. The warmth in her hug was special, filled with sincerity. If being in her presence was this satisfying, he couldn't imagine what it would feel like to stand before God. "It's good to see you again, son."

"Good to see you, Mother Walker." Around her, he was humbled. He didn't feel like the thirty-four-year-old CEO of two companies. He was a spiritual baby under her and gladly accepted the pecking order. When she came into the vestibule, even the pastor stood to the side.

"Well, hello, Abigail," Mother Walker said. They hugged and greeted each other. "Sho is good to have the two of you here with us today. Where is that brother of yours?"

"Oh, uh, he's at home, I guess."

"How about you?" she asked Don. "Do you know where he is?"

"No, ma'am, I don't."

Don wasn't sure why she was asking.

"I have a word for him." Chatter in the vestibule halted with the quickness of a finger snap. Chitchat converted to silence sprinkled with prayer.

"The God of Abraham, Isaac, and Jacob is the God of his father. The one that called him into being. The one that gave him the ability to think, to create, to be. That God has not changed. He has not forsaken him. He has not left him." She stopped with her eyelids closed. Don didn't know if he was supposed to respond. Not sure, he waited for direction. Abigail and Mother Walker had their eyes shut. After what felt like a minute or two Mother Walker held Don's hand, keeping her eyes closed. "Your brother has come to a fork in the road. He can go this way. He can go that way." She paused again. Nobody seemed to mind. She clearly set the pace in the vestibule. "One road is hardship. One is peace. Whichever way he go is gonna take a heap of help from the Lord."

Don wasn't completely following. Besides, the message was for Joel. Was he required to remember and convey the message in its entirety to him?

Abigail interrupted. "What does that mean?" Don scanned the crowd to gauge the reaction, glad it wasn't him interrupting, although he had the same question.

"Sometimes we get ourselves in holes we can't find our way out of. We keep digging and digging, thinking we're getting somewhere. Most of the time we're digging a bigger hole—don't have to be deeper, could be wider. We can't get out until we stop, look around," Mother Walker said, letting her gaze roll around the room, "and see that we're in a hole. To get out you need God. To stay in the hole and survive you need God." Her analogy was starting to make sense for Don. "Sometimes God allows us to get into a world of trouble so that we have to go to Him, no matter which road we take," she said. "I believe those are some of the most blessed people."

"Why do you say so, Mother?" Pastor Daniels asked.

"'Cause they have to seek God. Sometimes when we have a heap of choices, we don't always end up going the right way. When you don't have a choice, it's better." Mother Walker patted Don on his forearm. "You be sure and give your brother that word, you hear?"

"Yes, ma'am," he said before thinking again. He didn't know if or when Joel would surface. Maybe God was telling him to reach out to Joel? He'd attempted several times before, to no avail. Instantly he heard words boldly playing in his mind: *Forgiveness is endless. So should be your attempts at reconciliation. Whatever hinders you, set it aside for the cause of Christ.*

"We better move into the sanctuary. It's five after eleven," Mother Walker said.

"I'm so sorry. We didn't mean to disrupt the service."

"Noooo," Pastor Daniels said. "This is God's house. We're here to serve Him. We come prepared to have church decently and in order but when Papa shows up, we let Him have His way. Time is for man because we're temporal beings. God is eternal. Any time the Holy Spirit arrives, it's the right time." Amen rang throughout the church as the congregation flocked into the sanctuary. Mother Walker had gone ahead.

"That was a good message for Joel. It's too bad she didn't have one for you. I know you were hoping to get a word of encouragement," Abigail said.

"I did," he said, and left the response at that. He'd gotten a double dose of encouragement when he came only hoping for a single. God had Don in church on the precise day when He intended for Mother Emma Walker to share the message. God knew Joel wasn't going to be there so He sent someone to get the word for him. Don had to accept his purpose. If God was going to use him as a vessel to reconcile the Mitchell clan, then he was going to have to completely forgo pride, convenience, and personal desires. There were going to be times when he'd have to reach out to Joel and Tamara with unconditional love regardless of how many times they backstabbed him.

"Are you okay?" Abigail asked, maybe because he was walking slowly.

"I'm fine, just thinking." So many times he'd viewed himself as the second-class son who had to deal with adversity over and over. Realizing the gravity of his purpose, he began to understand that each challenge, hurt, and wrongful act committed against him was sanctioned by the Lord to strengthen his faith and to force him to understand the essence of forgiveness. Going to Robbins Island in South Africa and hearing about Nelson Mandela wasn't accidental. He needed to hear about the healing strength of forgiveness through a man who compelled his comrades to forgive, despite the inhumane treatment they suffered during apartheid. Embracing the hope of a future and being able to move forward depended on burying the pains of the past.

Not a single step or act was random; each was completely orchestrated in God's plan. Don had longed for reconciliation with his family, everyone, including Sherry. Now it was time to convert rhetoric into action. He and Abigail took a seat on one of the pews in the center of the church. Don began praying for guidance as he prepared to take on the most important challenge of his life, allowing God to use him as a tool of restoration in the Mitchell family. Forgiving and forgetting the hurts were his weapons, and he was to use them fearlessly.

chapter

48

Don pocketed his pride and blocked his own opposition. He went directly to Joel's house after dropping off Abigail. Joel had to listen. Don prayed along the way, believing he could reach a point of compromise with his brother. He didn't know how the conversation would flow and went ahead anyway. Three raps on the door and the housekeeper was standing before him. "Yes, sir, how may I help you?"

"Hi, I'm Don Mitchell. I came by to see my brother. Is he here by any chance?"

There was awkwardness. Only two visits to Joel's house in three years didn't facilitate family bonding. "Come in, please. I'll check to see if he's available." The housekeeper directed him to the room located off the foyer. "Please have a seat. Can I get you something to drink?"

"No, thank you."

Don waited about five minutes and Joel entered the

room. "I didn't realize DMI made house calls. What brings you by my house on a Sunday?"

"Mother Emma Walker."

"Who is that?"

"Do you remember the church lady from Greater Faith Chapel, the one they call Big Mama?"

"Oh yeah, her. She's good people. What about her?"

"I saw her at the church today, and she was asking about you."

"Really," Joel responded, standing near the door. He didn't seem relaxed enough to sit. Don wasn't deterred. Joel's comfort wasn't required for Don to complete his mission. "That's an interesting old lady," Joel said. "She's kind of eccentric if you ask me, but I like her. I'm not saying I agree with everything she says, but she's somebody I wouldn't mind having on my squad in the heat of a battle."

"Kind of like Shaq, it's better to have him playing on your basketball team than having to play against him in the post on another team."

"Yeah," Joel said, giving a slight chuckle, the window of connection Don was praying to get.

"Well, you must have left an impression on her. She was insistent that I relay this word of prophecy to you."

"I don't know if I want to hear it or not."

Don could relate. Mother Walker seemed to have a direct line to the Lord. She had good old-fashioned wisdom tempered with the Holy Spirit. When a person like that says "Thus said the Lord," somebody better pay attention. The downside was that once she gave the message, the intended receiver was then accountable. Sometimes ignorance was safer. So yes, Don could relate to how Joel was probably feeling. "I have to tell you so the next time I see her, my conscience will be clear," he said, hoping to get another chuckle from Joel. It didn't come, but Joel strolled to a chair, which was just as good.

"Do what you have to do. Lay it on me."

The stage was set for a huge revelation. Maybe he oversold the setup, because his message was only a few lines, paraphrased. Had Don known she was giving him an assignment, he would have brought paper and pen. Since he hadn't, he'd recall what he could, asking God to fill in the gaps. He didn't want Joel to lose a morsel of the message on his account. "She told me to tell you God hasn't changed. He has not forsaken you. He has not left you." Joel listened without interruption. "She said you're at a fork in the road, and you're going to need God to make your decision." He could have continued with the extra clarification Mother Walker gave Abigail about Joel's decisions continuously digging him a larger hole. Don opted to avoid confrontation and go with the condensed version. God would get part two to Joel if it was vital. He was certain.

"What does that mean? That's one thing about Mother Walker, she talks in parables and riddles when I'm looking for a straight answer."

Again, Don could have told Joel some answers only come through fasting and praying, or hearing from God directly. He would hold his comment. He had checked his pride and any seeds of confrontation at the door. Don was prepared to reach Joel by any means necessary. "I told you what she told me. My job is finished. The interpretation is on you, my brother."

"'Brother,'" Joel said. "That's not a term we use too often, not really at all."

Don realized this seemingly coincidental encounter with Joel had been perfectly orchestrated. Suddenly he was nervous, not sure what to say to capitalize on the moment with Joel. *Stop overanalyzing and speak* was the plea coming from within him, so he did. "There are many things in life that can be changed and some that can't. How you and I treat one another is one I believe can be changed."

"How so, big brother?"

"Let's start with setting aside our history. I know you have issues with me about Dad, and I've had my issues with you about him."

"I wouldn't call it an issue. You were his legitimate son according to popular belief. Your mother was married to him first. I've never had the same respect as his son," Joel said, leaning forward and letting his elbows rest on his knees and his chin sit on his clasped fingers.

"That's ironic, because I saw you as the favored son. You got to live your entire childhood with him. I grew up with visits, and they're not the same as day-in-and-day-out contact."

"Sounds like we're both messed up."

"Seems so," Don said, feeling his way through the quagmire of their relationship. It was so mangled. He wasn't seeking full restoration in one visit and would settle for establishing a solid foundation with layers of reconciliation to follow. "Where do we go from here?"

"You tell me, big brother. When I was a kid, I used to dream about having a family. Technically I have three brothers and a sister, but it's always felt like I don't have any siblings. None of you reached out to me as a child and I dreamed that you would. I watched you and Tamara play together when you'd come for your visits. I don't remember much about Sam. I do have memories of Andre from the time he lived with us, not many though. Honestly, you're the only one I really remember, and that's limited."

"We were kids trying to deal with the loss of our father."

"He wasn't dead."

"At the time he might as well have been. He wasn't home with us, and we were mad at you, and him, and your mother."

"That's mostly what I remember about Andre, how mad he was. He and my mother fought all the time," Joel said, peering down at his hands.

Andre was a topic Don wasn't going to broach; it was too toxic. To understand Andre's pain, they'd have to go all the way back to his adoption into the Mitchell family after his natural parents died. His emotional collapse was years in the making. The divorce, and what Andre saw as Dave's abandonment, had pushed him closer to the edge. Dad's attempts at reconciliation were discarded by Mother, but Andre was the one who felt the brunt of the pain. The fact that Mother initiated the divorce, after Dad's affair with Sherry, didn't seem to make a difference either in the end. Blame was almost exclusively directed at Dad and Sherry. Unfortunately, Andre's issues spilled beyond his anger toward their father and Sherry. Tamara was the ultimate victim of his rage. Don couldn't discuss Andre with Joel and switched to another topic. "What's done is done. I'm looking at today. What can we do to make this work for us?"

There was a time when Joel truly longed to have Don as a bona fide brother in both name and deed. Fast-forward to age twenty-six and the desire wasn't as critical. He'd survived without the love of his siblings. He wasn't opposed to forming a relationship so long as he was treated as an equal, regardless of age, birth order, mother, or position in DMI. His requirement was definite. Joel pulled his hands apart and let them clasp together again. "What do you suggest?"

"Can we start with working out a deal for Harmonious Energy? I'd like for you and your wife to have first dibs on the purchase. I respect the concept of family legacy."

"Harmonious Energy isn't my call."

Kumar made it clear no funds were being released prematurely to or for Zarah. Sheba and his mother had money and would gladly hand it over, but he wouldn't dare put their security at risk to get reestablished. Without cash from Zarah's inheritance, the money wasn't there to purchase her father's company. Without Harmonious Energy as the building block, there wasn't much value in keeping the West Coast division. A stand-alone division equated to a few grains of sand in the bucket, not enough for him to establish a dominant international presence. He was done with the concept. He would pursue other channels. This wasn't the end for him.

"Are you saying Zarah is the one I have to approach?"

"I guess that is what I'm saying."

Joel wasn't quite ready to have his family going directly to Zarah. On the other hand, she was in charge, her and their family legal team. They'd have to work out a deal without Joel. He'd step aside and figure out his next move. Becoming a member of the Bengali family was a mistake. Making the necessary correction quickly was going to be the best route for each person involved.

"What about the West Coast division? I have to discuss it with her too?"

"I guess so," Joel said, clenching his teeth.

"Let me be clear. You're okay with me discussing both Harmonious Energy and the West Coast division with her?"

"What choice do I have?" His best-laid plans were a disaster. Every indication and unsolicited piece of advice said purchasing Harmonious Energy, marrying Zarah, and overriding the board of directors were misguided. He hadn't listened and now he was sitting in the pit of his decision. Consequences were heaped upon his head with every passing day. He had to stop the fallout. He couldn't relive the past. It was already in the record book. A fresh start with a broader perspective was his goal.

"Then I'll set up a meeting with her and go from there."

"I'm sure you'll do right by her."

"Would you like to be included in the negotiatious?"

Joel paused, assessed his new perspective, and responded with "No." A clean break was best. He hadn't been any good for her. Zarah needed a fresh start whether or not she realized it, but that was a different discussion. Without him, she could receive her inheritance, buy her father's company if she wanted, and begin living her life. Maybe she could find happiness and build the family she desperately desired. He wanted that for her, just not with him. He had to concentrate on fixing his fractured world.

"We've taken care of DMI. Now, what about us? I'm serious, I want to form some kind of a relationship with you," Don said.

"You want us to go to ball games together and shoot hoops in the park?" Joel responded with sarcastic laughter.

"Maybe, why not? Seriously, we have to start somewhere. I'm not going to pressure you. I'll put the offer out there and the next move is on you. Like I said, I can't change our past—not even sure if I'd want to—but we're here now. This is our time to wipe the slate clean and make this whatever we want it to be as two grown men—not as Madeline's boy or Sherry's boy, as two men. It's up to you."

Joel nodded; he wasn't committing to a brotherly out-ing tomorrow but he was definitely in favor of explor-ing the possibility. He'd take time to set his household in order, clean up a few loose ends, and then take Don up on his offer. Maybe Don was correct and a Pistons or Lions game wasn't such a bad idea. "I don't mean to rush you, big brother, but I have to take care of some business."

"Okay, no problem. I'm good. I got the information I needed. Thanks a lot," Don said, extending his hand to Joel. There was a hesitation but Joel reached out toward him. Shake, embrace, release. Joel had no idea to what extent his relationship with Don would develop. He wasn't going to institute limits or requirements. Instead, he'd settle for letting a natural flow dictate what happened, something he wished a thousand times he'd done in his personal life. Corrections were on the way.

chapter
49

Don was gone. Joel's thoughts remained. There wasn't an easy way to do what had to be done. Zarah was getting stronger each day. Perhaps another month or two was more ideal. He could endure the inconvenience if it allowed Zarah to have a better chance at stability once he was gone. He meandered to his office, the room of solitude. He thought about the decisions he was most proud of, and they were equally balanced with those of tremendous failure.

He reclined in his desk chair, not really thinking about much except Zarah. He'd tried, sincerely, or so it seemed, to love her the way a husband should love his wife. No doubt he cared about her and wanted Zarah to have joy and fulfillment. He wasn't the man for her. She wasn't the woman for him. He knew it. His focus was on figuring out the most compelling way to get her to understand, gently. In case there was karma or truth in the philosophy "What goes around comes around," he'd handle the breakup with compassion. Building up goodwill wouldn't hurt. He'd call Kumar, and then they'd decide on the best way to inform Zarah about the divorce.

He picked up the phone to make the call without further consideration. Waiting would cloud his clarity and he hadn't been this certain in months about much. Satisfaction careened through his consciousness. After the call, he and Zarah could go for a quiet dinner, nothing fancy, just the two of them, as a peace offering. He'd stay around home for a week or so, then go back to Chicago to get the creative juices flowing. Maybe he'd get a rental downtown instead of having to crash at Sheba's. Lots of maybes with no urgency to commit, he thought as Kumar answered the call.

"Kumar, it's Joel Mitchell. We have to talk."

chapter
50

Don was sailing on a boost of hope. His meeting with Joel went better than expected; one sibling down, one to go. He exited the expressway en route to Tamara's apartment building. She was going to hear him out, no running away. Don found her building and crept down the street in search of a parking spot.

There was no rehearsing what he was going to say. His soul had already prepared the speech. He dialed her unit on the security keypad.

After several attempts, he heard, "Who is it?"

"It's me, Don, let me in."

She didn't buzz him in right away. He wasn't giving up. He was getting in whether she buzzed him or he had to ease in behind another tenant. He had to ring her several more times before Tamara finally let him into the building. Once he reached her apartment, he knocked repeatedly until she finally snatched the door open. "Why are you banging on my door? You are worse than Mother."

"Can I come in or are you going to let me stay out here in the hallway?" She gestured for him to come in, taking a step back with her hand gripping the knob. He could tell she wasn't thrilled with his dropping in. Don wasn't to be deterred and didn't allow his momentum to be diluted by her abrasive reception. "Thank you," he said, and entered.

"What do you want, Don?"

"We have to talk."

"About what? The last time we talked you were upset about me wanting to venture out on my own."

"Come on, Tamara. You know we talked about more than you venturing out on your own. I'm fine with you doing that. I took issue with how you were attempting to venture out, by undercutting me and what I was trying to do for the family."

"Are we going to rehash the discussion, Don? Because I'm not changing my mind."

"Tamara, I'm not here to rehash our disagreement."

"Good, because I'm going after the West Coast division. You can have the rest of DMI and the other three divisions." Tamara's phone rang. She kept talking. "I think that's more than fair."

"I think so too."

"What did you say?"

"I think it's fair too," Don repeated.

"Whoa, wait a minute. What did you say?"

"Take the West Coast division."

The phone rang again. Tamara ignored the phone and stayed engaged in the conversation. "Just like that, you're giving it up?"

"Actually the division isn't mine to keep or give away. It belongs to Zarah. I just spoke with Joel and he said to discuss the deal with Zarah. He's not involved, didn't even want to be there for the negotiations."

"Really, that's odd."

"I thought so, but stranger decisions have been made. So I'm not looking a gift horse in the mouth. In case he's sincere, you should reach out to Zarah and arrange a deal. I'm approaching her about selling her Harmonious Energy. If you want to combine the initial discussions into one meeting, we can."

"Sure, why not. Don," she said, plopping onto her sofa, "why the sudden change?"

He plopped down next to her. The phone rang incessantly. "Tamara, what is the deal with your phone? Aren't you going to answer it?"

"No, it's okay," she said, getting the phone and turning it off. She reclaimed her seat. "Now, what were you saying about changing your mind?"

He turned to face her. "I've been at odds with Joel most of my life. To be honest, I'm tired of fighting. Like it or not, we're blood. You and I have been tight forever. I refuse to end the war with Joel just in time to initiate one with you. I won't do it. If the division means that much to you, go for it. I won't stop you. My relationship with you is far more important than expanding DMI. As far as I'm concerned the company can shut down if it stands between me, you, Mother, and even Joel establishing a sense of family."

"Not everyone would step aside like you're doing for someone else to realize their dream."

"Don't pat me on the back yet. You might not like what's coming next."

"I should have known this was too good to be true."

"Well, Tamara, it's time for you to face your past, deal with what happened, and consider forgiving Mother." She went to get up but Don grabbed her arm. "You're always running. I want you to stop running. We can get through this together."

"Let me go, Don," she said, pulling away but sitting down. "Why can't you leave that crap from the past alone? Why do you have to push and push? For goodness sake, I'm back here, aren't I? That should tell you I've come an awfully long way. Let me move at my pace, not yours, and most definitely not Mother's."

"Forgiveness isn't about Mother, not totally. This is about you and reclaiming your strength. If you stay mad at the world—"

"Not the world," she said, interrupting. "Don't try to make it seem like my need to have distance from Mother, Joel, and Sherry is irrational. I have to protect my sanity and being around the bunch of them is hazardous to my psychological health. They have issues, ones I don't want to deal with. I love our mother, I actually do, but don't think I'm going to forgive, forget, and skip off into the sunset as her baby girl. That's not going to happen, not now, not ever, and you need to face reality."

"Have you considered therapy for the rape and for your anger toward Mother?"

"I don't need therapy!" she yelled out. "I'm not the one with the problem. Leave me alone and no one has a problem. How dare you, Don? You barge into my apartment, push me into reconciling with Mother, and when I won't, you recommend therapy as though I'm unstable. How many times have you recommended therapy to Mother?"

Don hadn't and wasn't going to lie. Mother needed therapy. He intended to tell her but hadn't gotten around to the task yet. Tamara wasn't going to believe such an explanation. No need to speak the words. He swallowed them and said, "None."

"Of course not, fix Tamara and everyone else will be fine. Uh-huh, I see how this is supposed to go, but I'm going to disrupt your plans. I'm not agreeing to counseling, forgiving, forgetting, or anything else on your list. I'm a grown woman, Don. I get to say what happens to me, not a long line of men dictating my life, starting with Andre. No, thank you, Mr. Peacemaker. I don't need help fixing myself. I prefer to deal with the past on my terms."

"Tell me, how successful has that been for you?" She had no response. "Get these problems behind you and stop wasting years," Don told her. Finding common ground with Joel wasn't simple. He didn't expect it to be any simpler with Tamara. He'd continue until either they were both exhausted from disagreeing or they reached a compromise. Day and night could come and go. He was planted on the sofa until then. He assumed Tamara's unwillingness to change was fueled by animosity and vengeance. "How twisted can we be? The very person you work so hard to avoid is the one you remind me of the most—Mother."

"I resent the comparison. Madeline and I are nothing alike. I don't need to be constantly reminded of her. You better go."

Accepting Mother was going to be a tough journey for Tamara. He understood that she wasn't remotely ready to invite God into her life. She'd have to confess sins, ask God to forgive her, and accept Christ, the son of God, as her savior. Huge steps for someone who'd been wronged. Tamara was so blinded by her pain that she couldn't objectively see her shortcomings or the need for someone in her life that had more power than her. Tamara didn't seem ready to give up her power to anyone or anything, not yet.

Abruptly, there was a heavy pounding on the door. Tamara nearly fell off the sofa. She ignored the noise. By the third round of banging, Don had to say something. Tamara didn't budge. "Who the heck is banging?" he said, getting up and going to the door.

"No, don't answer it!" she called out, practically tackling him. "Whoever it is will go away," she told him, frantic.

"Tamara," Don yelled, "calm down! Let me see who it is." She didn't calm down much; she was almost hysterical. "Who is it?" Don asked in a voice loud enough to be heard clearly.

"Tamara, who's in there with you? Open the door now so we can talk! Open the door!" a man screamed, continuously pounding on the door. Don was stunned to hear him shout Tamara's name in such an abrasive tone.

"You know this guy outside?"

"I-I—" she said with nothing following.

"You have to be joking. What is going on here?" Don asked. "You better start talking, otherwise I'm opening the door to find out from this guy."

"Don, stay out of this."

He jerked open the door despite Tamara's pleading. A man burst in, pushing past Don and going straight for Tamara. "Whoa, man," Don said, stepping between the guy and Tamara. Don hadn't seen him before; he was about five-ten, not stockily built but solid, with olive skin and shoulder-length black hair.

The guy began speaking roughly to Tamara in a heavy accent. Don could understand one out of every third or fourth word. From what he could tell, the guy was saying something about love and London. "Tamara, who is this?"

"Remo."

Who the heck is Remo? he wondered. Remo continued

raising his voice as if Don were invisible, speaking completely in Italian. Tamara argued right back at him. Don hadn't decided if he was going to intervene or let the argument continue. His decision wasn't final until Remo came around him and grabbed Tamara. Instinctively Don's right fist caught Remo on the chin and he dropped to the floor.

"Call the police!" Don shouted to Tamara. She ran to her phone.

Don had Remo pinned down on the floor with his arm pulled almost to the nape of his neck. Don tried to keep his gaze fixed on Tamara to make sure she was okay while handling Remo. At the most inopportune time, a cramp shot up Don's leg, causing him to writhe in pain and roll off Remo's back to the floor. Remo used the break to flee the apartment. Tamara wasn't going after him and Don couldn't. They'd have to wait for the police, who arrived ten minutes later.

"I understand there was an assault," the officer said. He took Don and Tamara's names and asked basic questions initially. "Can you give me the perpetrator's full name?"

"Remo Mancini. He's an ex-boyfriend from Italy who has followed me from Florence to Glasgow to Barcelona to Nice to London. No matter where I hide, he finds me."

Don was speechless. He had no idea Tamara was living in fear, running from one country to the next. No wonder she moved so many times. He had thought it was because of her relationship with Mother, but apparently it wasn't.

"What can I do? He's threatened to kill me if I leave him again, and I believe he will."

"Nobody is going to kill you, Tamara, not while I'm here." Don was flooded with memories instantly. As a boy, he couldn't protect his big sister when she was raped. As a grown man, he was ready for duty.

"We can certainly talk to Mr. Mancini and express that it's in his best interest to back off and stay away from you. What's his address?"

"I don't know. Once I moved from Italy to Dublin, I lost track and didn't care to ask."

"Is he an Italian citizen?"

"I think so but I'm not sure. We have both lived abroad and have more than one residency."

"Does he have an address in the U.S.?"

"I don't know."

Too much of "I don't know" left Don feeling helpless.

"Ms. Mitchell, we can take your report, but without more information we can't provide much more assistance."

"He's coming back to my apartment for sure. What else can I do?"

"You can file an order of protection restricting Mr. Mancini from coming near you. The problem is that we need an address to serve him the order, which you don't have."

The police stayed on a few more minutes. There was no more they could do.

"Don, what should I do?" she asked when the two of them were alone in the apartment.

"Grab a few items. You're coming with me."

"How can you be so willing to help me when I've been working against you lately?"

"How can you ask me that? You're my sister, no matter what. Now get your stuff and let's go."

Tamara didn't resist the help. She packed her bag and went with Don. He'd figure out the next step once she was safe and secure in his condo. Remo certainly wasn't getting in there.

The BMW floated along surreally. Tamara always knew Remo would find her, though she hadn't expected him to find her so soon and to be openly violent in front of Don. Her emotions were jumbled with embarrassment, fear, disgust, and the worst one, an element of helplessness. Here was a guy bent on having her with no regard for Tamara's desires or security. She searched her memory, trying to recall the time when he was the attentive, unselfish dreamer she fell in love with during her stay in Florence. Countless walks along the Via Roma, painting the future, dipping in and out of museums, shopping for sweaters and leather goods from the local merchants. Every bit of those times was long gone. Even the sweaters and leather were abandoned in her Italian flat when she had to flee the country, after Remo turned from Dr. Jekyll to Mr. Hyde the first time. She continued peering out the window until Don broke the silence.

"Don't worry, Tamara, you'll be safe with me. Remo

isn't getting in my house. Between me, the security staff, and the police, Mr. Remo won't show up there."

"Honestly, I'm not worried about him coming to your place. I'm just afraid of him finding me wherever I go. I am so sick of running!" she bellowed, choking down the swelling cry. Her tears were too stubborn to fall. Her helplessness was converting to determination. She yearned for a permanent solution. "I'm tired," she told him, letting out her surging rage.

"I'll figure out what to do. Don't you worry," Don said. "Mr. Remo has crossed into the right country to get dealt with."

Tamara was feeling the safest she had in years. They hadn't solved the problem with Remo but she was no longer alone in searching for a solution.

Don pulled up to the valet at his building. Inside, he stopped at the security desk. "I need you to make sure no one gets up to my unit without express permission from me, do you understand? No one."

"We got it, Mr. Mitchell."

"Particularly this Italian fellow named Remo. What's his last name?" he asked Tamara.

"Mancini."

"There you go," Don said, "Remo Mancini. He's about this high," Don told the guards, raising his hand to just below his nose. "Long dark hair, wearing a pair of jeans and a thin red sweater. If he shows up, I need you to call the police right away. He's dangerous."

"Is he armed?"

"I don't know," Don responded. Tamara hadn't thought about his being armed, another element to be feared. When would the nightmare end?

Don wrapped up his instructions at the security desk

and they got on the elevator. Everything between standing there and being inside his unit was a blur to Tamara. The adrenaline that had pumped through her earlier had put her on an emotional high. Now her body was crashing as fatigue set in. "Don, if you don't mind, I need to rest."

"Of course, the guest room is this way," he told her, walking down the corridor near the rear section of the condo. "Do you want me to wake you at a certain time or what?"

"I doubt if I'm going to be able to fall asleep. Resting is good enough for now."

"Okay then," he said as they reached the room. "Tamara, feel free to lock the door if it makes you feel safer. I'm here and you're going to be fine, but I understand and won't be offended at all."

She pursed her lips and gave him a soft nod. Knowing someone was in the struggle with her and understood her pain brought an element of comfort she hadn't previously experienced. She wasn't sure, but it felt like a touch of hope.

on wasn't confused about the next step. He had to get
extra security in place and put out a private search
for Remo. He was going to be the one stalked for a change.
Don was infuriated each time he thought about his sister
being hunted down by a crazed lunatic without help from
her family. Well, that was over. He was involved now and
Madeline would be too. He got her on the phone; the time
of day was totally discounted. Mama lion would want to
know.

"Mother, we have a situation here with Tamara."

"What now, did she run off with the entire company?
Good grief, did she leave you at least the Midwest division? My goodness—"

"Mother," he interrupted, "this isn't about DMI. This is
about Tamara's safety."

"What?"

"Apparently she's being stalked by this crazy guy named
Remo. He barged into her new apartment, and can you

believe he tried to grab her with me standing right there?"

"I hope you took care of him."

"Don't worry, I protected my sister," Don said, recalling the punch.

"Who is he?"

"Some guy she dated in Italy. According to her they broke up and he didn't take it well. All the moving around she's done in the last couple of years has been to get away from him, but he keeps finding her. She can't put an order of protection on him without an address to have the papers served."

"I can't believe this. I'm on my way home."

"Mother, wait, let me see what I can do."

"Now you're the crazy one if you think I'm going to be eight thousand miles away with a maniac on the loose in Detroit who's after my child. Save your breath. I'm on my way to the airport to catch the first thing smoking. By plane, train, or rowboat, you will see me in Detroit within twenty-four hours."

"You think that's realistic?"

"Believe me when I tell you I'm going to be there. I'll charter a plane if necessary. Let me get off this phone and get moving. I'll see you tomorrow, Son. I love you, and let Tamara know I'm on my way. Don't let her out of your sight."

"I don't think she's going to run this time. Where is she going to go?"

"I can't be bothered by her running. I'm coming home, period. No one other than God will delay me, and He'd even have a fight on his hands with me. See you soon," she said, and disconnected the call. Don was actually relieved to have Madeline coming home. Relaying information back and forth wouldn't have worked. Mother needed to be home. They all did.

chapter

53

Madeline had honored Tamara's wish and stayed away, but when her children were in danger, all deals were off. Nothing was more urgent than getting home. She had to move quickly. There would be nothing more frustrating than rushing to the airport only to find out the flight she desperately wanted had departed minutes before her arrival. She wasn't opposed to booking a private flight, but if a commercial flight was a few hours from taxiing down the runway and hitting the air, that would be her preference instead of getting flight itineraries registered, getting a pilot, and so on. Every free moment she had needed to be exclusively dedicated to dealing with this Mr. Remo. He'd picked the wrong daughter to stalk. He just didn't know the extent of his mistake. She'd make sure he found out.

Madeline tore out of the office after tossing a few items, including her laptop, into her purse. "Naledi, I have to go home. I'll have Don fill you in," she shouted, bolting for the door.

"Home for the evening? Then I shall see you tomorrow, yes?" Naledi said.

"No, I mean home to Detroit. Cheers," Madeline said without breaking her stride. The important business at home was her top priority.

Madeline was about to jump in a cab, then pulled back. She'd order a limousine with a privacy window instead. It might take an extra half hour for him to pick her up but she'd multitask. The privacy was going to be useful for the call she had to make.

The thirty-minute wait turned into forty as the car eased to the front of LTI, where Madeline was waiting, fuming by now.

"What took so long?" she asked as the driver opened the door for her to get in. "When I'm told thirty minutes, I expect thirty minutes or a call telling me you're running late, or that you jumped in the ocean, or something," she told him after getting in.

"Is your luggage inside the building?"

"No luggage, let's go. I'm in a big hurry." There was no further discussion on the matter. She was done with it and couldn't waste any more time with petty issues. The driver was in his seat and pulling off.

"Ma'am, my apologies for the delay. I'll have you at the airport right away," the driver said with an Irish-sounding accent.

Madeline had less than zero interest in chitchat. "Excuse me, can you please close the privacy window? Thank you," she said, eager to make her call. When the window was closed she scrolled through her electronic directory, stopping at the number she was seeking. She dialed and sank into her seat.

"Frank Mitchell here."

"Frank, it's Madeline."

"Madeline, well, hello to you. This is a pleasant surprise. What is this about? Wait, don't tell me. You've finally figured out that you married the wrong Mitchell man?"

Not a chance, she thought. If he lived to be a hundred and fifty, she could never see past his tactics, which were the purpose of her call. Certain business matters required a specialist, and that he was.

"I need your help."

"Talk to me."

"Some psycho is terrorizing my daughter, chasing her from country to country. He had the gall to barge into her apartment in Detroit and try to attack her while Don was standing right there." Retelling the story warmed Madeline's fury to the boiling point. How dare this Mr. Remo?

"Did Nephew take care of the situation?"

"He protected his sister, of course, but we have to go further. You know what I mean?"

"What did the police say?"

"Said they couldn't help without an address to serve the protection order."

"Oh, those don't work." Frank chuckled. "Women get killed every day by people under restraining orders."

"Now you understand why I'm calling."

"What would you like for me to do? Have someone talk to him?" Frank asked.

"I'm not interested in talking."

"The kind of talking I'm referring to produces results. Trust me, Tamara will be sleeping safely in her bed in no time, and Remo will be the one running," Frank said.

"That's what I want to hear. I don't want any more details, only results."

"Absolutely sure you want to pursue this?"

"I wouldn't have made the call if I didn't. I'm already prepared to pay your consulting fee or whatever title you're giving your services these days."

"'Consulting' has a nice ring and today's your lucky day."

"How so?" Madeline asked, half afraid to hear the answer. Frank was full of surprises, with the majority of them unpleasant.

"Since you and your children are repeat customers, I'm going to give you a break. Instead of my standard fee, I'll give you a fifty percent discount. After all, she is my niece."

"Thanks for the gesture but do what needs to be done. I'm good for the money."

"I know you are. My brother left you looking good with the money to back it up."

"I work hard. I'm responsible for Madeline, not Dave."

"Whatever you say. Are you ready?"

"For what?" Madeline asked.

"The digits to my account in the Cayman Islands."

"I know the routine, half of the numbers now and the rest later."

"You got it. I love doing business with you; repeat customers are my favorite. You'll hear from me when the time is right," he said, and they ended the call.

chapter

54

Tamara woke from her nap, wondering if she was in a dream. The confrontation with Remo seemed like a bad one. Now awake, the despicable incident was behind her. She felt better entering the living area. Don was reclining on the sofa reading a newspaper.

"I see that you're up. How are you feeling?"

"Better, I think. Was I dreaming earlier or did we actually have a fight with Remo?"

"We had a fight."

"That's what I thought," she said, sliding down along the couch to the floor. "I've created an awful nightmare, haven't I?"

"The only mistake you made was trying to handle Remo on your own. Tamara, you have chosen to be isolated from the Mitchells but the reality is, we're family. I keep telling you that when you have a problem, Mother and I have one too. We're not your enemies."

"I know you're not, but I've spent so much time avoiding my issues. I figured if I stayed away from the environment, I'd be able to forget about them and move on. Hasn't worked as well as I wanted, clearly."

"It's not too late for us to deal with our challenges and get on about the business of enjoying these lives that God has entrusted to us. I refuse to waste any more time angry at this family member and that one. It's pointless," Don told her.

"You're right," she said, toying with fibers in the floor rug. "I don't want to waste any more time either."

"You might as well know that I called Mother and filled her in on what happened. Before you bite my head off for calling her, I want you to know that I truly believe she deserved the call. She's been a good mother. I didn't say 'perfect,' but Mother has done the best she could for us. That's why I can accept her the way she is."

"You know how demanding she can be."

"You bet I know, but she means well. So if you're going to run away, you better get going, because she'll be here by tomorrow. She wants to see you as soon as she arrives."

Tamara wasn't opposed. As a matter of fact, she was relieved to have Madeline coming home. "For so many years I felt like I didn't need a mother if it had to be bossy Madeline." Tamara kept picking at the rug fibers, suddenly drawn back to age six. "Sitting here in this position, feeling helpless about Remo, makes me glad to have a mother like Madeline. I know she will fix this."

"Yes, I can imagine she's going to get heavily involved, let me put it that way."

"Normally I'd protest but not after today. If I ever want to walk the streets without having to look over my shoulder for Remo, I need to accept her help."

"Can't hurt, or at least I hope not." Don laughed and so did she.

Maybe it was time to really deal with her mother and form a new relationship—not necessarily rekindle what was tarnished when she was seventeen years old, but establish a new normal she was willing to accept.

chapter

55

Joel sat at the base of the winding staircase in his parents' home. His memories were positive; he hadn't had to endure the same fate as Andre, Sam, Don, and Tamara. Madeline and his father's divorce was before his time. Yet he'd seen the carnage left in the wake of the divorce. He hadn't suffered the exact same tragedies as his siblings, but he had wounds. He had to face facts. Divorce was disastrous to those impacted. Prolonging a dysfunctional union didn't lessen the pain, more like extended it.

Mother took a seat next to him. "What are you so eager to tell me?"

"I'm getting a divorce."

Sherry gasped and threw her hands over her mouth. "Joel, you can't. Zarah isn't strong enough to survive a divorce. It will kill her."

"There's no sense waiting. The marriage isn't going to suddenly improve. We have to end this charade. I have to end this." He was certain no time was going to be ideal.

Now was as good as, if not better than, waiting another two or three years. The contract called for three years of marriage. If no children were born, he could be released from the marriage and have the right to reclaim the West Coast division at fair market value. Joel didn't care. He didn't want to wait.

"You know I want you to do what's best for you, but I can't help but think about how overcome with grief Zarah was when she thought you didn't want to have a child with her. That's her dream, giving you a child. She's almost obsessed with the notion."

"Maybe, but we're not having a child together, not now, not ever. I want out, period."

"What can I say when you talk that way? I just ask that you be gentle with her. She's going to need support."

"I've already spoken with her father's attorney, Kumar. He oversees the Bengali trust and can help get Zarah back to India. He's expected to arrive in two days. I will babysit her every minute for the next two days until she's safely deposited in his hands."

"Doesn't she have a say? It sounds like you and Kumar have made the decision. How does she feel about this?"

"I haven't told her yet. I'm going home right after I leave here. I plan to tell her as soon as I get home."

"Are you absolutely sure this is what you want to do?"

"One hundred percent."

"Then I will support your decision," she said. "Please let me know what I can do. If it's sitting with Zarah, I'll be available. Don't hesitate to let me know. I'm here for the both of you."

Joel kissed his mother on the cheek. "I'll let you know if I need your help. Thank you," he said, kissing the other cheek.

"For what?"

"For not saying 'I told you so.' You and Abigail tried to talk me out of going forward with the marriage. My motivation was clouded, and I didn't fast-forward far enough to anticipate this outcome. It's done and I'm wiser having taken this scenic route to contentment."

"Are you content?"

"Not quite, but I'm headed in the right direction." He stood from the stairs. "Let me get out of here, Mom. I must talk to Zarah today and get this behind us. Gotta go, love you much."

Joel rehearsed his lines repeatedly on the way home. He'd spoken to Kumar in advance, and the news of a divorce wasn't well received. There wasn't much Kumar could do to change Joel's mind. Direct and gentle was the way to go. He called for Zarah as soon as he walked into the house. She came quickly.

"I'd like to take a ride this afternoon. Are you up for it?" Her stomach was queasy earlier but she seemed to be doing better. He guessed that she was fighting off some kind of a bug, a virus or food poisoning.

"Oh yes, I'd love to go for a ride."

"Are you sure you're feeling up to it?"

"Oh yes."

"Because you didn't seem all right earlier."

"It's nothing. I'm not ill, if that is your concern. Don't worry, I'm fine," she said, appearing to radiate with each word spoken to Joel.

"Okay, well, good," he said, feeling relieved. He couldn't deal with Zarah being sick again, not when he was handing her a divorce. "How soon can you be ready?"

"I can go now," she said, elated.

"But I do think you should see the doctor over the

next couple of days, just to be sure that you're all right." "I will."

His eagerness to share the bad news crumbled. Compassion dominated. He could wait until they were well into the ride. Twenty minutes later the Range Rover was barreling down I-75, heading for a park right outside of downtown. The setting was private and tranquil. He had to be careful not to end up in a location that was too romantic. That would be a cruel place to announce a divorce. Joel entered the park and found a parking space. Zarah was thrilled to be with him. She was a gorgeous woman with a good heart, the perfect wife for some other man.

"Zarah, let's get out and take a walk." She did willingly. He reached for her hand as they began their stroll. The walkway was nearly a half mile long, meaning he had about twenty minutes to break the news. No value to be gained from stalling. He opened his lips and let the speech flow. "Zarah, you are beautiful and very special."

"Thank you," she said, gripping his hand tighter.

"You deserve a husband who can cherish you, someone who is able to make you the center of his world." He paused, unwilling to rush the inevitable. "That's not me. My world is falling apart and I have to go away and figure out how to rebuild."

"I will go with you," she said.

"Zarah," he said, stopping their walk, "you're not going with me." Her zeal dropped. "I'm going alone, and you should go back to India."

"My place is with my husband. I will not go to India if you're here."

"I'm freeing you, Zarah. You are no longer obligated to me as a wife. I can't be the husband you want."

"I'm not complaining. You are the husband I want. I'm staying."

Joel was disheartened. She wasn't making this easy. He had to be more direct and bring this chapter in his marriage to a close. "Zarah, we are going to get a divorce."

"No, no, no divorce," she said. He kept a tight hold on her hand to help contain her reaction.

"We have no choice. You have not been happy with me. I truly believed we had a chance to make a real marriage after you began recovering from your illness, but I was mistaken. We're not good for one another. We have to separate."

"I don't want to. I can be a better wife. You will see. I can do it."

"You've done nothing wrong, Zarah, not a thing. You have been a wonderful wife. We just don't work well together, and I need a change. If you care about me, I'm asking you to release me from this marriage and let me go. You deserve better than this, and I want you to have it," he said as her emotion crested. He wrapped his arms around her shoulders and smothered Zarah into his caress, not one intended for romance, but an intentional act of affection. She wasn't the enemy. He acknowledged that she wasn't. Circumstances had brought them together and consequences were breaking them apart. It was time to part. Deep within her being, she had to know. He held her until the emotion subsided and they could return to the car.

Joel was worried about her stability and would stay with her until Kumar arrived in a day or two to take her home. The last nervous breakdown had frightened both him and her. Joel wasn't going to let her slip into fatal depression on his watch, not again. He would be with her all night into the day, fulfilling his final marital duty. The gesture was sincere. He owed her that much. A silent sigh of relief followed as they slowly made their way to the Range Rover. In a few days he'd take refuge in Chicago, opening a new chapter in his life. He was cautiously optimistic, reserving his sheer thrill for a time of celebration with Sheba. He'd see her soon, but for the next forty-eight hours Zarah required his undivided support and he aimed to deliver.

chapter
56

Tamara stood and sat repeatedly. She couldn't get comfortable. Mother had called, before boarding the flight yesterday afternoon, to give Don her itinerary. Tamara counted the minutes. If the two layovers went smoothly and the plane was on time, Madeline should have landed at six fifty, thirty-nine minutes ago. She could add a good hour and a half for getting luggage, clearing customs, and having the driver take her to Don's. From her rough calculations, there was close to an hour remaining. Tamara's anxiety meter was running hot. She was afraid but equally excited. Unable to make sense of her feelings, she didn't bother. She'd let them be, no longer locked in a box of guilt, shame, and fear.

Tamara went to get a cup of tea, certain Don didn't have a latte machine. "Where can I find the tea?" she called out to him, not sure where he was in the condo. He might have called it a condo, but the unit was another gigantic house compared to her last five flats. It was tough to believe they came from the same home. Their realities were an ocean apart. The ringing doorbell sent a shiver through Tamara. Remain calm, she thought.

Don answered the door and sure enough, it was Mother.

"I got here as soon as I could. Where's Tamara?"

"Here I am," Tamara said, coming from the kitchen.

"Are you okay? Did he hurt you?" Mother said, hustling toward Tamara.

Tamara didn't move. She couldn't decide whether to let Mother touch her or step away. In the split second before Mother reached her, Tamara remembered she was going to let the moment be uncontrolled until discomfort set in.

"He didn't hit me or hurt me. I was embarrassed more than anything."

"Mother, give me your coat," Don said, and she handed it to him.

"There is no cause for you to be embarrassed. You're the victim here." Maybe she was, but Tamara resented the title of victim. After the rape, she'd vowed never to be a victim again. No one would zap her power again. Remo had forced her to fail at keeping her one sacred promise. At times, Madeline had pushed too, but Tamara had always been able to maintain distance from Mother, until now. She knew Mother wasn't going to back off under the current circumstances. Tamara wasn't upset. Even at this critical moment in their union, she was the one controlling the visit. If she'd wanted to leave last night, this morning, or this afternoon, she could have. Tamara was where she had to be.

"Come in and let's sit down," Don said as the three went into his great room and found seats. Madeline waited for Tamara to take a seat and then sat next to her, leaving about eight inches of distance between them. Close, not crowded, worked for Tamara.

"I wish you'd told me or Don about this man stalking you. Every time I imagine you being out there scared and running, I get angry."

"Mother, I'm perfectly safe."

"You are now and will be permanently in a few days," Madeline said, letting her gaze drop.

"What do you mean? Was Remo arrested?"

"Not exactly."

"Then what?" Don interjected. The way Madeline responded seemed very suspicious to Tamara. Don must have picked up on the same vibe.

"I'm not going into details because I have none."

"Oh come on, Mother, what have you done?" Don asked, seeming very upset.

"I'll tell you this much. I retained a specialist to rectify our little situation."

"What kind of a specialist?" Don asked.

"Too many questions, Don. What you don't know won't hurt you."

Don laughed out loud, more like cackled. "Mother, we don't want to exchange one family problem for another. Please tell me that whatever you've done is legal."

"What I did isn't illegal. I retained a specialist. What the specialist does is out of my hands."

Don didn't appear to be satisfied with the response but let the line of questions rest. "Excuse me, I'll get the tea you wanted, Tamara. Anything for you, Mother?"

"Nothing for me, thanks," Madeline said, shifting her attention to Tamara. Instinctively Tamara wanted to leave the room with Don but was able to remain calm. The small space between her and Madeline provided the necessary safety net. Madeline patted her hand. "Really, how are you?"

What did Mother want her to say, that she was a wreck, that she hadn't slept a full night in years, or that she was tired of running? Instead she said, "I'm feeling better."

Thirty years of dysfunction weren't going to be resolved in one session on Don's sofa. Tamara understood restoration would be like losing weight. It had taken years to put the weight on, and it wouldn't come off overnight. She was prepared for some joyous and rough moments to come if she and Don were to truly make an attempt at becoming a family, not the one of her childhood, not the one before her father abandoned them, and not the one before the rape. She was looking at a family post-trauma, different but manageable. She was certain Don wasn't going to be a problem. Mother was her concern. She would want answers about why this and why not that. Some answers Tamara could give and others she didn't know.

Tamara wasn't delusional. The Mitchell family wasn't going to realize happily-ever-after any time soon. Lots of therapy, willingness, hope, and patience were required. So long as Madeline could let the three of them find their way at their individual paces, without intervention or pressure, Tamara was certain they could form a new normal in time. Inside, she was excited and relieved.

"Let's start with something we both enjoy, traveling. Why don't you tell me about South Africa? I hear it's lovely this time of year," Tamara said.

Mother must have gotten the hint about setting the tough issues to the side, because she said, "South Africa is lovely and so are you." The response lingered like the scent of a floral bouquet sailing through an open window in the springtime. Tamara was pleased to be home.

chapter

57

Joel had made his rounds, speaking with his mother, then Zarah, and he had one person left, Abigail. They'd had a strained encounter two weeks ago. She was worth his attempting to reach a truce before jetting off to Chicago.

He found her in the DMI office. "Abigail, can I come in?" he asked.

She beckoned for him to enter and kept typing on her laptop. "What brings you by?" she asked, tossing a quick glance at him and returning to the laptop.

"I wanted to share my big news with you." That got her attention. She looked up and fixed her gaze on him.

"What did you come to tell me, that you and your wife are having a baby?"

"No way, never, don't even play like that, just the opposite. I'm ending this before a mistake like that happens. No, I came to tell you we're getting divorced."

"Really? You're right. It is big news. I don't know whether to say 'congratulations' or 'I'm sorry.'"

He raised his eyebrow and pressed his lips together before responding. "Neither, it's bittersweet, but I won't bore you with the details." Joel definitely didn't want to insult her by going on about his wife. The purpose of his visit was to repair their friendship, not make it worse. "I'm also heading to Chicago."

"Permanently?"

"Not sure, for now I'm going to take it day by day."

"I'm sure Sheba will be thrilled," Abigail said, shifting her attention to the laptop.

"Chicago will be a good place for me to step away from the action and make a new start. I'm excited about the possibilities." Again, Joel was reminded that he wasn't there to rip open old wounds. Sheba was a sore spot. Abigail had seen her as a threat even before Joel married Zarah. Despite his best efforts to dissuade her, Abigail had wanted to make his relationship with Sheba a deal breaker in their friendship. He wasn't going to open the box of controversy.

"I have some pretty big news myself."

"Oh yeah, what, you're getting married?" he asked.

She shot a glance at him that sizzled like fire. "I'm resigning."

"Get out of here, you're joking."

"I'm serious. I've already given Don notice."

"Hard to believe you're getting out of here. You're one of the originals."

"Time for me to strike out from the nest and try my hand in another venture."

"Do you have another job lined up?"

"I don't have one, and I won't start my search for several months. I'm staying here for three months until they find a replacement. Who knows, I might launch my own consulting company. I can put the million dollars your father left me to good use. I have a few ideas stirring. The good news is that I don't have to decide a thing today. I can take my time and make the decision that's going to be best for Abigail Gerard. I like the sound of that," she said.

So did he. It was the same sensation he had ending the marriage. Freedom was cool.

"Who knows, maybe we can partner on a venture down the road; you never know. If the time is right and the deal is real, who knows?"

"Humph," she uttered, and let her gaze shift back to the laptop.

Joel wasn't dissuaded. His life would soon be wide open and the possibilities were going to be endless.

chapter

58

The call from Zarah was surprising, but with recent events, Tamara didn't rule out any scenarios. She took a private car along with a bodyguard to Zarah's. Madeline and Don had insisted that she not be alone until the predicament with Remo had been resolved.

Tamara had no clue as to what Zarah wanted. During the visit last week, Tamara had implored Zarah to stand up and show Joel she could be independent. She'd also suggested Zarah get involved in her father's former business and stop relying on men to dictate her moves. Zarah hadn't been receptive. Who knows? Maybe she'd changed her mind and decided to sell the division. Tamara would soon find out. She rang the bell. Zarah came to the door, which threw Tamara off. Joel or the housekeeper had answered on the other visits. Tamara couldn't help but notice how puffy Zarah's eyes were, like she was suffering from allergies.

"I was glad you called," Tamara said, "a little surprised, though."

"I'm very glad you came," Zarah said, sounding choked up.

"Is everything all right? You weren't feeling well when I was here last week."

"It is not all right," she said. Oddly, tears were streaming down her face without her making a whimper.

"Zarah, let's go sit and talk," Tamara suggested. Zarah led the way to the library. "What's wrong?"

"Joel has decided for a divorce."

Whoa was what she wanted to say. She hadn't dreamed he'd go this far. Tamara hoped her advice about Zarah taking a stronger stand in the marriage hadn't backfired. She felt awful. "Are you sure?"

"Most certainly. He's made arrangements with my family for me to return to India."

"Is that what you want?"

"I'm not certain. This is very sudden for me. My one wish is to remain Joel's wife and bear his children. If I return to India, my dream won't come to truth."

That amounted to two wishes, but who was counting, Tamara figured. She couldn't help Zarah with the wife-and-kids component. Having someone dictate whether she returned to India was a different animal. She could help there. Zarah needed an advocate, a Madeline kind of person in her circle, to help fix the unfixable. "I'm sure I don't need to tell you this, but you're an adult. You get to decide if you want to stay in the U.S., go to South Africa, or return home to India. That's strictly your decision, especially since your parents are gone."

"My father's attorney has decided."

"How can he? Is there an Indian law that says you must listen to him?" Zarah appeared unsure. It didn't matter; Tamara highly suspected there wasn't.

"Where is Joel?"

"He traveled to Chicago this morning," Zarah said, struggling to articulate her sentences.

"For how long?"

"He said two weeks, maybe four. He's allowing me time to get packed and moved."

Tamara really did feel for Zarah. She'd experienced that well of emptiness, not having clear direction or the support of close family to help shape her decisions. Zarah was alone in the world, except for an attorney. Tamara wanted to shake Zarah and tell her the future was a blank canvas and she was the solo artist. She could decide to go or stay, to work or not, to love or not. She was in control and couldn't do any worse than the men who'd erroneously mapped out the path for Zarah, the ones who'd left her abandoned, powerless, and frightened in the U.S. Tamara had an idea, though she was still not sure if her previous advice had contributed to the demise of Zarah and Joel's marriage. She continued anyway. "Have you considered staying in the States?"

"What would I do? I have no one here."

"You have me." The statement brightened Zarah's countenance. Chipping away at her frozen disposition was slow with Tamara's small ice pick of kindness, but it appeared progress was being made. "As far as what you could do, well, I suggest you buy Harmonious Energy. Before you say no, hear me out. This is your father's company, his legacy. There are no sons to carry his legacy forward into the future. You're it, and who better to take on the company? You said yourself that you worked with your father and understood his business. This is the time to show the world."

"I have no desire to show the world my abilities. Joel

was the one I wanted to please. In my culture, there is no failure worse than divorce. I will be shunned and disowned."

"All the more reason for you to stay in the States. People get married and divorced like buying shoes here." People find the perfect pair of shoes, fall in love with it, can't live without it. They take the shoes home, wear the pair everywhere all the time. One day, out of nowhere, the shoes don't fit anymore, don't look as good, and get replaced with the next great love. People survived. Tamara was confident Zarah could too.

"That is disturbing."

"Tell me about it, but at least you're not doomed if you do end up divorced. Trust me, divorce is not ideal for anyone." Speaking as a child of divorced parents, she'd experienced the trauma firsthand, but there was recovery. The past two days with her mother, small doses each day, were confirmation. Zarah could have the same chance at fulfillment. "Like I said, you should buy Harmonious Energy. Don will sell it to you for a good price so long as you're willing to cut an equitable deal for the return of DMI's West Coast division." Tamara was no longer interested in securing the company as an independent. She would trust Don with incorporating the division into DMI and allowing her to assume the lesser role of running the division. Clawing with him for the CEO position wasn't necessary. It wasn't a job she desired anyway. He did want it and she knew it should be his free and clear.

"I'm not interested in the division or the company if Joel isn't here."

This wasn't the perspective Tamara wanted to hear, but she respected Zarah as a grown woman capable of making decisions, right or wrong. "Let me be honest with you:

unless you take a stand, you're going to end up depressed and dead."

"Dead isn't a concept we believe in."

"Dead, asleep, reincarnated, or whatever. I'm not trying to demean your religion, but the fact is that you are only going to stay on this earth for a limited number of years. Unless you take charge," Tamara said, pointing toward Zarah, "your remaining years will be short. Tap into your strength. That's all I'm saying, and trust me, Joel won't be sitting around pining over you. He'll be in Chicago doing what he wants. The best way to get rid of the shame associated with your so-called failure is to succeed. Once you are successfully running your father's company, you will have enough clout to stay here or return home—your choice. So get your behind out of this house and get about the business of living. By golly, I'm demanding it." Zarah seemed stunned. "No, I'm joking. I can't tell you what to do or demand anything. Consider me a friend, and I'll help you as much as I can."

"I see what you say is true. I shall consider purchasing Harmonious Energy to honor my father's name. It is my duty if I have no husband," she said, gloomy.

Tamara stood to leave. Zarah wasn't the hugging type, which was good. When Zarah rested her palms on Tamara's and shook them vigorously, the hint of a smile showed. Tamara was relieved.

"Excuse me," Zarah said, "I believe my sickness hasn't gone." She rushed from the room with her mouth covered.

When she returned Tamara asked, "How long did you say you've been sick?"

"Three weeks, not every day, but many days."

"You should go to the doctor, just in case it's something more serious."

"My husband said I should go as well."

Tamara could detect the softening in Zarah's tone and jumped in to keep her from retreating into self-pity about Joel. "Tomorrow you call, today we go have fun," Tamara said and clapped her hands like a cymbal. She was extra jovial to give Zarah an emotional boost.

"Yes, I shall phone my doctor tomorrow and today we go. Thank you, Tamara, for being my friend. I am pleased," she managed to say before running off to the bathroom again. Whatever bug she had, Tamara sure didn't want it. Discreetly she searched for hand sanitizer while Zarah was gone. She didn't mind being a friend for life, but unto death was extreme.

chapter 59

"Zarah, Dr. Cooper's office is on the phone. They'd like to speak with you," the housekeeper came to tell her.

Tamara had suggested, during her visit yesterday, that Zarah see the doctor since her sickness seemed to be lingering. She'd left a message earlier and was pleased to get a call back rather quickly.

"Yes, Dr. Cooper, this is Zarah."

"Thank you for calling. I'm definitely concerned that you might be getting dehydrated again. Since you're recovering nicely, I'd like to have you come in for a thorough exam. How soon can you come in?"

"I can come without delay."

"Great, Zarah. I also have to ask . . . This may seem awkward, but have you considered that you might be pregnant? Morning sickness is quite normal during the first trimester. If you don't mind, I'll have you take the test when you come in."

"Yes, indeed." Zarah was mesmerized. To dream of

pregnancy was too much. She couldn't allow herself to be too anxious. The disappointment of thinking she was pregnant and finding out she wasn't would be the death of her for certain. She'd wait for the doctor to perform proper tests. Her destiny could wait a few hours for confirmation.

chapter
60

The weekend in Chicago ushered in a calm Joel hadn't felt in months, really almost a year. The nonstop finagling and scheming had taken a toll. He was fatigued. The sights along Grant Park, in the heart of downtown Chicago, allowed his mind to wander, no pressure, no obligations, to his father, to his family, to DMI, or to Zarah. He was free to explore the man he wanted to be, not the one his father had chosen him to be. Joel relaxed in the solace of the early autumn sky, pleased that the sun wasn't too hot or too cold, just right. So would his refurbished life be as well.

The phone buzzed in Joel's pocket.

He was reluctant to sacrifice the tranquillity of the moment and opted not to answer the call. Another minute swept by and the phone buzzed again. Curiosity got the best of him and he glanced at the inbound call. It was his home number. Must be the housekeeper, he figured.

By now, Zarah and Musar were either in India or well on their way.

He answered the call. "Joel speaking."

"Joel, I have important news to share," Zarah said. He hadn't heard this kind of zest in her voice since their three days of wedding festivities took place in India about five months ago. She sounded like a different person. The split was proving to be as much in her best interest as it was in his. "Joel, you must know that I'm pregnant. We are having our first baby. The gods have shown me mercy."

"What did you say?"

"The gods have blessed us with a child."

Joel wanted to drop to the ground and wallow. His shock kept him vertical. He was beyond stunned. He didn't have a response, but the anxiety burning within expressed his sentiments wholeheartedly. Worst luck in the world, he thought. What were the odds? Fewer than five intimate moments in five months and he'd created the title of Dad. Joel was disgusted.

"How do you know that you're pregnant?" He wasn't going to get alarmed before there was a fire. Joel intended to get the accurate, thorough details before reacting. Zarah was so desperate to remain his wife. He wouldn't have been shocked to find out that she'd made up the story to get his attention. Their marriage was over and she'd have to accept the truth and not make outlandish, life-altering claims.

"Dr. Cooper ran the tests. I am six weeks along."

Joel was clinging to the belief that Zarah was exaggerating out of desperation, not manipulation. His belief was fading quickly. The certainty was clanging deep within. He sensed she was telling the truth and his wish for hope sank.

The Chicago air seemed to tighten around his throat and choke the freedom from him.

Six weeks ago, he guessed, was the night his fate veered off course. Right before her breakdown, he'd felt sorry for her and comforted her as only a husband could. So much for pity; who was going to comfort him now?

"When will you be home?"

When he'd set the Lamborghini on I-94 heading west to the Windy City, both his address and his concept of home changed. The Zarah Bengali chapter in his life was complete. With her crushing news, he had to reassess what home meant and where it fit into his life. He had been blessed to grow up with his father in the home, a gift every child deserved. On the other hand, Don grew up without their father living in his home. They had still been able to maintain a rapport. Maybe Joel's options weren't as limited as he initially believed. He'd have to work out a plan.

"I'm not sure when I'll be there, but I am coming soon. We need to talk about our future." The baby's future was the only one of concern for him, but she didn't need the extra commentary. She'd find out how he wanted to proceed soon enough, about the same time as he found out. "Take care of yourself. Get plenty of rest and fluids. I'll see you soon."

"Yes, I'm pleased. I look forward to your arrival."

Joel let the dialogue linger. This day would forever be etched in his memory: the day when the decisions of his past overtook him and beat down the hopes of his future. He limped to the car, letting the final remnants of freedom ring, not sure what tomorrow was going to hold. Zarah had prayed to her gods. Perhaps the time had come for him to pray to his. It wasn't like he could get himself out of this. He wasn't asking God to make Zarah un-pregnant. Asking for direction and guidance would be the core of his prayer. No one else could help him come to terms with his bind. He'd begin his prayer as soon as he was inside his car. God didn't need the extra time; Joel did.

Broken

Patricia Haley

MAKES YOU GO *HMMM!*

Now that you have read *Broken*, consider the following discussion questions.

1. Tamara is the oldest living child of Dave and Madeline Mitchell. Estranged from her family, she's been gone for nearly fifteen years. Do you think her unexpected return was a plus or a minus for the family?

2. Did Madeline make the right decision when she left Detroit and DMI so that Tamara could come home? Was Tamara selfish in wanting her mother to go, or was she justified in wanting the space to make her reentry into a dysfunctional family environment?

3. Madeline and Tamara seem to be making amends, albeit slowly. Considering the years of separation and the horrific memories, do you think Tamara and Madeline can truly reconcile? What will be the most critical factor? Can Madeline and Tamara work together at DMI?

4. What do you suspect Joel will do now that Zarah has informed him about the baby? Will he stay in Chicago to sort out his feelings and options? Will he proceed with the divorce anyway, or will he opt to stick out the marriage for three years and then be eligible to buy back the DMI West Coast division? Will Joel give up Sheba? (Note: For more insight into their "undefined" relationship, read 1 Kings, chap-

ter 10, concerning the biblical drama surrounding the Queen of Sheba's visit to King Solomon.)

5. Now that Zarah is carrying Joel's child and holding ownership of the DMI division that Joel wants, how do you think she will use the situation? Is she a business threat to Joel, Don, or DMI? Will Tamara influence her?

6. If Joel does decide to return to Detroit and to his marriage, will he also make another attempt to wrest control of DMI from Don?

7. Thanks to a nudge from Tamara, Abigail finally became fed up with being second best in the Mitchell men's lives. Was Tamara correct in saying that there will always be a Mitchell standing between Abigail and the lead position in DMI? Do you think Abigail will really leave DMI in the end? Can she truly walk away from Don and/or Joel?

8. Where do you see the relationship with Naledi and Don going? Is he truly free of his feelings for Abigail?

9. What role in the company does Tamara deserve? Does Don need to worry about her? Will Don ever be at peace with managing the company, or will another attack or takeover by members of the Mitchell family always be looming?

10. Uncle Frank is a very colorful character and quite consistent. As of now, he's been retained to deal

with Remo. On the outside chance that Uncle Frank is unsuccessful, do you believe Remo will end up back in Detroit for Madeline to handle directly, or elsewhere in the world posing a constant threat to the Mitchell family?

11. If Madeline returns, will Sherry stay? Can Sherry, Madeline, and Tamara all work together? Will Madeline or Sherry ever remarry?

12. What message was Big Mama, Mother Walker, conveying to Don for Joel?

13. The *Chosen* series is loosely based on King David's character and the family drama surrounding him. A mighty Biblical warrior, King David had God's favor and a distinct purpose, but his life was not free of mistakes, sin, and tragedy. Yet he is remembered not for his shortcomings, but for his love for God and his ability to forgive and forget. What's the difference between forgiving and forgetting? (Note: Does forgetting mean wiping away the memory of the offense or does it mean letting go of the hurt, anger, bitterness, rejection, guilt, etc., that was felt/experienced when the offense occurred? See chapters 46 and 47 for Don's perspective.)

14. Who benefits most from forgiveness, the offender or the person offended? Forgiveness is liberating; it enabled Tamara to begin letting go of her lingering anger and pain. Is there anyone you need to forgive in order to move forward? What's stopping you?

Acknowledgments

Thank you to my readers. You are the reason God has me do what I do. I hope *Broken* encourages you to use your talents, discover your purpose, and embrace the message of forgiveness. May you be inspired to use your life to the glory of God and serve as a blessing to others. Much love to each of you.

Thanks to all my family (Haley, Glass, Tennin, Rome, and Moorman) for the constant support, including my tall, dark, and handsome husband, Jeffrey, an amazing daughter, brothers, friends, Little Sis, and an extended circle of loved ones. As always, I honor the memories of my father, "Fred," beloved brother Erick, and father-in-law, Walter.

The hardest part about writing my books is completing the acknowledgments section. I am blessed with such incredible support, so it's easy to inadvertently leave someone out. I wish I could call everyone by name, but I will fall short.

So, with much love, I say thank you to my entire group of supporters, those who constantly cheer me on. You know who you are. May the Lord bless you abundantly in return.

With a grateful spirit, there are some that I must highlight because they've been a gift to me. My advance readers get applause for consistently providing feedback that makes my stories stronger: Jeffrey, Emma (John), Laurel, Dorothy, Tammy, Aunt Ada, and Renee. Special thanks to my agent, to the Simon & Schuster team, to many book clubs, media, and booksellers. I give a loving shout-out to Myrt Yarbrough as she retires; thank you for giving me my first big push in Waldenbooks during my self-publishing days. A special thank-you to Shirley Brockenborough, Maleta Wilson, David Almack-CLC, Marlene Bagnull, and Sirius Web Solutions. Thank you to my Delta Sigma Theta Sorority sisters, especially the Schaumburg-Hoffman Estates (IL), Valley Forge (PA), Rockford (IL), Chester (PA), Milwaukee (WI), and Louisville (KY) Alumnae Chapters, Omicron Chi Chapter (Stanford), and the 2011 Midwest Regional conference committee. Many book clubs and ministries have shown me much love, but I have to personally thank a few who have blessed me tremendously with years of support: First African–Sharon Hill, Circle of Hope–Jones Memorial, Women of Wisdom–Bethany Baptist, Women of Character (FL), Sistas Empowered and Making a Difference (DE), Enoch-Pratt Library (Shirley), and Rockford Public Library (Faye and Staci). Much continued success to LAABP (Carmen Steward). Lastly, I greatly appreciate the ongoing prayers from my New Covenant (Trappe, PA) and Beulah Grove (GA) church families. Only God can return to you what you've given me.

P.S. Happy fiftieth birthday to my husband, Jeffrey Glass, who is my best friend and the love of my life. Happy seventieth birthday to my beloved mother and hero, Fannie Haley Rome. Happy fortieth to cousin Eugene James. Many continued blessings to Uncle James Tennin, Aunt Lela Haley Dockery, and Uncle Jim Haley for being in the "eighty-five years old and over club." Happy twentieth wedding anniversary to my cousins Will and Kimberla Lawson Roby. Congratulations to Adetutu Bakare, Bradley Wright, and my cousins Matthew Tennin and Bethany Tenner on their college graduations.

Author's Note

———

Dear Readers:

Thank you for reading *Broken*. I hope you found the story entertaining. Look for other novels in the *Chosen* series.

Please join my mailing list, drop me a note, or post a message on my website. I look forward to hearing from you. You can also join me on Facebook (Patricia Haley-Glass).

As always, thank you for the support. Keep reading, and be blessed.

www.patriciahaley.com